STANDING ON THE BEACH

STANDING ON THE BEACH

A Mystery

M.J. CODY

ETOWN PRESS

Cover: Marcia Barrentine Design

To D.A. who took me there.

HE CAME THROUGH THE DOOR like he lived there. The old men looked up from their plates, grumbled and shifted uncomfortably eyeing each other slyly. Jimmy Ketah shook the rain off his cowboy hat, planted himself at the counter and watched Norris pour him coffee.

Rita saw it through the kitchen order window. Said to Joe one thing. Trouble. Joe said you don't know, slapping gravy over the pork chops and wiping the excess off the rim of the plate with the corner of his apron.

The Tick Tock was one of the oldest cafés in Seattle, part of the St. James Hotel built in the thirties, remodeled in the seventies, and hardly bothered with since. Rita scanned the room. The Tick Tock was practically a private club for retired drifters, merchant marines, longshoremen, salesmen, loggers, displaced cowboys. She could see the lonesome forms of the exiled littering the lobby all day and long into the night watching television. That is, when they weren't in the café or in the back room playing hold 'em.

Funny how there weren't any women, but then women weren't inclined to roam for a lifetime unencumbered or settle for cracked Naugahyde couches, coffee tables stained with the modern day hieroglyphics of cigarette burns and cup rings, and a nineteen-inch Sony that worked if you hit it just right.

The question was: why would Rita's kid sister waste her time waitressing in a dive like theirs when she could fix herself up and move on to any restaurant in the city? Norris had worked for a month at The Bistro in the market, one of those artsy-fartsy places swarming with Boeing engineers and Microsoft millionaires. Norris could have snagged any one of those men and be set for life but came back to the Tick Tock with no explanation.

Norris was talking to the Indian now. She was smiling. He was grinning. Rita took a drag on her cigarette. Norris picked the oddest people to be nice to. Hell, her best friend was that queer fellow from their hometown, Warren Bartholomew. Now there was a number. Tall as a birch and thin as one too. A mop of dark wavy red hair that belonged on a young man, yet Rita knew he had to be in his late forties. He was in the class behind hers. He was nice enough, even though Rita couldn't begin to understand him. Once in broad daylight she thought she detected a bit of makeup just around the eyes. Rita looked away, ashamed. She asked Norris about it later and Norris shrugged and said, oh, probably.

"A flaming queen he is," Shorty Henderson had announced in a loud booming voice the first and last time Warren ever came into the Tick Tock. Rita was so unnerved she dropped a milkshake into the dishwater, while everyone else in the cafe laughed. Except Norris. Anyway, Rita didn't want to know about that. At least Warren was a friend for Norris, someone to spend time with although Rita thought it was a shame an attractive person like Norris wasting her time with one of *those*.

Shoot, Rita had introduced her to lots of great guys. What was wrong with Kyle, the hunky beer truck driver? He was kind of loud, now that she thought about it, but Norris could have at least gone out with him. Bet he was a lot of laughs.

Rita told Joe that Norris was a psychological cripple from her husband driving off the bridge like that. Joe grunted like always, swiping his sweaty red face on his sleeve. He didn't want to discuss things. He just wanted to cook. He told Rita to mind her own business even though he knew she never would.

Rita was stuck right where she was because she and Joe owned the place. But Norris? Rita worried that Norris would never remarry, get on with a decent life. She could understand Norris hiding out for a while after the accident, recovered, safe here with the old timers, no pressure, no threats, the free rooms upstairs. But it'd been almost three years. That was enough time to get over anything. A normal person wouldn't spend so much time alone in her room. Painting for god's sake. How could she live like that? Canvases and paints all over, not a decent place to sit except the unmade bed, the heady aroma of turpentine so strong Mr. Timmons had to be moved to the second floor. Norris did have a few shows at those galleries in Old Town but what was the point? It might be romantic for someone younger to live like that with paint-splattered jeans and that mass of blond hair going every which way but trying to be an artist wasn't something a thirty-five-year-old woman should do.

Rita lit a new Virginia Slim from the butt of her old one—it was her place, let them arrest her—and watched the smoke linger around the deep fat fryer and trail through the order window into the cafe. She briefly tried to imagine a different life, a place that didn't reek of old men and hamburger grease, but put it out of her mind. Things were as they were and there was no use thinking about them being any different. Besides, she'd never leave her Joe.

Norris was the one who should wake up and smell the coffee.

Norris was emotionally shipwrecked, that's what she was, as hopelessly adrift as any of those old timers playing cards and sucking down Jim Beam in the back room.

Rita watched Norris clear the tables then head back to the counter where the Indian still sat. Rita didn't appreciate him taking possession of the counter like that making the regulars uncomfortable. Rita tried to motion Norris to move him on but she didn't take the hint. He sat at the counter all that miserable rainy afternoon and let Norris pour him coffee.

The next morning, Norris quit her job, packed a bag, and followed Jimmy Ketah to Juneau.

Rita had a fit. Rita said she was crazy chasing after a man like that, but then Rita didn't know much about Norris.

THE AIR TOOK HER BREATH AWAY. A hint of fir, a hint of ocean, air as clear and sharp as ice. Norris stood at the airport curb, Jimmy Ketah half sitting on a cement planter beside her watching the highway, his long legs stretched out in front of him in Levis and scuffed moosehide cowboy boots. They'd been waiting thirty minutes for their ride and she was glad he didn't fidget. Gladder still he didn't talk. She knew he'd be steady and quiet and it suited her fine. In fact, everything about him suited her, even though boarding the plane a moment of panic overtook her like a summer storm.

Rita's reproaches echoed, stinging, raining down. Rita treated her like an invalid and now that she had gone, was furious she could walk. At least Joe kissed her goodbye and wished her luck, pressing a hundred dollar bill into her pocket with his clumsy rough fingers. Maybe she shouldn't have left them so suddenly but all of Rita's admonishments could not convince her she was guilty. She was only afraid she was stupid.

She could have listened to Rita and waited but waiting was a sickness she'd as soon be over. Jimmy Ketah was like a savior, Jesus come to redeem her, though she doubted Jesus would be that good in bed.

Norris smiled to herself. She was brand new. She was awake. She was standing at the airport in Juneau with a stranger.

Storm clouds slid toward the mountains and Norris shivered as a renegade scudded across the sun. Jimmy reached for her hand and pulled her to sit next to him on the planter closing her hand in both of his.

"Cold?" he asked and blew on her hand then tucked it between his legs, hunching against the chill. He looked up at her and smiled, a funny lopsided grin from under his cowboy hat. It was a simple gesture, as ordinary as a blade of grass, and she loved him. She loved the thought of him coming to her last night, down the hallway past Rita and Joe's apartment, unseen, unheard, tapping on her door. She hadn't invited him but knew he would be there. From that first moment in the café she knew everything would change. She could feel her life shifting. Had she conjured him?

Just that morning she had looked across the room at the old men eating, crouched over their plates, absorbed. The men with their gray hair and bald heads, their gnarled hands, their rheumy windswept eyes, the dribbled food down shirtfronts. She looked at them fondly and wistfully. So many lives treading emptiness. Looked at them and thought: any day now I'll leave you. Whispered to herself: any day now.

Her paintings, once her refuge, now well received and sometimes fawned over, had become remote, rote. She appreciated Candace and Merilee, the gallery owners who supported and launched her. Ever enthusiastic and so terribly glad to see her but were they real friends? Friendship in the art community could be elusive and Candace and Merilee were part of that most dangerous echelon, the Art Elite. They were perfect: the clothes, the accessories, the shoes. They drank in the best places, frequented the best restaurants, knew everyone worth knowing. Norris had no illusions about the precariousness of being an artist. She was one of the worker bees who made their life possible. As long as they liked her work, as long as it sold, she was worth something to them. The minute she stopped producing, would she be history? In a way, that's why she was back at the Tick Tock. No pretensions. She had worked at The Bistro and made good money, met people, yet felt always on display with an emanating underlying pity as though something more was expected of her. She preferred the seclusion and anonymity of the Tick Tock. She would rather hear the tired stories of the old men than the refined chitchat of the terminally chic. She didn't want the hip, cool, turned-on, plugged-in world. She wanted . . . Something.

And Jimmy had arrived as though on cue.

She'd opened her bedroom door to him and they stood on the threshold smiling. It didn't take a minute for clothes to come off, a half-dressed staggering lunge to the bed. God, she'd missed that. Lying with her, spent, he scanned the room. Seemed at home in the unconventional. He was curious, observant, and something else. If she glimpsed a darker current beneath his tender, cautious surface, it didn't matter.

She wasn't afraid. She had nothing to lose.

Rita could never comprehend the depth of her sudden attachment to him. He was deeply familiar, yet completely new.

Norris couldn't explain it. She'd known him thirty-six hours and counting, but knew more about Jimmy Ketah in an instant than she'd known about Bailey in all their married life. She leaned against him.

The pickup barreled to the curbside, smoke billowing from underneath, traveling on its own cloud, the muffler hanging.

"Need a lift?" the driver asked, hanging out the window and beaming like a fool.

"Right on time, buddy," Jimmy said as if he meant it, tossing their bags into the rusted bed.

"Norris, Smitty; Smitty, Norris."

Smitty was as big as a walrus. Norris tried not to stare but there was something amazing about a big bull stuffed into the cab of a red '57 Chevy pickup, the blubbery torso crammed behind the wheel, his head barely an inch from the roof, skinny legs shooting out to the pedals like they belonged to somebody else. A red kerchief was tied around his huge head in a useless attempt to keep his outlaw hair restrained.

"Glad to meet you," he said, leaning across the passenger seat and offering a huge puffy hand from the frayed sleeve of his denim jacket. The fingers were slightly tapered, as tight as sausages, the fingernails too long, yellowing and grimy underneath, his voice as gentle and shapeless as his grip.

"Nice to meet you too," Norris said, marveling at how a man that big could be soft as dough.

"Where's Danny?" Smitty asked once they were settled in the cab, Norris in the middle, her knees wedged away from the gearshift.

"Guess," said Jimmy.

"Damn it, Jimmy," Smitty said, shaking his walrus head, clenching the steering wheel.

"King County Jail was getting to be his second home. This time I let him stay."

"You shouldn't of done it," said Smitty, controlling anger.

"Best thing."

Smitty calming down, recovering. "You got a new crew mate then?"

"Looks that way."

"Well, she's better looking than Danny. Can she fish?"

"She'll learn," said Jimmy, smiling out the window.

"Can she change a gill net on a forty-degree roll with the ocean coming in her face?"

"Can you?" said Jimmy.

"No. Just asking."

"So she won't be able to do everything Danny could. At least I won't have to bail her sorry ass out of jail every time I turn around."

"You hope," said Norris, making both of them look at her for a second before they laughed.

They were on the expressway headed toward Juneau away from what they called The Valley—the suburbs that sprouted around the airport, cut out of nowhere, lying on the marshy flatlands of the receding Mendenhall Glacier. Jimmy said the glacier was to her left, between the mountains, hidden in the clouds. She took his word for it.

The highway followed the lowlands of Gastineau Channel and Norris watched the passing meadows, the high grasses riffling in the wind, cottonwoods in the background unfurling against the jolt of mountains thrust vertically from the sea into the clouds. These were remnants of ancient continents rammed together. Batholiths mixed in with young mountains still forming, raw mountains sprung abruptly and violently like geologic jack-in-the-boxes. In a few thousand years this place would be like Norway: craggy, dramatic, almost tamed. Now it was merely tremendous.

The clouds moved fast now, closing in, spilling down the mountainsides like runaway sundae topping, everything getting darker. She half-listened to the men talking. Something about Jimmy's grandfather. Something about a one-eyed dog.

"There's Freddy's," Smitty said, jarring her out of bliss. He was pointing at Fred Meyer's, a sprawling warehouse of a store sprung from the scrub brush of the mud flats, a store no different from thousands in the lower forty-eight. A one-store strip mall with plenty of parking.

"Nice," she said, as they passed by.

"We've got a Costco, Walmart, and the mall too," he said. "You need to find someone, but don't know how to get ahold of them? Your best bet's to sit in Freddy's parking lot. Sooner or later they'll show up. Saturday nights, the place is busier than a casino."

"Too bad we'll be in Angoon Saturday," said Jimmy. "We could have double dated. Maybe take in Costco, get some free food samples. Make it a really big night."

"Smart ass. Some of us don't get to hop a plane out of town any time we want," Smitty said, staring straight ahead.

"OK, I'm sorry. They're the best. A shopper's paradise."

Smitty was smiling now. Norris couldn't decide whether it was touching or pathetic the way he seemed to love those stores.

The rain came in a burst, clattering on the pickup roof, the driver's windshield wiper barely able to keep up with the deluge, the other flailing. They were suddenly in blurry darkness, the expressway ahead scarcely visible, a river of gray.

The squall of heavy rain passed quickly leaving them in mist. As they approached the marina, Norris could see a few of the city buildings but the heart of Juneau lay tucked around the corner. Here, she saw the sprawling waterfront at the end of the expressway, a Holiday Inn, the Totem Motel, a big mistake of a building referred to as the Plywood Palace, the arching bridge to Douglas Island, Juneau's other suburb across the channel.

By the time they parked above the marina the rain had gone. Blackberry vines glistened at the grassy edges, sunlight skipped on the water. Across the channel, the storm engulfed Douglas Island like a conjuror's trick. There in the sun one minute. Gone the next.

Jimmy tossed a soggy box of engine parts to Smitty and grabbed their dripping bags. They headed down the narrow, rain-slick catwalk to the dock, the ramp steep with the low tide. The catwalk creaked and swayed under Smitty's weight and Norris held tight to the rail expecting the ramp to collapse or shoot out from under them like a torpedo. The ramp held and they made their way to the boat, the dock bouncing with Smitty's unhinged gait.

They stopped in front of a black and white thirty-six-foot custom-built trawler, rigged for gillnetting with its booms and cables and masses of nets. A workboat needing paint. A fine boat. Norris hadn't considered what his boat might look like. She simply was prepared to adjust to anything. Anything that was different. Away from the routines of the old men and Rita's watchful, judgmental eye. Away from the person she'd become.

Jimmy hopped aboard and dumped the bags then gave Norris a hand. The deck was a tangle of nets, cable and rope, and where it was uncluttered, rain lay puddled like iridescent drops of glass. Norris took in the pungent smell of the marina—the mingling of diesel, creosote, saltwater, fish.

Smitty handed Jimmy the box of spare parts and turned to go, said in a low voice, "Ole's got the fish for Eden." "Fuck," she thought she heard Jimmy say. But Smitty was already leaving.

"I'm meeting Dix at the Red Bear. Don't forget Grandpa Jack. It sounded urgent."

"Grandpa Jack's idea of urgent is picking up Doritos and cigarettes," said Jimmy.

"Yeah, well, some people never understand the importance of Doritos. Later." Smitty waved, lumbering off, his massive back to them, his jeans barely hanging onto a behind the size of a mosquito.

"Thanks," Norris called after him.

"No problem. And watch out for that guy," he said, half turning back and shouting. Off he went, bouncing down the dock on his flattened tennis shoes, little wavelets slapping against the hulls in turn.

"He liked you."

"I liked him too."

"Good," said Jimmy, kissing her quickly and almost stumbling over the bags in a rush of sudden heat. Unbalanced, she tripped in the rigging and hit her head on the corner of the fish hold. Jimmy pulled her up.

"Shit, are you OK?" Jimmy said touching the corner of her brow above the eye.

"OK," she said.

He opened the door to the wheelhouse and tossed the bags inside.

"It's not much but it's home," he said, drawing her inside. Jimmy kicked the bags aside and pinned her against the window. The urgent matter of a proper welcome.

She was crammed between the wheel and the captain's chair, sliding toward the deck, awkward, uncomfortable, crushed against him, on fire.

"Back from Seattle already?" shouted the old fisherman staring at them from the boat in the adjacent slip. He had a pipe in his mouth and trailed a rope as though he were walking an invisible dog.

"Who's your lady friend?"

"Norris, meet Ole Johanson. Ole's a dirty old man and one lousy fisherman," Jimmy said loud enough for Ole to hear.

Norris waved backwards, half smashed against the window.

"Well, I'll leave you kids to your chores," he said, as he disappeared into his cabin leaving the invisible dog behind.

"Some chores," said Jimmy, leading her down the few steps into the tidy galley, past the head to the cabin.

NORRIS LAY WITH HER HEAD against Jimmy's bare chest, a chest as smooth and lean as a teenager's. She listened to his heartbeat and the lapping of the water against the hull, watched the orchid blush of sunset turn to plum.

Above the door to the galley hung an exquisite Tlingit mask. Raven. Watching them. Jimmy kept things neat. Much more orderly than she. The bunk opposite had its three-stripe white Hudson's Bay wool blanket tucked taut and trim. The books aligned on the teak shelving had a precision she would never achieve. Even his maps and paperwork were orderly. He must have grimaced at her room with the down quilt thrown haphazardly over her never-made bed, the stacks of books on the floor, the postcards and pictures stuck in the mirror or tacked anywhere that took her fancy, the vases of flowers everywhere, some long dead, the colorful fabrics laid over armchairs. He didn't seem dismayed though. Said it was a Matisse interior. She'd laughed and said that was a nice way of saying chaos. Excellent chaos, he'd said and kissed her.

Jimmy touched her face as though he were blind trying to memorize her. She shut her eyes as his hand trailed down her throat, across her shoulder and down her arm, the left, where he traced her long jagged scar like a river.

WHEN SHE AWOKE IT WAS DARK. Jimmy sat on the edge of the opposite bunk ripping the tags off half a dozen pairs of new white cotton socks he'd apparently bought in Seattle. "Hungry?" he asked.

"Famished," she said, getting up and whisking the covers off the bed and around her shoulders all in one swoop, warding off that special bone-chilling damp particular to living on water.

"We could make oatmeal, open a can of split pea soup, or we could go over to Eden's for her killer chili," he said, placing the socks into a drawer as Norris closed the door to the head.

"Chili," she called back through the door, combing her long hair away from her face with her fingers, vaguely wondering who Eden was.

She glanced in the small round shaving mirror hanging above the sink and saw that she was flushed with happiness. She looked healthy, gray eyes shining, almost blue. Steelhead, her father had once remarked. Eyes the color of steelhead.

Norris never thought of herself as anything but passable. Sometimes a little better, like those outdoorsy horsewomen you'd find in *Town & Country* magazine. Today though, she saw someone she'd never seen. Ravishing, she thought, amazed.

When she headed back to the bunk, Jimmy was on his way out. "I promised Eden some fish. Be right back."

"OK," Norris replied with a slight feeling of dread watching him leave. Who was this Eden? She could see him talking to Ole through the porthole and by the time she dressed, he was back.

"Beauties, huh?" Jimmy said flopping two Coho into the sink, eight- to ten-pounders. She touched their firm silvery scaly sides trying to remember how long it had been since she'd been salmon fishing. The mouth of the Columbia the summer before Bailey died she thought, recalling the smell of the tiny fishing town, Chinook. The fish rot at the river's edge.

"I offloaded most everything to the tender from the last run. Eden'd kill me if I forgot her fish," he said as he wrapped the salmon in newspaper.

"Why didn't Smitty just give them to her?" asked Norris.

14

"Smitty and Eden don't exactly get along. It's a family thing."

Jimmy unhooked the Zodiac from the stern and let it fall, splashing into the water. He jumped in and Norris followed. He fired up the outboard and they spun out into the channel, skittering across the glassy surface, a fly on ink. The lights of the bridge above reflected in the water, shimmering and swaying in their wake like a Chinese lantern parade. In a few minutes, they tied up at a deserted dock down the channel. They made their way carefully up the unlit dock to a two-story houseboat that looked primed to slide into the channel. Norris eyed the rail-less catwalk connecting the steep pitch of the embankment to the parking lot and was glad they'd come by water.

A hand-carved wooden sign above the door read "Edensaw." Jimmy tried the door and rang the old-fashioned bell by the side of the door. He started to clang it again and Norris nudged him, pointing to a scrawled note taped to the window: "Gone to Anchorage. Back in a few—Eden."

"Great," said Jimmy. Norris thought they'd leave. Instead, Jimmy took his keys and unlocked the door.

"I'll pop these in the freezer and be right back," he said, gliding toward the kitchen and leaving her in the doorway staring into a living room awash in the glimmer from the street lights on the bank behind her. The wood plank floors were painted a high-gloss black. The furniture looked like vintage Craftsman, wood and leather. But it was the art that held her. A wall of Tlingit masks, an abstract soapstone statue of a deer on the coffee table, woven baskets, a Chilkat robe on the far wall. Norris was tempted to go in, look at the robe up close. From where she was, it looked real. Museum quality. The ornate black border, bear in the center, the yellow and aqua, the fringe. An authentic vintage Chilkat robe must be worth a fortune, thought Norris. And one's hanging here? She started to take a step inside, but it felt like trespassing and Jimmy was already back. She'd ask him about it later.

"Sorry about the chili. You're in luck though," Jimmy said, locking up. "I think it's gizzard night at the Bigfoot."

"Yum."

"No, you'll love them. Guaranteed," he said as he pushed her playfully down the dock toward the Zodiac.

Norris hardly thought so. Then again, she didn't care.

THEY STEPPED BRISKLY IN THE CHILL AIR, almost running arm in arm the three blocks from the Bigfoot to the Red Bear where they would meet Smitty. That is, as briskly as they could stuffed to the gills on deep-fried chicken gizzards and fries.

The Red Bear Saloon was like most small-town working-class bars in the Northwest: crowded, noisy, cedar shingled on a far wall, scattered with men of all shapes and ages in flannel shirts, jeans, and work boots. Norris scanned the familiar room and winced when she spotted her. At the far end of the bar like they always were, this one pushing fifty, but how could you tell, desperation is such an incalculable thing. There she was, the inevitable barfly, the husky smoker's laugh, playing dice with the bartender, an eye darting to the entrance on the lookout for that special someone who might change her life. It would never happen. There but for the grace of god go I, thought Norris, turning away.

They wound their way through the tables to Smitty near the back in a booth with a thin, graying man called Dix. There was a hush in the bar as she passed, and

Norris guessed it wasn't merely the presence of a new woman in town but the collective assessment of just what kind of woman she was. A white woman with Jimmy Ketah. He was in home territory, was apparently known and liked, yet even with the more liberal influence of government workers in town, it was still basically redneck frontier country. Well, they were entitled to their opinions. And she doubted anyone would say anything to Jimmy Ketah.

The bartender, a big balding bruiser with a long handlebar mustache and a T-shirt that said "Free Mustache Rides," brought a pitcher of beer to the table. "On the house," he said as he clapped Jimmy's shoulder. "Anyone who brings good-looking women into this joint gets free beer." Jimmy introduced her to Calvin Bean and Calvin's bright blue eyes danced as he kissed her hand in a formal cartoonish manner. He winked as he headed back to the bar leaving no doubt that he was serious about the T-shirt slogan.

It didn't take long for Norris to be fatigued. She'd spent plenty of time in such places and found neither comfort nor need any more. She told Jimmy she'd go back to the boat if he didn't mind. He said he'd go with her. She said no, she'd find it—all she had to do was walk downhill and she couldn't help but run into the channel. Right?

"Right," he said and borrowed Smitty's truck to take her back.

He showed her how to light the small pot-bellied stove, how to start the engine if she had to, showed her his 1923 Winchester shotgun hidden under the bunk, the shells on the shelf behind, showed her how to load it, just in case. They stood on the deck and Jimmy held her pressed tight against him, watching the sky. Jimmy said he'd changed his mind and wouldn't go back, but

Norris said it was fine, Smitty and Dix were expecting him. What was an hour or so apart when they'd be inseparable the next two weeks fishing? In fact, they'd probably be ready to kill each other with all that togetherness. They laughed and kissed a long goodbye.

She watched as he loped up the ramp, now almost level on the incoming tide, the weak light at the top of the ramp illuminating him for a second as he passed through. He got into the pickup, waved, and disappeared in a curling trail of exhaust, the lonesome glimmer of a single red taillight dissolving into night.

It had been a long time since she cared whether anyone came or went and a moment of melancholy flooded through her. Norris looked up at the deep black sky shot through with a million brilliant stars, and thanked whatever it was that brought Jimmy Ketah to her.

She had no idea she would never see him again.

3

NORRIS WAS ON THE BUNK in a tangle of blankets. She thought she hadn't slept but wan sunlight woke her. The anger of waiting up all night for Jimmy Ketah was gone and dread lay in her stomach like buckshot. And the awful dream, dark, smothered in the sound of wings.

She played last night over again in her mind. They'd kissed good-bye. He said he didn't want to go. She'd insisted. He'd said he'd be back in a couple of hours. He hadn't returned.

Before dawn, in the dead of the sickening blackness, she'd decided to take the first flight back to Seattle. Now, in the morning light, she knew she'd have to find him first.

She didn't think Jimmy Ketah was the type to leave a woman and even if he were, she was certain he wasn't the type to abandon a boat. That's right, she thought. Calm down. It's just one night. He was with friends he hadn't seen in a while, give him a break. She could talk herself into believing he was fine for a few minutes, maybe even manage an hour, then the sickness and panic would return.

She wished she knew Smitty's last name or where he lived but hadn't a clue.

She peered through the porthole to see if Ole was up

yet and looked out on an empty slip. She jumped back as though zapped by an electric fence. The idea of the old man being there was a comfort. Someone to confide in. Someone to help her sort it out. She sat on the bunk and wanted to cry but she'd cried enough last night and crying would not find him.

She would go back to the bar. Try to trace Smitty or the man called Dix. Resolved, she threw on a navy blue wool sweater of Jimmy's over the clothes she'd slept in and headed out the door into the early morning chill.

She crossed over the expressway and followed one of the main streets into town. It meandered around the base of a hill and ended up at the foot of one of the monster state capitol buildings that gobbled up several blocks. Downtown was a mishmash of utilitarian 1970s boxes, flashy contemporary edifices and a few historic structures reminiscent of the 1890s Gold Rush. Buildings nestled against the mountains, rambling up the steep foothills, downtown receding quickly to a residential gallery hanging on the hillsides, a balcony of late-nineteenth-century wooden homes.

It was easy finding the Red Bear. Juneau was small, navigable on foot. You were either downtown near the harbor or uptown, squashed against the mountain. The bar was closed. She stood on the sidewalk trying to think what to do. She scanned the empty streets hoping an option she hadn't considered would appear. Percy's, the local drugstore/café, was open. She could go get a cup of coffee or she could go to the police.

Percy's was full of regulars starting out the day. Mostly men reading the paper over coffee and pancakes, steak and eggs. Some were clean-shaven, comfortable in suits and ties. Some weren't. The busy buzz of breakfast almost reminded her of home. Home. If she weren't so weary she'd laugh. She found a booth and slid in.

"You from the ship?" the waitress asked, coffee pot in hand. "Gayle" the nametag on her blouse read. She must have been in her thirties but it had been a rough ride. Her longish too-black hair was pulled off her face by a pink plastic hair band. A pretty face beleaguered with makeup.

"The ship?" asked Norris, unable to take her eyes off Gayle's luminescent lavender eye shadow.

"The Nordic Queen?"

It took Norris a moment to decipher.

"Oh, no. I'm staying with a friend."

"Bad night?"

"You could say that."

"I didn't think you looked like the cruise ship type."

No, she guessed she didn't with no make-up and no sleep and no shower still in her jeans and turtleneck she'd slept in and Jimmy's too big sweater. Norris self-consciously pulled a strand of flyaway hair behind her ear while Gayle poured her coffee. As soon as she was gone, Norris slipped into the ladies' room.

The face in the mirror startled her—pasty pale, her hair still French-braided but a disaster, her eyes as lusterless as slate. Then there was the shiner. Last night it was merely red and a little swollen and she'd forgotten about it. Now it was an ugly bruise. She touched the brow and winced. It didn't look too obvious as most of the bruising was right on the bone under her eyebrow, although there was deep purple discoloring along the lid that looked as though she'd applied exotic eye shadow. God, she was a sight. She washed her face with cold water and pinched her cheeks to bring up some color. She pulled her hair back and re-braided it. It wasn't clean, but at least it was tamed.

She returned to her booth, took a gulp of coffee, put a couple of bucks on the table, and left half waving, not wanting to be trapped in conversation or questions.

Norris walked past the police station three times and couldn't muster the courage to walk in. Jimmy had been gone only overnight, she told herself. She couldn't report him missing yet. She waited, undecided, and walked on past the Baranof Hotel and down the hill. There looming behind the library was a behemoth cruise ship. How'd she miss that? She walked through the waterfront park nearly empty in the early hour and stopped a moment to gape at the ship moored at the pier. A policeman holding a coffee to-go cup eyed her curiously before he crossed the street to his car. She moved on.

She walked uphill through town past the shops and bars, concentrating on nothing. She was quickly above the commercial district and walking past houses where the thought of people getting up, showering, dressing, brushing their teeth, dragging whining warm kids in pajamas out of bed, all with the certainty that today was no different from any other, made her ache. Where was he?

Her mind raced with possibilities, none of which were good. She stopped in front of a Russian Orthodox church in a small yard enclosed by a picket fence. The church was like a doll's house, painted a pristine white with Prussian blue trim, the copper dome gleaming in morning sun. It seemed inviting. A friendly place of shelter. Perhaps she could find solace in the icons and symbols, the organized myths of religion. She would welcome anything to help her mind settle. Even other people's beliefs. Religion touched her deeply when she was young. It didn't seem to help at all later. The organizing of it, the rituals, the sermons, the battle of ideas seemed hypocritical. The world was teeming with holy wars. Norris believed in something but whatever it was didn't require a group to sanction it, didn't require dressing up and going to church on Sundays. She opened the wooden door.

Inside, the smell of incense and ancient wood enveloped her. She started toward the icons on the wall and wondered if it would be blasphemous to light a candle and pray when the double doors at the back opened. As she slipped out, she barely got a glimpse of the robust, barrel shaped, red-bearded man carrying a kitten.

Norris hurried down the steps and out through the gate hoping whoever it was, probably the priest, hadn't seen her. She half-ran up the street not caring where she was going. Just away. When the pavement ended, she took a flight of stairs straight up the hillside to the next terrace of houses and paused to catch her breath. She turned and looked behind at the spectacular channel. Yesterday she would have been exhilarated but now found the sun glinting off the water cruel, the mountains jutting straight out of the sea terrifying, the sky so blue it could cut you, the air so clear she could hardly breathe.

How long had she been gone? Maybe hours. Maybe not. She made her way back to the boat hoping Jimmy would be there when she arrived. She somehow knew better but she could hope.

Ole's boat was still gone. Jimmy's boat still empty.

She stood in the galley useless and blank. She tried to convince herself that he'd soon be there with a good excuse or Smitty would show up with explanations. She went out on deck and concentrated on him walking down the dock. She shut her eyes and willed it. A raven mocked her from the spar of the *Misfit*, a fifty-two-foot sloop three slips down.

She tried to read, tried to draw, tried to eat. She sat at the end of the pier and watched the gulls drop mussels on the rocks at the water's edge then swoop down in a hurry to beat the ravens to the exposed flesh in the broken shells. She decided to try the bars again and walked along the expressway, silently cursing city planners and highway builders. Apparently it never occurred to anyone that someone might want to walk from the old marina to town. She waited for a lull in the traffic and darted across the highway to the median, waited for another opening and ran most of the way to town thinking she might now learn something. She came around the corner and found the town transformed, teeming with tourists trotting here and there in quick little groups, taking photos and pointing video cameras, surging into and out of shops.

"Weird, huh?" said Gayle, the waitress from Percy's, outside the entrance taking a cigarette break. "Thirteen hundred of them this round. They're getting their last-minute T-shirts and authentic Northwest Indian crafts made in China before they have to get back to the ship. They don't really look at anything, but then they don't have to, do they? They've got it all recorded on their video cams." Gayle took a pleasureful drag on her cigarette. "Don't look so forlorn, they'll be gone before you know it."

"Do you know Jimmy Ketah?" Norris asked.

"Sure. Most everybody knows Jimmy," said Gayle.

"Have you seen him lately?"

"Maybe three weeks? Jimmy's a great guy. He'd help you out if you were in a jam." She was staring at Norris's black eye.

Norris covered it up. "Oh, this. I fell in some rigging, hit my head."

"Uh, huh."

"I really did. I'm staying on Jimmy's boat. He didn't come back last night."

Gayle took it in. "No kidding."

"Do you know his friend Smitty?"

"Big guy? Mammoth hands?"

"Yes."

"No. I've seen him around, but he hardly ever comes into Percy's. Not like Jimmy."

"How about a man named Dix? Thin, older?"

"Oh, sure. Dix has been a regular for years. Called The Professor. Teaches at the junior college in Douglas. He lives down the street, up above the Gold Rush Mercantile, but he hangs at the Red Bear mostly. You want to come in for a cup of coffee? You look like you need it."

"Maybe later," said Norris. "I want to see if I can talk to Dix."

"If there's anything I can do, I mean, if you're in trouble or something . . ."

"I'm fine."

"If you say so." Gayle was looking at her eye.

"I tripped, really."

"Sure. It can happen," said Gayle, unconvinced.

"Really. I'm fine. Thanks."

"Anytime."

Norris left Gayle stubbing her cigarette out on the sidewalk and threaded her way through the crowds to the Gold Rush Mercantile to see if she could find Dix. She found the door to the upstairs apartments next to a life-sized wooden chainsaw-carved statue of a miner holding a gold pan. The green door with red trim matched the bright façade of the store. Inside, another matter. The one light bulb high in the entry had burned out so she left the door partially open to daylight. She climbed the stairs and asked a woman bundled in a sleeping bag on the landing if she knew where Dix lived.

"Number three," the woman said in a mush since she had no teeth.

25

Norris walked up a flight, found number three and knocked. Knocked again.

"If you want The Professor, he's not in."

Now she tells me, thought Norris. "Do you know where I can find him?"

"No. Not that I'd tell you, being you're a stranger."

"Suppose I'm a friend of his."

"Suppose you're not," she said shrewdly.

"Well, I don't actually know Dix," Norris confessed.

"Told you!" the woman said in a burst, pointing a finger at her.

"I'm looking for Jimmy Ketah and thought Dix might know where he is."

"You got a problem."

"What do you mean?"

"Nothin'," said the woman pulling the sleeping bag around her tight.

"Do you know where Jimmy Ketah is?"

"You find The Professor, he'll tell you." And that was it. She crumpled her lips tight and said no more.

NORRIS SPENT MOST OF THE DAY going from bar to bar hunting for any information on Jimmy, Smitty, or Dix, and now pulled open the glass doors of the police station. The lobby was a twenty-by-thirty utilitarian room with too-bright buzzing overhead fluorescent lighting, a matching pair of faux leather brown couches, one with the surface cracked and a shank of foam protruding like a festering wound. Well-thumbed magazines spilled across the coffee table.

She stood before two large windows dominating a side wall. The left said Motor Vehicles, Traffic Tickets, Licenses. Norris chose the right: Complaints, Disputes, Reports.

A strawberry blond sat sorting papers, head down at a desk under a shelf filled with stuffed animals and potted plants. The woman looked up and Norris was momentarily jarred that she was so fresh-faced. Freckled. Young. If she didn't know better, Norris would guess she'd stumbled into a dorm room rather than a police station.

"Can I help you?" the strawberry blond asked.

"I need to file a report for a missing person," said Norris, her heart pounding, her mouth dry.

What she wanted, the bright-eyed, scrubbed-faced young woman said, was an RTL.

"An RTL?" asked Norris.

"A Request to Locate?" the young woman clarified.

"Yes," Norris said.

Norris finished filling out the form at the coffee table and handed it back through the slot at the bottom of the window. The woman picked it up and scanned it.

"You forgot to put a phone number where we can contact you."

Norris was a throwback, didn't have a cell phone.

"OK then." A look of astonishment, reading, "Staying at the old marina huh? Tell you what, you call back in a day or so. The best thing to do is to go home. People nearly always show up."

"Thanks," said Norris, wanting to believe her.

THE MUSEUM SAT ON A SMALL LAWN trimmed with flowerbeds of marigolds, flanked by two totems. Norris paid her admission and walked through the museum trying to concentrate, trying to find something that would take her mind away. A sculpture. A painting. An exhibit. She cruised by the logging and mining displays then turning a corner saw a photo of a Chilkat robe much like the one she'd seen at Eden's. Eden. Maybe she was back from Anchorage. The note had said 'a few.' What? Days? It'd been a few days . . . No. Only one. How could it seem so long ago and only be a day? Regardless, she had to go. She'd launch the Zodiac and go to Eden's.

"Leaving so soon?" the attendant asked, alarmed as though Norris had found the museum wanting.

"I'm sorry, I forgot . . . I have an appointment," Norris said lamely.

NORRIS COULD SEE THE PIECE of paper on the trawler from the ramp. Taped to the transom above the door, flapping in the breeze. Jimmy! she thought, and began running. She scrambled onto the deck and tore the note off the door. "Miss Reed," it read, "Please contact Juneau Police Department." It gave a telephone number and an extension. Heart beating, Norris flew off the boat and down the dock. She crossed the highway, nearly getting run down by an SUV passing a cement mixer, and ran into the Totem Motel, where she thought she'd find the nearest phone.

As she opened the door, a middle-aged woman vacuuming the lobby scowled at her then went to the counter and handed Norris the desk phone. The woman pretended not to watch, fiddled with the vacuum as she carefully listened in.

"Did they find him? . . . OK I'll be there," was all the woman got to hear.

When Norris rounded the corner a block away from the police station, she saw a large Indian man holding the entry doors for an Indian woman, possibly in her forties, impossible to tell.

"Smitty!" Norris called and waved, nearly jumping with happiness. The man looked right through her.

Norris was momentarily confused then felt foolish, watching them disappear behind the building to the parking lot. It wasn't Smitty. Or if it was, maybe he'd been arrested and didn't want her to see him. Maybe that's what had happened. Smitty and Jimmy had gotten in trouble and were in custody.

Relieved, Norris went to Complaints, Disputes, Reports. The desks behind the windows were now full of women visiting with each other, filing, typing, answering phones. She could see the strawberry blond watching her but it was a sharp-featured brunette who told her to go out the first set of doors and up the stairway to find Alex Tanner in Criminal Investigations.

At the top of the stairs she found a warren of partitioned cubicles and began to walk down the aisle looking for his door.

"Can I help you?" asked a weaselly-looking guy in uniform, posturing like he was in charge. His uniform pants were too short and his mousy brown patch of hair looked as though he'd plastered it down with fresh spit.

"Alex Tanner wants to see me."

"I bet he does," he said slyly, looking at her with a greasy smile. Then, coming toward her, confiding, "You're the one down at Harris docks with the Indian, right? Guess Alex's got some news for you."

She took a breath. "Actually, he didn't say."

He smirked like he knew something she didn't, which, of course, he did. It made Norris uncomfortable knowing he knew anything about her. Especially where she was staying. "Is he in?" she asked, edging to the hall.

"You think I keep track of him?" he said, casually picking a tooth with a fingernail. He found what he wanted and looked at it.

29

"What's up, Farley?"

The weasel jerked to attention and Norris turned to see a stout man in tan slacks and a crisp blue dress shirt. He was as trim and solid as a fat man could be. Close-shaven, meticulously so with plenty of cologne that reached Norris at ten paces. There's something repellant about certain well-fed close-shaven men, she thought. His nametag read V. Humboldt.

She explained she was looking for Alex Tanner and was directed down the hall and around the corner. Second door on the left.

She knew Humboldt and the creep were watching her. She picked up her pace. The confinement of the police station made her uneasy with its too-warm interior, the depressing lighting, the cubicles, the anticipation of an inquisition where she would probably be thought of as nothing more than a foolish woman. Jilted. She could already hear Rita saying, "I told you so" and could see the smarmy smiles on those two out front. She resolved to turn the corner and keep going as soon as she was out of sight. She'd follow the exit signs and leave without anyone knowing. She couldn't face anyone right now. She'd talk to Detective Tanner later. She wondered how long it would take them to discover that she'd never talked to him. Would they care? After all, she was the one who filled out the missing report. She hurried down the hall.

She passed Tanner's office and saw the exit door at the end of the hall. She ran toward it, already relieved. She pushed down on the door bar handle. It didn't budge. She tried again. Locked. She hit the side of the door and wanted to cry. She started back down the hall and ducked into the ladies' room to collect her thoughts. She leaned against the inside wall. What was she doing? She'd come here for help and now she was panicked. She was avoiding what made her afraid, the seriousness of what she might learn, an outcome she couldn't face. One thing was certain: she couldn't stay in the ladies' room. The smell of the deodorizer was sickening.

She made her way back down the hall to Alex Tanner's door. She stood for a moment, heart racing, irrationally wanting to escape, do this tomorrow, anytime but now, yet not wanting to pass by the two men out front again. She spotted the drinking fountain and took a long cool drink. She put her face into the stream of water and let it flow.

"Enjoying yourself?"

Norris wiped her face on her sleeve and turned to see a man in jeans and a black polo shirt leaning in the doorway, holding a coffee cup. He smiled.

"Detective Tanner?" she asked, making a not very broad leap in deduction since his coffee cup had "Alex" written across it in Gothic script. He looked at it and smiled.

"Investigator Tanner," he said.

He had a kind, informal style, and the trim, well-proportioned body of a baseball player. In his early forties, he was nearly handsome with a slightly crooked nose, closely shorn brown hair gently receding, amber eyes almost green. A wholly likeable face. Not a face that she would imagine belonging to a cop. Not that she'd ever thought about it. He simply seemed different. Nothing at all like the two out front, Humboldt and Farley. This one was relaxed, open, someone who could be a friend. Norris needed a friend. But she doubted Alex Tanner was it.

"What can I do for you?"

"I'm Norris Reed. You wanted to see me?"

His expression changed. He motioned her to come inside his office.

The room was unexceptional—a metal filing cabinet, adequate shelving, a military-issue metal desk and green faux leather-seated metal-framed chairs. Nothing fancy or even interesting save the dog calendar on his wall—a setter with a pheasant in its mouth, courtesy of Janof's Hardware.

"So you found Jimmy," she said.

It took him aback.

"The officer out front, he . . ." she started.

"Farley has a big mouth. Sit down, Miss Reed."

It was Mrs. actually but she didn't correct him, never used it. "Did you find him?"

He didn't answer.

"Do you know where he is?"

Alex sat down staring at his desk as though it was the most compelling thing he'd ever seen.

"Yes," he said.

"Are you going to tell me?"

He came around and sat at the edge of the desk in front of her, one foot dangling, the other planted on the floor. He contemplated the carpeting. Norris couldn't bear looking at him so looked at the floor too.

"If you know where he is, please tell me," she said, barely audible.

He looked at her carefully. Norris looked up. Now she was sorry he had that readable face.

"He's in the morgue," Alex Tanner said quietly.

The shock struck like a cobra. Quick pain. Circuits blown. Blackness. An awful, long silence.

"Can I see him?" Her heart pounding.

"He's already been identified."

"It was Smitty then."

"Do you know him?"

"We just met."

"Would you mind telling me what your relationship is to the deceased?"

"We're friends."

Alex nodded.

"Lovers. I came up here to fish with him." She took a breath, "I need to see him."

"His nearest relative has already identified him. There's no reason for you to."

"Smitty isn't a relative is he?"

"No." Alex didn't want to finish the sentence. "But his wife Charlotte is."

Norris stared at him as he carefully aligned the pencils on his desk.

"Jimmy's wife," she said quietly, the air knocked out of her.

"Can I get you something to drink? Coffee? Water?" asked Alex quickly, jumping off the desk as though he were sitting on stove.

"Water," mumbled Norris.

Alex grabbed his coffee cup and hustled out the door.

It hadn't occurred to Norris to ask if Jimmy Ketah were married. He didn't seem married, not that she knew how married seemed. Maybe it was ex-wife. No, not the way Alex Tanner had said it. He was embarrassed for her. She was grateful he left. She considered leaving before he came back but decided no matter what the circumstances were she had to see the body. Finish it.

Alex brought the water back in his "Alex" mug. Her first instinct was to pour it over her head so she could wake up. She drank it instead. A long moment went by.

Then Norris asked softly, "Can I see the body?"

"I'm afraid not. It's in Anchorage awaiting an autopsy," he said.

"How did he die?"

"Not pretty."

"A car wreck, what?"

33

"He was murdered. He was stabbed and then bludgeoned. Or bludgeoned then stabbed. We won't know exactly until the autopsy's done."

"I have to see him."

He hesitated.

"Please."

"I don't think so," he said.

Norris stared at her hands, lifeless in her lap. "I need to."

Alex watched her. Crumpled. Deflated. Barely breathing. He slowly reached into a folder lying on his desk. He slid a couple of photographs across the desk to Norris without a word.

She looked. Photos of a man lying face down in an alley wearing jeans and a blood-soaked plaid shirt, no shoes, only socks. Dark stains lay like a halo around his head, a rivulet flowing from his ear to a small puddle beside his elbow. She tried to detach.

"I need to see his face."

"I'm afraid that's impossible," he said firmly. They stared at each other, Norris defying him. Belligerent. What difference could it make?

"He doesn't have a face," Alex said, handing her another photo, this of the man turned over, where a face should be, a featureless pulpy mass.

Norris shut her eyes then looked again. She studied both photographs carefully.

She would have screamed, would have torn the place apart, would have collapsed. But the dead man in the photos was not Jimmy Ketah.

4

ALEX HAD WARNED HER ABOUT the face but hadn't said there weren't any hands.

"It's not him," Norris said, barely getting it out before she ran, groping her way down the hall to the ladies' room where she vomited into the sink. Scraps of chicken gizzards swimming in bile. Yellow vile liquid, coffee-tinted. She stood gripping the sink, dry heaving. She wished she could stop but the spasms kept coming. Then Alex was there turning on the cold tap, wetting a paper towel, holding it out to her. She stopped heaving but didn't have the strength to move. Her arms trembled, still gripping the sink.

"You OK?" he asked.

She couldn't speak. Couldn't let go of the sink.

He took her shoulders and carefully turned her around. He washed her face like a kid and she started to cry. She couldn't help it. It wasn't the shock of seeing the body in particular. It was something else. Release. The relief of it not being Jimmy. The cop's tender touch. The stupid wet towel on her face.

"I'm fine, I just . . ." choking back, embarrassed. She took a dry paper towel and wiped her face. She tried to recover but he looked so tragic she was overcome again. Alex reached out and pulled her in, letting her sob.

She caught her breath and composed herself.

"It's not him."

"I know you're upset and that's what you want to believe."

"It isn't his body. The arms . . . That looks like his shirt but they're not his socks."

Alex looked at her.

"I saw him put on brand new socks before we left the boat. White tube socks with a red stripe at the top. Those man's socks were dark. And short."

"Maybe you only thought you saw him put on new socks. And the angle of the body was all funny jammed against the bank like that. Something like that can . . ."

"I should look at the photos again."

"I don't think that's such a good idea." He was being kind. He was almost pleading with her.

"Please. I'm sure I'm right."

Alex held the door open for her.

"How long did you say you'd known Jimmy Ketah?" Alex asked.

It was ridiculous. She considered lying. Two days would sound so implausible. A few months or a year maybe. But two days? She would lie. What would it hurt?

"Two days," she said.

Alex looked at her quizzically. Was he going to laugh? No.

"Must have been some two days."

"Yes."

"Are you into rough stuff?"

"What do you mean?" she asked.

He was looking at her eye.

"Oh, that," she said, touching her eyebrow. "I hit my head on the boat last night."

Alex nodded.

36

Humboldt shuffled papers around his desk pretending not to watch as they left the ladies' room and rounded the corner to enter Alex's office, Alex guiding her through the door with his hand at the small of her back.

"I wouldn't mind a piece of that," said Farley, leaning into Humboldt's office.

"You're sure you want to do this?" Alex asked, retrieving more photos from the manila file.

"I'm sure."

He handed her photographs.

This time, the naked body on a slab at the morgue. The face was covered with a piece of cloth, but the garish bloody stumps of the chopped-off hands were exposed. Norris made herself look carefully at the body, waxy and pale. Not human. Slightly yellow and lavender tinted with deeper purple bruises on the chest and arms. The puncture under the rib cage that must have hit the heart. Somebody knew how to use a knife. So how come the face was a mass of pulp and the hands were chopped off? She looked away. Back to the chest. To the feet, now naked without the socks. There was no doubt about it. Even though their frames were similar, she knew every inch of Jimmy Jack Ketah and whoever this poor man was, it wasn't him.

"No," she said.

"You're sure?"

"Positive."

"It has to be."

"It isn't. Jimmy Ketah has long, elegant fingers and toes. This man's body is too compact, not lean enough."

"You've only known him two days."

Norris looked at Alex. Could he sleep with a woman and not know her body? She doubted it.

"I've got witnesses who say it's him."

"They're wrong."

37

"I'm sorry you think so," Alex was losing patience, putting the photos in the folder.

Humboldt stood in the doorway. "So his feet are too stumpy for you and his dick's too short? Maybe things shrivel up a bit when you die."

Alex bridled. "Look, Miss Reed, the case is already closed. We picked up the punks who did this not more than an hour ago."

"We've got a positive ID and Jimmy Ketah's wallet was in his back pocket. Got his cell phone too. What more do you want?" said Humboldt.

"Where's his down vest? He had on a green down vest. And his socks?" said Norris.

"Socks?" Humboldt said, raised his eyebrows at Alex.

Alex was quiet.

"Why would they cut off his hands?" she asked.

"Maybe a white supremacy thing," said Humboldt.

"Who knows," said Alex.

"Doesn't it seem strange? Overkill?" asked Norris.

"Nothing seems strange anymore," said Alex.

"Hell, one of 'em has green hair," said Humboldt as though that were explanation enough.

"It doesn't matter does it?" she said. "It's probably a convenience. A fact of life in Alaska. Indians die. All they have to do is drink until somebody gets plastered enough to shove a knife in somebody's ribs. Happens all the time. Right?"

"Sometimes they use baseball bats. Or freeze." Humboldt said, snorting a burst of laughter.

"I'm sorry I took up your time," Norris said, leaving as fast as she could. She stopped at the door.

"It's not him."

Humboldt stood in the doorway, arms crossed, watching her retreat.

"Nutcase," he said.

A BREEZE CAME IN OFF THE CHANNEL. Norris stood in front of the police station wanting to run but unable to move. Her body felt heavy and large, an immense useless thing waiting for a command that she could not muster. Two uniformed officers joking with each other burst out of the doors and gave her the once-over as they skirted around her on the way to their patrol cars. One of them looked back at her with an uncomfortable questioning gaze on the verge of scorn. Norris covered her eye with her hand and hustled downhill to the pier. She leaned on the rail and stared into the milky green glacial water.

Alex Tanner could be right. She was distressed. Numb. She couldn't bear to have that corpse be Jimmy. Bailey, her husband, was enough. Jimmy couldn't be gone too. She wouldn't let him.

Every time she thought of Bailey, her heart clenched as though he had a grip on her still. She'd been through it a thousand times: Bailey did what Bailey had to do. It had little to do with her. At the time, they all said it was an accident. They stuck to that story still.

Before Bailey died, Norris knew their marriage was in trouble, but every time she thought of divorce she felt sick. She wished she could pick up and leave. She wished she could smother him in his sleep. Instead, she was paralyzed with faith. She always believed in him and he always let her down. It was almost laughable. His last embarrassment was the checkout girl at the local market three blocks from their apartment. She was blond, giggling, and wore lipstick the shade of bubblegum. Norris hoped she was over seventeen.

After eight years, love turned to habit. Habit became addiction. Norris hated the very thought of separation—the tears, the anger, the recriminations, the explaining to parents, the whole ugly mess of it.

In a way, Bailey solved all that. One fine autumn morning after a pleasant outing together at a U-pick orchard, he coolly, calmly, drove off the Wenatchee Bridge. It could still stop Norris cold, the terror of the splitting rail, that flight in slow motion. The sudden bewildered silence and nothing but sky, a flash of senseless thought that she'd left the iron on at home, apples everywhere, falling. She was reaching for Bailey and the next instant they were plunging waterborne and he was gone. She drifted for a mile or two in the heavy fall runoff, tangling and spinning with logs and debris. A cataract caught her and sucked her under. But a Douglas fir wouldn't let her go. She was caught in its branches, buoyed up and out of the water, the tree like some demented porpoise, her arm nearly ripped off at the shoulder. She lay on its back holding on with her good arm and let it take her where it might.

She was fished out, stitched up, sent to Rita and Joe.

An accident, they said. A terrible accident but Norris suspected not. Bailey wasn't the type to have accidents. He simply couldn't face it anymore: thirty-two years old and still catching Double-A ball. Two semi-successful knee operations and not a chance in hell to make it to the Major Leagues. And it was just like Bailey to take her with him. He never could stand being alone.

She listened to the sympathetic mourning murmurs with stunned silence. She couldn't lash out, share the burden of his final act. She had no one to confide in. Not the baseball wives, who had little in common with her but their primordial preference for a certain type of male. Not his parents, or hers, who idolized him. Yes, a terrible, terrible accident.

She knew there wasn't anyone to blame. Not their parents, the hometown crowd, a lifetime of hope attached to him. Not the promoters. Not the foolish groupies ready to do anything to snag a ballplayer, married or otherwise, their ticket to somewhere, anywhere, out. Not the starry-eyed young boys asking for autographs, treating the players like heroes, feeding their cockiness, making them believe they were gods when most of them were just boys themselves. Not the hype of sports on television that made them all yearn for an impossible thing, made everything else seem vague and thin. She knew all this, but in the end blamed no one but herself.

When her arm healed, the anger was gone. Sympathy came and sadness emptied her out. She was nothing. In desperation, she drank everything she could lay her hands on and slept with anyone who was convenient. She had resented them all, including Bailey's teammates whom she inevitably found in her bed but took their selfish charity and was grateful for it. She took everything anyone had to give hoping someone would numb her pain. After a while, in some raw corner of her besotted rotting brain, realization took hold like a tumor: all the vodka and men in the world wouldn't obliterate a single thing.

She began with sketching the café life. Rita and Joe. The old men—a diary of sorts connecting her to the living. She'd majored in art at college and she began to revive the pleasure that had buoyed her throughout the long baseball seasons with Bailey on the road. She couldn't grasp it now.

Norris looked out across the channel—maybe Bailey had it right. A solution flooded her brain. How long could you survive in glacial water? Three minutes? Four? Night would be best. No one to see you. No one tempted to save you. She ran away from the thought, up the street away from the water, running until she was out of breath, panting as she leaned against a wall. Two doors down, she saw a bar and made for it.

What the hell, she thought. Another old solution.

"What can I get you, darlin'?" the bartender said in a singsong drawl like he was in some western town. Alaska was as west as you could get, but this far north, what people thought of as the true West was east. The West of the imagination was cowboys and horses, plains and ponderosas—Texas, Wyoming, Montana. This was the great wooded Northwest, rainforest fishing country, timber country, where mole people were shrouded in the mossy dense forests of their damp lives. This wasn't Big Sky country. This was Big Rain country.

Most people didn't understand the distinctions between the Northwest and the West. Those huddled west of the Cascades, riding the shores of the Pacific, had more in common with Ireland or England than they did the vast thundering forlorn sage-brushed wheatlands of their east-of-the-mountains counterparts.

Maybe Norris should go to Montana. A sky like that could heal a person, she thought. With a landscape that open you couldn't help but let the wind whip you as clean as bone. The thought of being as pure as a wind-dried skeleton cheered her for a moment. But she wasn't in Montana. She was water logged and sodden in a miserable overbuilt frontier town.

"Ma'am?" the bartender said.

Norris went outside leaving him shrugging to his lone customer hunched over a shot of rye. She backed against the brick wall. Lord, she could use a drink. Not this time, girl. Work to do. She walked three doors down to the Red Bear. The bartender still hadn't seen Smitty but Dix was sitting at the back table.

Dix looked gray, his face pinched and grave in the low light. Hadn't he slept either? He absently stirred a cup of coffee. Dix looked up. His eyes were rimmed in red.

Was he crying? Hung over? High?

"I'm Norris. We met the other night?"

He shoved a chair out with his foot, an unspoken invitation to sit. Italian loafers without socks. Expensive. Worn.

"Hell of a thing," he said rubbing his eyes with the back of his hand. "Tough on you, huh?"

"Did you see the body?" Norris asked.

"Nope. Smitty and Charlotte came by."

"What did they say?" she asked.

"What could they say? Smitty lost his best friend."

"And she lost her husband."

"Yeah. I don't suppose she was too broke up."

"What do you mean?"

It dawned on him. "Jimmy didn't tell you about Charlotte."

"No."

"No need to. Charlotte and Jimmy parted years ago. She's been living with Smitty since, hell, I don't know. She and Jimmy married when he got back from the Gulf. Parted early. Charlotte wasn't anything to Jimmy more than an irritating sister he couldn't shake. And had to support for the rest of his life. They have one kid, an eleven-year-old girl. Charlotte and Smitty have two, three, I don't know, who can keep track of kids?"

Jimmy has a daughter. What next? "Do you know where Smitty and Charlotte are now?"

"Probably back in Angoon. They live out at the village in Jimmy's old house. They could have caught the two o' clock. Or they could be shopping. Charlotte likes to shop."

"The two o' clock?"

"The afternoon floatplane to Admiralty Island."

"Do you think they'd mind if I talked to them?"

"I don't think they'd bend over backwards to oblige

you. Smitty'd be all right, but just try to get to him without Charlotte. She keeps him on a pretty tight rein. And Charlotte? Well, she never was happy with Jimmy but she's the type who doesn't want anyone else to have him either."

"What about the daughter?"

Dix laughed. "Oh, she'd talk to you all right."

"I tried to find you at your apartment yesterday and a toothless woman told me you'd know where Jimmy was. It may have been my imagination, but she seemed like she already knew about the body."

He tried to keep it light, but the laughter was sucked out of him. "She likes to talk. Besides, I usually do know where he is. You shouldn't pay any attention to her. She's confused. Wet brain."

He reached for his coffee and his sleeve inched up revealing red scratches on the inside of his arm as though an angry cat had attacked him. Norris tried not to stare. He pulled his sleeve down. Shooting meth? Cocaine? Heroin? Maybe it was a cat. Norris didn't know. Norris was beginning to believe she didn't know anything. She'd come to a strange land with a stranger.

A couple of strung-out men with greasy hair under hooded sweatshirts came into the bar and headed straight for the bathroom. Dix eyed them and excused himself. "Sorry. Friends I need to see."

Dix shuffled to the bathroom in his worn loafers, his stonewashed gray jeans loose on his slim frame. The sun was full on her from the high windows but Norris was cold.

5

NORRIS ENDED THE CELL CALL and leaned over, pressing her forehead against the table. She'd wanted to talk to Rita but hearing her voice had made Norris speechless. Telling Rita would make it real. She dialed Warren and let it ring. She hung up, glad for once that he still lived in the eighteenth century. No computers or cell phones or answering machines for Warren.

She dialed the number she'd found in the phone book and written on her hand. Jimmy Ketah, Angoon. An older woman answered.

"Is Smitty there?" asked Norris.

"Oh. Let me see," said the woman, yelling Smitty are you here with no answer back. "Nope. He must be out."

"Is Jimmy there?" asked Norris, berating herself the minute she'd said it.

A pause. Clicked off.

Stupid, stupid, stupid, thought Norris. They'd heard of his death and her asking for Jimmy was too cruel. She knew the body wasn't his. Apparently they didn't.

She punched in the number again.

Picked up. Silence.

"I need to talk to someone about Jimmy," she said quickly before they could cut her off, which is exactly what they did.

Through the window, she could see the throng scuttling from shop to shop in the drizzle, some older couples wearing matching shirts under their raincoats. So they wouldn't lose each other? Her stomach lurched. If only she and Jimmy had had matching shirts . . . I'm going mad she thought.

"You doin' OK?" asked Gayle.

Norris tried to smile, handing her the cell phone. "Thanks for the phone. I thought you said the tourists were headed back to the ship," said Norris.

"Hon, this is the afternoon bunch. Only eleven hundred on this one."

A man entered wearing an olive drab Army issue raincoat and black wool beret with a yellow and red striped Army Delta Force pin fastened to the side.

"Don't ask," said Gayle, nodding toward him and leaving Norris to deliver a coffee refill to her customers.

The man waited in the aisle between the café booths and the drugstore shelves alert, listening to something only he could hear, then darted to the magazine racks where he began to berate the magazines for misconduct. Norris wished she were closer and could hear. Whatever it was, he was adamant. He scolded, gesturing in small clipped motions. When he was finished, he straightened up and sat at the cafe counter where Mimi, a pixie of a waitress with kewpie doll lips, served him orange juice without asking. He furtively looked to each side before he pulled a tightly rolled newspaper from inside his raincoat and carefully laid it on the counter where he read it with his index finger. That done, he tapped the article with his finger sharply, rolled it back up and slipped it inside his raincoat. He pulled out a twenty-dollar bill and brandished it toward Mimi.

"Twenty dollars! No cops!" he said and brusquely shoved it back in his inside pocket. From his pants pocket he retrieved a quarter and laid it neatly on the counter.

He made his way to the door stiff and erect in the manner of an army commander just having finished inspection. Halfway to the door, he passed the freestanding gumball machine where he stopped, frowned, and quickly gave it a smack on its glass head and walked out the door.

"That's Mick," said Gayle, now next to Norris again. "We call him Captain Paranoid. He thinks he's persecuted by the CIA or the FBI or some mysterious government agency. Whatever, it's all spies and subterfuge to him. Totally off his rocker but harmless. Welcome to Juneau. Hey, how about that cup of coffee? Or better yet, something to eat."

"Thanks. Maybe later," said Norris.

"Sure. Did you have any luck?"

"Dix was at the bar, but I haven't found Smitty yet. Do you know if Jimmy had a place in town?"

"Gee, I don't know. Let me ask Ray," said Gayle. She went to the far end of the counter and talked to a middle-aged Indian man in a shiny black satin jacket emblazoned across the back with a burning cross.

"Ray says Eden's," called Gayle.

Of course Eden's, thought Norris. Jimmy had the keys.

THE BOAT FELT WRONG. The books and dishes in the galley seemed to be in the same place and her drawing pencils and watercolor paint set sat untouched on the shelf behind the table. She carefully lowered herself down the steps into the galley. There was the faint scent of . . . a man's cologne. Brut. There was no mistaking it. Bailey used to wear Brut. The back of her neck tightened. She didn't move, sniffed again. Now it was gone. Or she was used to it. She walked into the galley and grabbed a butcher knife. With her left hand, she banged a pan on the stove. She made her way noisily to the cabin, pretending to be in conversation, hoping to stir whoever might be hiding in the cabin. No sound except the slight creaking of the boat as it adjusted to the incoming tide. She stopped and listened by the head. This is not too bright, she thought. If there is someone with bad intentions in there, I've trapped him. I'm toast.

"Hello," she called. "Anybody home?" changing her tone, making it seem like she was an innocent, had merely stopped by to visit. Perhaps that was the best way. Then whoever it was could graciously find an excuse for being there rather than bash her brains in and dump her overboard.

"Hellooo," she said again and stepped into the empty cabin. Relieved, she sat on the bunk and leaned back against the bulkhead. You dope, she thought.

THE ZODIAC'S OUTBOARD MOTOR responded on the third pull. Norris hated rope-pull two-stroke engines. That's why she never mowed the lawn. Not that she'd ever had a lawn. Except when she was a kid and for some reason her sister Rita always did the mowing. At least she knew how it worked. They'd had plenty of experience with outboards growing up. Lived on a lake. Summer picnics to islands, water-skiing, fishing. Norris cleared the marina, increased speed and spun out onto the channel, skimming the evening chop.

She walked up the dock to Eden's houseboat and rang the bell. Eden's note was still taped to the front window but she rang the bell and knocked anyway. She checked the side windows to see if she could see anything. Nothing had changed since she'd been there with Jimmy two days ago. Two days? It couldn't have been only two days.

She tried a likely key from the ring of keys she'd taken from the boat. If he were planning on ditching her or hiding out here, wouldn't he have taken the keys? The door opened and she slipped inside quickly, shutting the door behind her.

She called out. No one answered back.

The wall of masks in the living room kept watch as Norris made her way silently through to the bedroom. It was sumptuous compared to the white-walled almost museum starkness of the living room. The walls were a deep red matching the Persian rug. A queen-sized bed was covered in a rich patterned tapestry of golds and blues, luscious and seductive like something out of *The Arabian Nights*. Norris gingerly opened the closet and found a few silk kimonos, vintage dresses and dozens of shoes from expensive hiking boots to hand-stitched Italian heels.

Norris tried to imagine her. Art collector? Artist? Whoever Eden was, she had taste and she had money and she was eccentric. And she was a direct link to Jimmy Ketah.

Norris retreated to the living room and out the kitchen door to an enclosed porch where she found the freezer that Jimmy must have used. She opened the lid and saw the fish bound in their newspaper wrappers just as Jimmy had left them. Norris touched the paper and closed the lid. Oilskin jackets, rain gear, a Navy pea coat and a couple of flannel shirts draped on a row of hooks next to the back door. There were fishing poles and nets, hip boots and rubber knee high boots in two sizes. His and hers. Just outside the porch door on the landing were steps descending to another, newer dock under

construction and a stairway up to a new addition. The
door at the top was unlocked. She turned the knob and
walked in.

The room was in the midst of renovation. A
bathroom was being added and the skylight windows
were a gaping hole to the sky covered with visqueen. A
twin bed with a red wool Hudson's Bay blanket was
against the wall opposite the window. A long table at
one end was strewn with the tools of Jimmy's trade.
Unfinished masks lay across the table and on the lone
dresser. Frog. Bear. Eagle. Raven again but a different
expression from the one on the boat. Norris smiled to
herself. She'd asked him who did the mask on the boat
and he'd said, oh, someone. She'd known. She'd said uh,
huh and he smiled drawing her to him. Norris fingered
the masks, the tools, drew lines in the sawdust of the
cedar. Jimmy's room.

He hadn't been there recently. Norris looked out the
window to the channel. "Where are you?" she said out
loud. She suddenly felt fatigued. She sat on his bed and
leaned back, watching the rain patter the visqueen
above. She almost considered she'd made a mistake. No.
It wasn't his body. It wasn't.

She fell asleep and woke to the sound of a door
closing and footsteps coming up the stairs. She lay still
and listened, her heart thundering in her ears. The
footsteps stopped halfway up and then retreated. The
porch door banged shut and she heard an outboard start
up. She ran to the window in time to see a fairly large
man in a red baseball cap and black slicker speeding out
of sight in a dull green skiff. Get out now, you fool, she
thought to herself. Rushing down the stairs, a lingering
scent of Brut.

6

ALEX LOOKED AT HER HALF SMILING. He took notes but she had an idea that he was doodling.

"Was there anything missing?"

Not that she could tell. Did she recognize the man? No.

"The so-called intruder could have been staying at Eden's," said Alex. "The way it looks to me, you were the trespasser. You have no way of knowing that the man followed you or even knew that you were there."

"But the cologne."

"A lot of men wear similar colognes. Your imagination's got the best of you. Why don't you call it a day and get some sleep? Would you like me to drive you to the marina?"

"Thanks, but there are a few things I need to do first."

"The bars again?"

"Yes," she said almost defiantly. "That body is not Jimmy."

"I double checked with Smitty and Charlotte. They're real certain the body is him."

"I don't know why they're doing this," she said and left.

He was right. Brut was fairly common. She could picture Bailey in their bathroom, splashing it on and slapping his face with vigor, smiling at himself, leaving her for another night out with the boys. You know how

51

it is, babe, he'd say. And she thought she did. Didn't begrudge him time with his teammates. Until she found out how it really was. Those supposed nights out with the boys. How many women was it? One, two, ten? She asked a couple of the players who she thought were her friends. It wasn't their place to tell her, was it? Some sort of code of honor among them. The wives played the game too. Ignorance is bliss. Roger was the one who finally told her. Roger Cooke, the big lunk of a pitcher, the only one of the old group who made it to the Majors. He told her Bailey was out of control, one in every town, you know. Bailey vehemently denied it. Accused her of sleeping with Roger. And when it was all over at the end of summer, apple picking season, the lingering scent of Brut in the closet, in the bathroom, on the pillowcases . . .

I'll leave my name and number at the Red Bear, she thought, then go back to the boat and try and get some sleep. Then she remembered she didn't have any number to leave. Alex had a point. She was tired and maybe she wasn't thinking too clearly. She crossed the street and went the two blocks to the Red Bear anyway and was glad to see the bartender, Calvin Bean. He was concerned, looked at her curiously when she asked if he'd seen Jimmy.

"Jimmy? Didn't they tell you?"

"I'm sorry, I meant Smitty."

"Smitty. Naw, he hasn't been around. For a minute there, you had me freaked. I mean, like you thought Jimmy was still alive or something and you were going mental on us. How about a beer?" He poured a draft of Alaskan Amber before she could say anything and slid it to her with a flourish. He kept his blue eyes locked on her. She smiled and drank slowly, swiveling her bar stool around to keep an eye on the crowd. She drank half and called it quits. Sure, he'd give Smitty a message the next time he saw him. Was she positive she didn't want to stick around, have another beer? Try the famous Smoked Porter? You never know who might wander in. No, she said, thanks. If there was anything he could do, and he meant it. He had the afternoons off, they could go out to the glacier or something—she could use some distraction. Thanks, she said. No. But thanks.

The beer made her light-headed. She'd walk it off. Maybe get something to eat. She wandered up the street and came to a group of stoned teenagers huddled on the corner playing a game of dare with their lighters. Who was the coolest? Who could leave his hand in the flame the longest? They eyed her as she approached and she couldn't tell if they were friendly or menacing. She took an abrupt right, away from them, and walked into the alley. Half a block away, yellow police tape cordoned off the area. She walked toward it.

"Had to see where they killed him, huh?" It was the cop Farley sitting on the back step of the mercantile eating chow mein out of a Chinese carton. She was riveted to the dark red stains on the concrete. "That's why I'm here. Gotta keep the tourists and the curious away. Couple days and the blood'll be faded, nothin' to see."

They hadn't told her the man who was supposed to be Jimmy was killed right there in town, two and a half blocks from the Red Bear, behind the mercantile. "See that rock over there? That's what the punks bashed his head in with. Bits of skull and hair on it. Some brain matter." He took a big bite, the noodles half falling out of his mouth. "I can let you past the tape if you're real nice to me."

Shut up, shut up, shut up, she thought. Roaring in her ears, her heart pumping so fast she thought it might explode. Without answering, Norris ran back to the corner nearly knocking down one of the teens.

"Whoa," said a skinny bad-complexioned kid as he regained his balance, the kid's soft hand on her arm, his middle finger tattooed with a cross. She mumbled thanks and hustled up the street where she threw up into a window box. She wiped her mouth on her sleeve and walked fast, looked at nothing, only the ominous Mt. Juneau ahead of her, pressing tightly behind the town, snow still on top, thin streams of spring runoff cascading down its towering sides. Why hadn't they told her it happened so close? Did it matter? Or didn't they want her to know?

She walked uphill until the street gave out and took a wooden staircase straight up to the next tier of houses. She was three or four blocks higher than she had been before, on the spine of a foothill, the last row of houses huddled high above the city, their backyards plunging into a river-cut ravine into sudden wilderness. She hadn't realized the houses were perched on a ridge. From below, they looked as though they hung on the mountainside. She followed the road along the ridge past the houses as it wound back into the ravine, away from the city, a narrow pass between Mt. Juneau and Mt. Roberts. She tried to shake the image of the dark stains in the alley.

She kept walking. The rhythm of movement gave her solace. Every time she stopped, she began to sort possibilities. Thinking was not something she could manage right now. Thinking immobilized her. She would walk away from the questions she could not answer.

She followed the road and came to a wooden cantilevered bridge tucked against Mt. Roberts' side, a drop to the ravine and the engorged roaring river below. At any other time she would have been afraid of the loose planking, paralyzed by the glimpses through the gaps to the river below. Right now she was so fearful of everything else, she didn't notice.

She descended on the road that soon turned to gravel and meandered along the valley floor through sparse woods of second growth fir and alder. Above on the mountainsides she could see partially hidden in the timber the ruins of old gold mines—tin buildings and fragments of sluices, the rusted remainders of another time. She walked to the end of the road and took an overgrown trail up the mountain. Not thinking. Just moving. She came to a mine entrance nearly hidden in the foliage and remembered Jimmy had told her there were more miles of tunnels snaking inside the mountains than there were roads in Juneau. She entered the opening and could see the rough burrowing cut off six feet in front of her, the old mine shaft blocked. For a moment she was disappointed the shaft hadn't gone further for her to explore, a distraction, a strand of childish adventure unconnected to the real world. Suddenly a blast of air enveloped her, the wind sucked from somewhere inside the mountain, whipping around her, musty and organic, the breath of the dead. She gasped her way back out to daylight not wanting to be caught in the dark, a tomb.

Outside, the leaves on the bushes and trees shuddered beside her in the strange deathly wind. Norris shuddered too. And ran.

Norris checked the bus schedule at the side of the covered shelter. She had seven minutes to wait. Gayle had told her the easiest way to get to the Fred Meyer was the bus. Why take a taxi and spend twenty bucks when the bus would get you there for two? Hadn't Smitty said the best place to find people was Fred Meyer's? The simple plan: find Smitty, talk to Smitty and all will fall into place. Jimmy's somewhere and you're going to find him.

A three-year-old boy bent over, picked up a piece of shiny gum wrapper from the gutter. His mother yanked him back abruptly nearly tearing his arm out of the socket and threw the wrapper back. The boy started to cry.

"Quit," she said and coughed a wracking cough. The child stood very still. Norris wanted to take the boy away, find him a safe place.

A raven cut across the sky and landed on the lamppost across the street. It looked at the gum wrapper then fixed its eye on Norris and sat there like it had nothing on its mind other than to watch her. Norris felt an icy prickling. She'd almost decided to find a taxi when the bus appeared.

It was half full and most of the passengers seemed to know each other. The simple exchanges of longtime friends were like an assault. Norris moved to the back of the bus behind two rangy handsome sullen Indian teens plugged into their iPods, their long unmanaged dyed red hair trailing down their black T-shirted backs. Norris concentrated on the small gold hoop earring in the lobe of the boy in front of her. Here, with nothing but the remote tinny plunking from his iPod, she could breathe.

The first stop was the hospital, a clean, modern, low-lying building that looked more like a condo village than hospital. Norris wondered if the body was first taken there. She forced the image out.

They traveled the old Glacier Highway, a rutted route under construction skirting the mountainside. It looked like a road under constant construction. A road harassed by nature. Winter flooding, mudslides, sinking, shifting. Jimmy had told her Juneau had the largest uplift in the world. Twenty thousand years ago, southeast Alaska was buried under 2,000 feet of ice but when the last Ice Age ended, about ten thousand years ago, the ice began melting rapidly. With the weight off, the land bounced back like a sponge. A very slow sponge in our measure. In geologic time, a flash. In a scant hundred years Mendenhall Glacier had retreated more than two miles from the Gastineau Channel and was picking up speed.

The bus lumbered away from the mountain slope and onto the meadows of the mud flats crossing over Lemon Creek running gray and dirty with the heavy silted mountain glacial run-off. She wondered if it ever ran lemon yellow.

They turned off the highway onto a narrow asphalt back road leading into a degenerating residential neighborhood. The place had all the fragmented trappings of a striving middle class gone sour—lawn furniture torn and stained and broken, weather-battered boats on rusted trailers, sad-eyed dogs tethered in muddy grass-splotched yards, tire-less cars on blocks, satellite dishes green with mold. Norris wondered why the bus had taken the diversion from the highway. As they rumbled around a corner it was obvious. Behind the last row of houses through a scramble of berry vines and stunted firs sat a prison, Lemon Creek Correctional Center. Aluminum-sided buildings with great mad coils of razor wire looped haphazardly around the perimeter of the complex.

No one got off and no one approached from the prison.

Out of the forlorn detour and back onto the highway she could see Costco in the distance stuck on the scrub-brushed landscape, Fred Meyer next stop.

Norris stood near Fred Meyer's entrance watching. Cars and pickups came and went; the electronic doors never rested, opening and closing. A popcorn machine and a clown with balloons for the kids in front. People in; people out. Tons of groceries, tons of consumer goods piled into trunks and back seats. And not a sign of Smitty.

After what seemed like hours, the bustle became a blur. The constant motion and never-ending whoosh of the doors made her edgy. Norris went inside, picked up a disposable cell phone and roamed the acres of aisles. Nothing interested her. Shopping seemed a foreign thing. She couldn't fathom all the stuff people had to have. The sheer volume seemed impossible. And what people didn't buy? Where did all that go? She'd read somewhere that every child born in America created two hundred times the disposable waste of any other child on earth. Norris watched the people pushing their loaded carts and believed it. She imagined never needing anything ever again.

She bought her phone and went outside.

One ring. Two.

"Bartholomew here."

"Warren, it's me."

"Norris! Where are you? Having fun with your new man?"

"He's gone." She barely choked it out, tears welling, her throat constricting. The shoppers bustled by, the clown at the entrance dispersing candy and balloons. Norris didn't want to cry on the phone. Lose it.

"Didn't hang on to him long, did you, toots?" Warren said flippantly.

"Warren, he's missing gone. They have a body but it's not him."

She could hear him take a deep drag on his cigarette. The long whoosh. A moment to think.

"Who has a body?"

"The police.

He could hear the circus music in the background. "Norris where are you?"

"I'm at Fred Meyer looking for Jimmy's friends." She could almost laugh.

"Are you certain you're not at a circus?"

"There is a clown. And a trained dog act in the parking lot. I'm going insane."

"Of course you are. Slumming at shopping malls. Police and bodies and things. What makes you think it isn't Jimmy?"

"I saw the photos. It wasn't him."

"Photos. Oh, Norris."

"Everyone says it's him including his best friend and his wife. But it isn't."

"Wife, huh."

"Separated."

"Grab your things, get in a taxi or dog sled or whatever they have up there, go to the airport and come home. All that fresh air can't be good for you."

"I have to find him."

"How do you propose to do that? I presume the police think you're out of your mind."

"Actually, they do."

"Well then."

"I don't know how I'll do it. I just have to. I can't do anything else."

She spotted a red pickup at the far end of the parking lot. "Hold on . . ." she said, as she ran to the curb for a better view and saw a makeshift market selling velvet paintings of whales, elk and Elvises along with ceramic flowerpots, plaster animals and Madonna yard ornaments. Smitty drove off with several ornaments in the back of the pickup.

Norris forgot she had the phone in her hand and could hear Warren's tinny voice trying to get her attention.

"I just saw Smitty drive off with a pickup full of plaster Madonnas and moose," she said.

"Is the plural of moose meese?"

"Warren, this is serious. I need to find Smitty," she said, wondering where the pickup stayed when Smitty was back on the island.

"No. You need to come home."

"I can't." And rang off.

THE BUS WAS COMFORTING in its anonymity, two others on board—a man who looked too old to be an Eagle Scout but dressed in the uniform just the same and a scowling woman in a gray coat and plastic rain hat. The Eagle Scout was in back, the woman up front watching her with an eagle eye. That woman ought to be the Eagle Scout, thought Norris.

She got off at the marina and walked down the dock in the rain. Darkness descending.

7

HER BACK HURT. Norris shifted and hit her elbow on the corner of the table.

"What the . . .?" She realized she was slumped over the table in the galley. She pulled the hair out of her eyes and squinted in the sunlight. A bowl of split pea soup barely touched crusted and discolored around the edges sat in front of her.

She shoved it away.

She picked up a paperback and tossed it onto the shelf behind her. She'd read and re-read the same paragraph for hours and had no idea what it was about. She took the bowl of soup to the sink, thought about taking a shower and changing her clothes, instead went outside to the deck. It was the kind of fresh morning that someone might say was full of promises. Norris ran a finger under her eyes, wiping the sleep and mascara. Her black eye was healing, numb now and yellowish-green, almost gone.

Ole's slip was still empty next door. Gil, the big blond hippie fisherman on the *Misfit*, was waving. She waved and quickly ducked back inside. If she lingered, he'd lope over with his hearty enthusiasm and a cup of coffee. He was a nice man and she could use the coffee, but she'd already learned he had no perception of what a brief visit might be.

"TICK TOCK," SAID RITA. "Tick Tock Cafe . . ."

"Not again," Norris heard Joe say in the background before Rita slammed down the receiver. Norris shoved her new cell phone in her pocket and walked down the aisle of the souvenir shop to a rack of post cards. She'd write Rita and Joe. Every time she called she had no voice. She missed Rita and Joe with a hollowness. She could use their steady rooted calm but knew too that their ability to comfort was fundamentally flawed. If they gave you solace; you owed them. Their capacity to see another side to things was blinded by their faith. Things were as they were and you didn't question. You did not try to be something you weren't. You did not doubt. And if you did, your pastor would set you straight. They had big hearts but not without a price.

Norris selected a couple of post cards and proceeded to the cashier. A middle-aged high-strung mother on the verge of anorexia hustled her five-year old daughter out of Norris's path in disgust.

"They shouldn't let these homeless people in the stores," the woman seethed to the woman next to her.

"I wonder what's wrong with her?" said the other woman.

"Mental illness," the anorexic guessed. "We need to get these people off the streets."

Norris pretended not to hear and put her two postcards and the correct change on the counter.

"You must have lots of friends," said the cashier.

Norris looked at her blankly.

"I mean, this is the third day in a row you've bought the identical two postcards."

"Is it?" said Norris.

The cashier gave her a look and Norris took the postcards.

"Have a nice day," said the cashier.

All three women watched her go.

Outside, Alex Tanner was leaning into the window of a squad car, talking with a uniformed officer. Norris crossed the street hoping he wouldn't see her.

"Miss Reed!" he shouted.

Too late.

He crossed the street after her.

"Let's go get something to eat."

She kept walking. He caught up.

"You look like you could use a good meal. I'll buy."

"I'm fine."

"You don't look fine. Get in. I'll take you home," he said, steering her toward a black Crown Victoria sitting at the curb.

"Is this a police state?" resisting.

"You got that right," he said, opening the door for her.

 She hesitated.

"I've heard quite a few reports about a homeless woman in a navy blue sweater wandering around town."

"Is it that bad?"

"Yep."

They drove to Food Town. Alex got out and ordered her not to move. Norris was too tired to argue.

He came back with an armful of groceries and drove her to the marina.

WHEN SHE STEPPED OUT OF the shower, she could smell the toast and coffee. She put on clean jeans, a clean turtleneck sweater, a pair of Jimmy's new socks with the striped tops and walked into the galley where Alex was slipping an omelet onto a plate.

"Eat," he said.

She did. Slowly. Then stopped.

"Not enough," he said.

"I'm full," she said, shoving the plate away.

"Do I have to come here three times a day and feed you? Make certain you're eating?"

"No. I'll eat."

"And sleep.

"I promise I'll eat, but sleep has a life of its own."

"You'd be better off if you headed back home to Seattle."

"I can't yet."

"Making any progress?"

"No." She stretched out her leg and showed him her stockinged foot. "These are the identical socks that Jimmy had on that night. See? Brand new. White. Red stripe." He squeezed her foot and put it down, smiling to himself. She knew he didn't believe her. But he was kind and she'd take that. She wouldn't go back home like he told her, though. Home. Back to Rita and Joe and the old-timers and their tired stories and their chicken fried steak with mashed potatoes and gravy every Wednesday night. She looked at the sink and saw that he'd done the dishes.

She thought about being indignant but was grateful.

"I'm making it tough on you aren't I?" she said.

"A little."

"Everyone thinks I'm crazy."

"Pretty much. I don't want to have to put you under house arrest. We have vagrancy laws you know."

"I'll eat. I'll try to sleep. I won't wander around town anymore scaring women and helpless children . . . And thanks."

"Hey, somebody has to watch out for you. Call your family," he said. "Call your friends. You shouldn't be handling this alone. Go home."

From the deck, she watched him walk down the dock. Out of the corner of her eye, she saw the weasel Farley atop the parking lot. Before Alex had climbed to the top of the ramp Farley had driven off.

8

NORRIS LIFTED THE MASK OF RAVEN off the hook above the galley door and turned it over and over in her hands. On the inside corner was the small inscription JJK. Jimmy Jack Ketah. She smiled. The mask had a serene playfulness as though it might come alive. Norris had long admired Tlingit art. The almost woodcut simplicity was vigorous and sure and endowed with the mystical, yet didn't strike her as being sinister as did the kachina dolls of the Hopi or some of the fierce Aztec imagery. Tlingit art was divine and playful storytelling, mostly depicting the clan crests, manifestations of animals—Eagle, Bear, Frog, Wolf, Salmon, Killer Whale, Raven—Raven and Eagle/Wolf being the two main groups from which all the clans derived.

Each clan had their own myths, legends, and histories involving their crest and each clung voraciously to the right to tell these stories through their art. The Tlingit were famous for their masks and cedar boxes and totem poles, but even the most common utilitarian objects were works of art. Baskets and bowls, eating utensils, fishing gear, canoes and paddles, house fronts, screens, corner posts, clothing and ornaments—all wonderfully adorned.

Norris loved that insignificant things—a bone sewing needle, an antler fishhook, a button—would be carved or painted. A little smiling seal fishing lure. A bear face on a spoon handle. Even the colors seemed inspired. The bold black formlines of the abstract figures against the reds, blue-greens, and yellows. The images reminded her of aboriginal Australian art, the way the black outlined an X-ray vision of the skeleton, the ribs and structure rather than the whole.

She'd seen some modern masks and totems and although striking, she wondered if the artists had kept the strict restraints of their culture or whether they were copiers, fanciful independents, immune to the old-fashioned notions of insult and offense for using a crest in a story not one's own. Norris had no way of knowing if Jimmy was an outsider or a traditionalist. The way this mask looked though, she was certain he belonged to Raven.

She put the mask to her face and inhaled, trying to find a scent of him. She held it with both hands, shut her eyes and breathed the cedar in. She felt each stroke of the blade, the detail of the carving, the contours and valleys trying to reach him. For a moment, comfort in this fine thing. Then bereft. She put it back. She stumbled blinded by tears to the shower.

The water washed over her. She crowded into the corner of the stall and let the hot water scald her back. It felt good. Scouring. Steam rising. She stayed until she ran out of hot water.

She lay on the bunk, pulling the covers over her naked body. She tried to remember every moment she'd spent with Jimmy. The way he watched her that day in the Tick Tock, the funny way he would grin at her, the comments about the smudges of paint on her arms. She knew the moment he came through the door that something extraordinary was about to happen. She was glad he'd liked her paintings. The landscapes of myths, he'd said then laughed. Don't you hate it when people interpret your work? he'd said. No, actually, Norris found it amusing. Especially the significant, hushed pontifications. Sometimes a field was simply a field, a river just a river, no undercurrent, no thread, no mystery, just a shape or color that had taken her.

She loved lying in the moonlight with him, enfolded, her room transformed to some otherworld. She hadn't felt that way in years. Or ever. Charged. Electric. Blessed. Life with her husband Bailey had been stalemated for so long. No emotional attachment anymore, not that there ever had been. They were young and the sex was good. They were attracted to the possibilities of a life they imagined. The Major Leagues. A summer life. The smell of grass and kids and . . . why had she stayed with him? She didn't know. It was all so humiliating. That everyone knew. She supposed she'd never guessed there were men like Jimmy Ketah out there. A clear sharp pain knifed through her.

Time watched her. She could feel it waiting. She lay on the bunk and listened to the lapping, listened to the movement of traffic on the expressway and the bridge. People going places. Another dimension. She held the mask of Raven to her chest, shut her eyes and prayed for a moment of grace. Just one moment.

She heard the engines reverse, close in. She sat up and something close to joy sprung. Ole was back. Through the porthole she could see the old fisherman's red sweater as he guided his boat toward the slip. By the time she'd dressed and was outside, he'd already maneuvered in. He tossed her a line and she tied it off on the cleat then made certain all the bumper floats were in place.

"Hello, there," he shouted above the engine's noise.

She waved.

He shut down the engines and hopped onto the dock in his signature knee-high yellow boots.

"That feels good," he said stomping the boards of the dock. "Solid ground. My sea legs are a mite wobbly."

Norris didn't remind him he was still on water and not yet on solid ground.

"Where's that good fer nuthin' Injun?" Ole asked, lighting his pipe.

NORRIS AND OLE SAT IN THE BACK booth of Andy's Bar and Grill, a dark den of a place that Ole claimed had the best T-bone steaks this side of Texas. Ole'd never been to Texas but it struck him that Texas should have the best steaks in the world when actually it was probably Japan. Norris wasn't about to point this out. Nor would she mention that her steak was full of gristle and as tough as leather and the salad suspect. At least three or four days old, she thought, rinsed in bleach to keep the brown off. That was the trouble with being a waitress. You knew trade secrets.

"You ever taste a steak like this?" Ole asked, sopping up the bloody juice with a roll.

"No," she said truthfully.

Ole gobbled up every scrap of food on his plate, a good appetite in spite of the story Norris had told him. He sat back nursing his J&B and sucking on his pipe.

"Will you look at the photos?" asked Norris.

"Missy, I won't. If you say the body's not Jimmy, then by damn, I believe you. Now, we need to figure out what to do and seems like the first thing is to find Smitty."

Norris was so grateful for a comrade, she lunged across the table and kissed him on the top of his head.

"You gonna eat that steak?" he said.

NORRIS PAID THE TAXI DRIVER while Ole grumbled.

"I still say we take my boat. You're throwin' your damned money away," he said.

"We don't have the time," she said, heading into the airport terminal.

"Ten hours."

"Jimmy said twelve to fifteen hours."

"Depends. Wind, tides. Thirteen maybe."

"Still too long."

"Angoon's been a village on that island for a thousand years, it ain't going nowheres."

Norris found the "Wings" counter, a commuter airline on the lower floor of the terminal among a handful of others. She stood behind two young Tlingit women in jeans, sweatshirts and Uggs who piled their purchases from Fred Meyer and Costco onto the scale. Packages of pampers. Bulk bags of oranges, onions, cases of canned goods, sodas, candy bars, chips. Several other tribal members, men and women, milled and chatted in the lobby.

"Next," called the efficient young man as though there were a huge line when Norris and Ole were the only ones waiting. He took a pen out of his pocket protector and held it poised, waiting.

"Two round-trip tickets to Angoon," Norris said.

"The flight's been delayed," he said, tapping the pen on a roster for the flight.

"Excuse, me?" said Norris.

"Doesn't look like the flight'll get off the ground. Fog on the outer islands."

"When's the next one?"

"Well, we'll go as soon as the fog lifts."

"Any idea when that might be?"

"Could be an hour, could be tomorrow. We wait and see. All we can do. If the flight's cancelled, you're automatically on the morning plane. Still want the tickets?"

She paid for the tickets and joined Ole who'd found a bench against the wall.

"We might not get out today. There's fog on the islands."

Ole brightened. "Then by damn, let's get on home and rev up the *Sea Witch*. She'll get us there."

"We should at least wait until the flight is cancelled for certain," said Norris.

"By then it might be too late to cast off. We should go now," he said, urging her.

"You're afraid of flying, aren't you?" asked Norris.

"I am not. I just don't see the point is all."

"You don't have to go along."

"I know my way around the island. Got a pal out there like I told you. You need a guide. I'm it. I just don't see why we have to fly."

"There's nothing to it. You'll like it. Relax."

"I am relaxed. What makes you think I'm not relaxed? I'm damned relaxed. Let's go get us a drink. They'll announce the flight in the bar."

"OK, but first I'm going over and ask any of those people if they know Jimmy or Smitty."

"I wouldn't if I were you. Wait till we get on the island. Don't want to give yourself away."

"What do you mean?"

"Queer folks, them," he said nodding toward the Tlingit.

"Ole, they're just like anyone else."

"No they ain't," he said.

THE WINGS AGENT STOOD at the lobby door and checked off the roster on his clipboard as a squat man in Carhartt overalls and thick leather gloves rolled a stacked dolly out to a waiting van. The counter agent made a show of announcing over the P.A. system that Wings Flight 360 to Angoon was now boarding. No one needed the announcement. They were already out the door.

Everyone crammed into the van, the six Tlingit, plus Norris and Ole. In the lobby, the tribal members had been talking to each other. In the van no one spoke. A man in his fifties with two missing fingers drove them across the tarmac, down the airstrip along an access road past warehouses and tied-down planes, past rusted equipment and plane carcasses to the airport ponds. They reached the dock at the far end of the airport where they boarded the De Havilland floatplanes, the Beaver and the larger Otter, workhorses of Alaskan bush piloting. The Tlingit crowded into the Otter, leaving Norris, Ole and the extra cargo to be loaded into the Beaver.

They taxied out on the landing strip waterway, a man-made lagoon gouged out of the wetlands. They glided down the glassy runway, high grasses at the water's edge. The larger, more powerful Otter overtook the Beaver and got in position for takeoff. It cleared and disappeared. The Beaver revved, shaking. Norris sat in front, next to the pilot, with Ole in back. The pilot opened a small plastic container about the size of a film canister and shook out a pair of neon lime-colored foam earplugs onto his palm. He handed them to Norris and demonstrated in mime, showing her how to knead them into a smaller shape to place in her ears. The Beaver roared and shimmied and they were airborne. Norris looked back at Ole. He was staring at his feet.

The first glimpse of the outer islands made her gasp. Pristine forests to the sea. Waves crashed white against the crystal aquamarine water of rocky shorelines. The intense blue-green of the shallows faded gradually into the deep

Pacific blue of Chatham Strait. Across the strait, she could see another necklace of islands before they gave way to open ocean. Huge, high cumulus clouds tumbled on the horizon in the clear sky. Norris felt a surge of hope.

They left the mainland and flew along the western coastline of Admiralty Island. Twenty minutes out, almost half the distance to Angoon, they passed over a clear-cut, a disaster of mud, slash and stumps. Mountains covered with once-dense rainforest were now bare as far as you could see, scarred and patchy like mangy fur. Logging roads crisscrossed the patchwork bare hills and deep rivulets of runoff carved their way through the barren hillsides, sending gushing torrents of water unchecked, taking the shallow topsoil with it, choking streams and rivers that ran like cafe latte down the mountainsides into the blue-green sea. A village of trailer houses sat lined up against the western hillside raw on the acid red soil. She could see a dog walking and a larger building with a flag out front. A school? There were a few trucks going back and forth from the cut at the top of the mountain through town to the mill at the shore.

They soon flew beyond the clear-cuts and into old-growth forest, government-owned parkland stolen from the Tlingit. At least it was untouched.

Norris wanted to cling to the romantic notion that tribal caretakers would manage their lands more sensibly than the shortsighted capitalists who had ravaged most of the nation in a scant hundred years. White men like her father and uncles and grandfather who couldn't fathom that the rich forests they saw before them would ever run out. They'd long lost any sense that the earth was a sacred place and they were part of the whole. The aboriginals must innately understand the equation. The fragile nature of their lands. The interdependence of ecosystems. They had myths and legends and rituals

73

keeping the links alive. Jimmy had told her she was wrong. The dollar was a strong god.

She was looking at Jimmy's territory now. His homeland. She tried to imagine what it felt like being aboriginal to the place. Not settlers, trappers or pioneers like her people. Norris searched the alpine meadows for deer or bear or elk. She scanned the shorelines, craggy and exposed for wildlife. She saw nothing.

They lowered altitude.

"The tide's going out," the pilot shouted over the roar of the engine, loud enough for Norris to hear through her earplugs. "They get twenty-foot tides out here. Tremendous change."

Norris looked below at the narrow channel where the sea was running swift like a river.

"Angoon," he shouted again, pointing to the peninsula on her right. Norris looked back at Ole. He had his hands clasped in his lap and his head down, asleep or deep in prayer.

The village sat on a small peninsular hook of the island. It was dotted with rows of two- and three-story cedar frame houses, larger than she expected, most needing paint, reminiscent of a nineteenth-century Russian village—the influence of early Orthodox presence.

The plane closed ten feet off the surface of the water, past the town, past a long wooden building that looked like a motel and past a copse of small cedar where someone had built a large home fronted all in glass. She saw their reflection flash as they sailed by.

They touched down and taxied to the dock where the Otter had already unloaded. Its passengers milled, waiting for their cargo.

A stocky woman with a crew cut, a wind-weathered face, wearing tan overalls with an embroidered name "Meg" under a Wings insignia, waved to the pilot, all smiles. She grabbed the lines and secured the Beaver to the dock as Norris unplugged her ears and put the earplugs in her pocket. Ole was already down the wire ladder from the back seat exit and on the dock. Norris climbed out.

"I see you're headed back on the afternoon flight," the pilot said.

"You sightseeing?" asked Meg.

"Looking for a friend," said Norris.

The others on the dock looked their way.

"Maybe one of the villagers could give you a lift into town," said the pilot handing the boxes from the hold to Meg. He said it loud enough for everyone to hear and no one volunteered, everyone suddenly preoccupied with finding their cargo.

"We can walk. It's only a short hike up the trail over there," said Ole.

"I'll take you," said Meg.

In the short drive to town, they learned that Meg was divorced from her pig of a husband, who god knows how got custody of their daughter. After summer, she was going down to Seattle and straighten out a few things, including the lie that she was still on drugs. She was clean. Had been for a whole month. Got this job and he could just shove that unfit mother bullshit. The butterfly tattoo on her neck pulsed with outrage.

"Sure you don't want me to wait?" asked Meg, dropping them off at a weatherworn shack.

"We'll be fine. A friend of mine," said Ole.

"Good luck. If you need some company, I'm at the motel, room four," she said, as she drove off in her rusted Toyota, disappearing in the dust.

They walked up an overgrown path, Norris swatting at mosquitoes. Ole knocked on the door then entered.

"Henry?" he called. "Henry, it's me, Ole. You here?"

It was a one-room shack with a pot-bellied wood stove, a table with two chairs and a bed partially hidden behind a tattered blanket hung on a piece of rope. Nobody home.

Ole walked down the well-worn path to the outhouse.

"Hey, you old moose, come on out here, you got company," he shouted, rattling the door. The door swung open. No Henry.

They heard an outboard motor start up and ran down the path to the dock in time to see a sixteen-foot fiberglass broad-beamed outboard speed off. They shouted and waved, running along the shoreline. "Henry always was deaf," said Ole, as the boat skimmed out of range. "Where's he getting off to on an outgoing tide? Too late for fishing. Probably going crabbing or some damn thing."

They walked back to the house and stopped beside the woodshed where Ole noticed a chair sitting against the wall with a fishing net bundled by its side.

"Looks like Henry's doing some mending. Right in the middle of it," said Ole, fingering a large needle stuck in the net. Next to the chair on the edge of a stump sat a half-empty cup of coffee. "Still warm," said Ole picking it up. "Afraid the old coot's getting absentminded as well as deaf."

Norris and Ole walked down the dusty road to town. That is, the general store/post office/gas station. They walked onto the porch past two kids slurping popsicles on a wooden bench. The girl had cherry red smeared all over her mouth, and the one-eyed dog sitting at her feet watched her carefully, nose glistening wet, quivering in anticipation of a bite. The kids had high pink chapped cheeks and looked like they'd pulled their clothes out of a rag bag. The boy, about nine, had filthy orange jeans and a never-to-be-white-again, overlarge sweatshirt hoody. The girl, maybe eleven or twelve, wore a green turtleneck under a big black T-shirt with an illustration of a puffin on the front over purple spandex leggings and remarkable yellow and green polka dot socks with purple sneakers. Their rusted bikes leaned against the wall. The kids eyed them carefully as they entered the screen door.

Inside, Norris asked the woman at the counter reading a magazine if she knew where they could find Smitty.

"Mel," the woman called to the back without answering them.

"Mel," she repeated, getting up from the chair as though that would give her voice more volume.

A short Tlingit man with black horned-rimmed glasses and a bad complexion emerged from the back room.

"They want to know where Smitty lives," said the woman.

Mel thought about it.

"Sorry," he said.

The woman was quiet.

"How about Jimmy Ketah?"

Mel shook his head.

"This is a small village," said Ole, "Are you sure you don't know 'em?"

"Must be wrong village," Mel said.

"Wrong village, me arthritic mother. You people are hiding something," said Ole, anger rising.

"Sorry we bothered you," said Norris, nudging Ole out.

"They know damn well where they live," said Ole. "Them in there's probably relatives."

"I know. Now what?"

"Beat the crap out of 'em," said Ole. "I should have brought the .357, that would have got their attention."

"You have one?" asked Norris, somewhat amazed.

"Naw, but I damn well ought to. I wonder how they found out we was coming? God damned smoke signals. I knowed we shoulda come by boat."

The kids were still on the porch, the mutt licking the last of the girl's popsicle.

"You guys know where Smitty lives?" asked Norris.

"Sure," said the boy before the girl elbowed him.

"No," said the girl shoving the boy.

Mel opened the screen door. Without a word, the kids grabbed their bikes and pedaled off, the back wheel of the girl's blue bike squeaking against the rusted metal of the fender.

Mel shut the door.

"Nice, friendly place. Told you they warn't normal," said Ole.

Norris and Ole wandered through town and out onto the ferry pier catching the furtive glances of people avoiding them, disappearing behind window curtains, changing directions, falling silent as they passed. Ole called out to a man working on a fishing net. The man walked into his shed without a word.

"Get the feeling we're not welcome?" said Ole. "I was afraid we might get the cold shoulder, but never seen a whole village clam up."

They walked down a wooded path out of sight of the village and heard the wanky screek of the bicycle before the girl caught up to them, feet sliding in the dust to stop rather than use brakes.

"What's it to you?" said the girl.

"What do you mean?" said Norris.

"She means how much are we willing to pay to get the information we need," said Ole.

"Five bucks," said Norris.

"Get real," said the girl.

"You tell us," said Ole.

"A hundred," she said.

"Forget it," said Norris.

"Ten," said Ole pulling out a bill.

She grabbed it quick. "Third house from the pier, blue with yellow trim," and she was gone.

A BENT-BACKED OLD WOMAN with long gray braids answered the door, not opening it fully. No, she didn't know where Smitty lived.

"How about Jimmy Ketah?" Ole said.

She shut the door.

Ole and Norris walked off the porch and down the path back to town.

Norris glanced back and thought she saw Smitty at the window as he let the curtain fall.

9

THE GLACIER SHIMMERED ON THE HORIZON. A jewel of ice translucent, an apparition. You couldn't make such a thing, nor paint it. It was unlikely. Pure imagination stuck in the far-distant gap between the mountains.

The Beaver banked for the approach to the airport lagoon. Norris saw the white airport van waiting. And the black Crown Vic.

They made a perfect, almost splashless landing on the glossy green surface. They motored toward the dock where Alex stood surefooted, heavy-handed, a cop, waiting.

The plane sidled up to the dock and Alex tied off the struts. The pilot jumped to the dock and Norris waited inside for Ole to climb down the wire steps first.

"Anything I can do for you?" the pilot asked Alex.

"I need to talk to the lady," Alex said, waiting for Norris to emerge from the plane.

"Enjoy your trip to Angoon?" asked Alex as Norris stepped onto the wire ladder.

"Very nice," Norris said.

"We've had a few complaints."

"Complaints?" asked Norris, jumping to the dock.

"Seems like you were harassing a few people," said Alex.

"How could we be harassing anyone if no one would talk to us?" said Norris, her hackles raised.

Ole and the pilot dropped back, letting the two of them settle what needed settling.

"You're disturbing people. People don't like to be disturbed. We're kinda like bears in hibernation up here. We're fine and content unless someone interferes. Then . . . well, then, things change."

"Have we broken any laws?"

"No. Officially it's not our jurisdiction."

"Then I don't see what the problem is."

"Look, I can't tell you where you can or cannot go. But folks don't appreciate strangers asking questions."

"Folks? Or you?"

"I've been real patient with you and tried to smooth things over with most everybody in town. But my advice: head on back to Seattle. There's nothing you can do here." With that he abruptly left her on the dock. His sedan did a U-turn and spun out, tires squealing.

Ole raised his eyebrows at Norris.

The pilot busied himself with paperwork.

A young airport shuttle driver leaned against his van chewing on a matchstick trying to seem like he hadn't heard.

They walked up the catwalk and climbed into the van, Norris and Ole in the back. The driver turned to look at them. "What was that all about? Do you mind my asking?"

"We've been looking for a missing Indian and nobody likes it," said Ole.

"No, I guess not," said the driver. "Seems like a futile deal."

"Yeah, but I figured somebody would say something," said Ole. "Even one of my old buddies bailed out on us."

"A couple years ago they were looking for a missing woman. Forest Service botanist or something," said the driver, a kid not more than twenty-five. "Last place she had contact with was a village in Yakutat. Do you think anybody'd talk? Not a one. And she wasn't even one of their own."

"Did they ever find her?" asked Norris.

"Oh, yeah. She turned up in Whitehorse with a geologist for Exxon. No big deal. They'd taken off for a week. She'd told her roommate but the roommate went on an assignment out to Kodiak and didn't think to tell anyone. By the way, my name is Eric," he said extending his hand backwards with a business card. "If there's anything I can do, let me know."

BACK AT THE MARINA Ole put an arm around Norris. "Buck up. We keep shaking the tree, somethin's gonna fall out. Hey, how about dinner? I'm going to Andy's. You know how those steaks are."

"You go ahead without me. I'll fix a salad or something."

"Salad's not food. Red meat'll do wonders. Put iron in your blood. Make you strong." He rolled up a sleeve and flexed his biceps. Great pecs for a seventy-three-year-old man.

Norris laughed.

"Atta girl. Sure you won't join me? Steak and whiskey?"

"I'm fine."

"Suit yourself."

NORRIS STARED AT WILTED LETTUCE and closed the tiny refrigerator.

She sat on the deck and watched the rainbow patterns of the diesel and oil suspended on the water change and mutate with the incoming tide. She watched a heron glide low down the channel heading south. High atop an adjacent mast, a raven watched her.

She was still sitting on the deck, back against the nets when the van driver Eric wandered up.

"Permission to come aboard, captain," he said, startling her. "Took a chance you might be lonely," he said holding up a six-pack of Bud and two Subway sandwiches as he boarded.

"I won't be very good company."

"Oh, come on, have a beer, eat, relax. Tell old Uncle Eric all about it."

She smiled. Old Uncle Eric. He was barely old enough to buy the beer. The kid made himself comfortable, sitting beside her. He handed her a sandwich and cracked a can open. Handed her a cold one and took one for himself.

"So what's the deal with the cop?"

She told him as succinctly as possible. Relishing her sandwich, ravenous, even if it was pepperoni.

"You mean the Indian that was stabbed the other night? You knew him?"

"No," she said. "That's the point. They say it's Jimmy Ketah. It isn't."

"You sure?"

"Positive."

"Whoa. You only knew him a couple of days. I mean, the cop could be right. You're upset and all. And besides, you were only looking at photos. That saying, 'a photo never lies,' is bull. You could take a picture of just about anything or anybody, change the lighting and angles and swear it's not the same. Especially with Photoshop and stuff. Not that I'm saying the cops manipulated the photos, only that it's possible.

"Maybe," she said.

"I got an idea: let's think about something else," he said leaning toward her and blowing a strand of hair out of her eyes. He smelled good, like the outdoors, like sea air. He was so close, looking at her, eyes sparkling. "Come on, you need to loosen up," he said, taking her arm and pulling her toward him.

"That may be, but I think I should do it alone," she said, trying not to sound too shrewish but tough enough to make him leave.

"Really?" he said, smiling in disbelief.

"Really," she said, getting up and brushing crumbs off her jeans.

"Well, I tried," he said, getting to his feet.

"And a very nice try it was," she said, shoving him toward the edge of the deck.

"Maybe next time," he said, jumping down to the dock and taking the six-pack carton she handed him. "Sure you don't want me to leave these with you?" he asked, holding up the carton with the remaining cans.

"I'm sure. Good night, Eric."

She watched him until he was out of sight. Instead of being angry with him trying to take advantage of her situation, she felt more alone. She couldn't believe that was possible.

"N-O-R-R-I-S. NO-O-ORRIS," she heard him calling down the dock. The bunkside clock said two a.m. Ole was just getting home. She threw on a pair of jeans and a sweater and went out. He staggered from side to side down the dock in his red sweater, pea coat, and yellow rain boots. He reached her boat and tried to get on board, stepping in air. Norris leaped onto the dock and steered him careening to his own.

"Someone else, Norris," he blabbered. "A man. Rock. Not him."

He was saturated with drink and sweat and smoke. It was all she could do to get him on board. He kept slipping down. She kept pulling him up. "Waco. Ask him Norris."

"Ask who?" He almost nodded off. "Ole. Ole!" she shook him.

"Mmmiii. Saw Wac . . ."

He was incomprehensible. A mumbling stumbling drunk. She dragged him to his bunk. She sat him on the edge and shoved him. He fell over onto his back.

"Sleep it off, Ole." Put a blanket over him.

"Important . . . Waco," he mumbled reaching for her arm. He was out. He snored heavily, the saliva slopping at his mouth with each exhale, his arm stretched out still reaching for her. He lay there on his back, his arm flung out. The snoring reduced to whistling wheezes.

Norris tried to remove his boots, but they were stuck. She wondered if he ever took them off, shut out the lights and let him be.

IN THE MORNING, THERE WAS NO sign of movement next door so Norris decided Ole'd need breakfast when he woke up, sure to have a hangover. She'd go to the store and maybe he'd be awake by the time she got back. It felt good to have resolve even if it was only a trip to the grocery store. And the bakery, she thought. She had a vague notion where it was. The bakery would be good.

She might even be hungry.

NORRIS CROSSED OVER THE EXPRESSWAY, groceries in hand, and could see the flashing lights. Three squad cars, an EMS unit in the parking lot and a Coast Guard cutter dockside. A handful of police officers and a few onlookers were at the edge looking down on the docks. Norris walked across the lot and through the crowd.

Below were two uniformed officers cordoning off the area. Their dock neighbor Gil was there, pale, stricken. EMTs stood back as a Coast Guard rescue crew pulled on a rope. A diver was in the water. They pulled on the rope and soon a rubber boot broke the surface. Attached to the rubber boot was Ole.

They pulled him out like they were fishing. A big dumb old red-sweatered yellow-booted Ole lure.

10

HUMBOLDT WAS IRRITATED. Alex Tanner edged Norris aside, away from the scene, leaning over her protectively. He was saying something but she couldn't hear. She kept watching the scene, Humboldt and the creep, Farley. Humboldt coughed up a gob of spit and sent it flying over the edge of the ramp to the water. A small crowd of fishermen, dockworkers and the morbidly curious kept asking questions. He motioned to Farley manning the police tape to move the onlookers back.

"Nothing to see here. Keep moving." Farley said, puffed up in charge. He winked at a teenager in tight jeans. "We've got it under control," he said, "Nothing you need to know."

"Let's go get some coffee," Alex said. She didn't respond. "Norris? Coffee?"

She wasn't able to tear her eyes away from the lumpen form that used to be Ole.

"We're going to Percy's," Alex said to Humboldt as he guided her away.

The coroner's people were already swarming over Ole. Norris stopped for a moment to take a last look at him lying on the dock before they tucked him into the body bag. An accident, the police said. Norris wanted to believe it. Ole could have stumbled outside and slipped with his foot tangled in the rope like that. But when? Wouldn't she have heard something? She winced at the photographer's flash. She followed Alex out of the crowd.

"You left your groceries," Humboldt called after them. Dropped at the top of the ramp. Milk, eggs, bananas, oranges, almond croissants. Humboldt kicked at the food with his foot.

"HI," GAYLE SAID BRIGHTLY, recognizing Norris.

"You two know each other?" asked Alex.

"Oh, sure, old friends. I'm Gayle."

"Norris," said Norris.

Alex ordered coffee, scrambled eggs, bacon, hash browns and whole wheat toast for both of them. Norris protested, wanted only coffee. He ignored her.

Norris cupped her hands around the coffee cup. Comforting, that bit of warmth. All of a sudden she was so tired she thought she could fall asleep right there. Alex was telling her she should go back to Seattle. She half-listened. No way would she leave now.

As she'd watched them untangle Ole's foot from the rope, the water sliding off in perfect droplets, she'd had this small stirring awareness. Fear hovering beside her. Fear compelling her forward. Better than the incomprehensible void. How could she explain that? Now, she had a new objective. She'd track Ole's bar rounds to find out what it was he tried to tell her. Alex would say to leave people alone, but how could she? Jimmy was out there somewhere and she had no doubt it was all connected.

She stared at her coffee. Gayle brought their food and Norris dared to say it. "Ole knew something."

"Here we go. Now Ole was murdered," said Alex.

"He tried to tell me something last night. He was drunk

and rambling. He mumbled about a man and a rock. And Waco. Then he passed out. Does Waco mean anything?"

Alex smeared his toast with jam. "Waco is a place in Texas."

"You know damn well Waco is one of our more colorful drunks," said Gayle, passing by.

"Maybe that's who Ole talked to," said Norris. "If you ask around in the bars . . ."

"Uh, huh."

"If someone went to the trouble of obliterating that man's face and hands, they evidently didn't want the body ID'd. This Waco must have told Ole something and they had to get rid of Ole too."

Alex didn't answer.

"I get it," said Norris, leaning back in the booth, disgusted. "If Ole was murdered then you might have to reopen Jimmy's file. You might have to ask some uncomfortable questions. That would be so inconvenient."

"That's not the way it works."

"But that's exactly what you're doing. Ignoring any challenge to what you've already decided. The punks bludgeoned Jimmy. Ole had an accident. And me? The whacko making trouble."

"Unless Jimmy killed them both," said Alex.

Norris stared at him.

"For your information, although I don't have to tell you a damn thing, I don't think Ole Johanson stepped off the dock on his own." said Alex.

Norris was thrown. Maybe he was on her side. It would be nice to have someone believe her.

"Why don't you tell me about it?" Alex said.

She looked at him blankly.

"You and Jimmy. What were you up to? Drugs is my guess. You had an argument. He hit you . . ."

"I fell. I told you that."

He didn't acknowledge her. "And you decided not to go along. The plan being: Jimmy faking his own death. But he took off. Left you behind. Now you want to find him."

"You've got to be kidding."

He wasn't.

"Where'd Jimmy Ketah get this kind of money?" He pulled a piece of paper out of his jacket pocket and slid it toward her. A list of bank deposits. She scanned down. All the entries were under twenty-five hundred dollars with a larger deposit last fall of $31,000. There was nothing unusual. He must have sold some art. And last summer's fishing season.

"Everybody knows he fishes," she said.

"Looks like you two caught a lot more than salmon. Check the next page."

She turned the page and $150,000 jumped out at her. Deposited a few days before he met her and a withdrawal of $150,000. The day he disappeared.

"Who withdrew it?" asked Norris.

"None other than Jimmy Ketah. That's what Anita Dorr at First Bank says."

Norris' eyes began to blur. It didn't make sense. Alex watched her.

"So maybe we can reconstruct a little. Want to try?"

"There's nothing to reconstruct. I don't know what's going on," Norris said, getting angry.

"Easy. Don't get excited."

She was excited. She was furious. He acted like her friend. Now this. "You've known this from the beginning. What were you doing? Waiting for me to slip up? You said the body was Jimmy, case closed. Now you're telling me you think Jimmy faked his death and disappeared?"

"I'm merely trying to get to the truth. I think a drug

deal went bad and he was at the wrong end of it. I simply don't know where to put you."

He let her absorb it. "Now, I'd like you tell me who you are and why I've never seen you before and all of a sudden you come to town and I've got two homicides on my hands in a week and you know both victims."

"I told you that I met Jimmy in Seattle. We came up here to fish. He disappeared. End of story."

"Nope. I need background. I could take you in for questioning but this seems nicer."

"You harassing my friend, Alex?" Gayle asked, refilling the coffee.

"It just comes naturally, Gayle."

Norris said nothing.

"Anytime. I'm not going away. It's more pleasant here but like I said, we could go down to my office."

She thought of the police station and Humboldt and Farley. No thank you.

"Nothing much to tell. Grew up in a small logging town sixty miles northeast of Seattle. Father and mother deceased, a sister, married, running a derelict hotel and café in Seattle, the place I was working when I met Jimmy."

"And your husband died in a car accident."

She looked at him. "Yes."

"Were you driving?"

Stared at him. "No."

"Then what?"

"Working at Rita and Joe's. I told you."

"Drug habits?"

"Do I look like I have a drug habit?"

He was waiting.

"No."

"What do you do in your spare time?"

"I paint."

"Pictures?"

"Yes, pictures."

"You didn't make a living painting, so you became a waitress."

"I waited tables all through college. And it just came naturally. No thinking. You can go anyplace anywhere and find a job."

"Good place to meet people. All kinds. And one day you met Jimmy Ketah."

"Yes."

"Did you know Danny Jenkins?"

"I only heard the name, Danny. I have no idea if that's who you mean."

"He lives in Seattle. You probably ran into him."

"Oh, yes. I know everyone in Seattle."

"Danny gets around."

She didn't answer.

"How long had you known Jimmy before you came to Juneau?"

"I told you."

"You met him one day and left with him the next, just like that?"

She could see Rita's frowning face.

"I guess you had to be there. There was something about him."

"Like a quick hundred and fifty thou?"

"Jimmy's not an idiot. What kind of stupid drug dealer would put money like that in a bank account?"

He was baiting her. She resented his cross-examining. His shoulder walkie-talkie crackled. She couldn't decipher it. Some code number and a garbled request.

"I'm on it .10-4," he said, pulled out his wallet and left money on the table.

He was the most curious cop she'd ever met. Well, he was the only cop she'd ever met, except, of course,

Jim Barton in her hometown. But that was different. Jim was a fixture. Famous for foiling a bank robbery in their small town. Written up in *Detective* magazine.

Alex turned back at the door. "By the way, could you stick around a few days? I need to follow up on a few things."

"I thought you wanted me on the first plane back to Seattle."

He shook his head and left.

Gayle came to the table to clear up.

"Cute, huh?"

"What?"

"Alex Tanner. Some hunk, right?"

"I guess so."

"She guesses so. Girl, you are something. I'd jump on that." Gayle in a fluster. "Oh, gross. I forgot. It's not exactly a time to be joking around about men is it?"

"What do you know about him?"

"Single, widower. Plays it close to the vest. You know, hard to read. Sometimes real nice, sometimes cold as ice."

"Mostly cold. I'd stay away from him," a man said. "Mind if I join you?" He wasn't waiting for an answer. He was already sliding into the booth. Tall, sandy haired, forties, in shape, aviator sunglasses, smiling, confidently reckless.

"Drew Murdock," he said, extending his hand across the table.

"Norris Reed," she said, taking his hand and looking at Gayle who was shaking her head and already pouring him coffee.

"Drew is our resident helicopter pilot, flies for Winston's. Welcome back."

"Thanks. What'd I miss?" he asked, looking at Norris.

"You heard about Jimmy Ketah?" said Gayle.

"Yeah. I can't believe it."

"You knew him?" said Norris.

"Long time. If it weren't for Jimmy, I wouldn't be in Juneau. Did you know him?"

"Yes," said Norris, her eyes stinging with tears.

He noticed, took off the sunglasses. Blue eyes.

"Norris came up to go fishing with him," said Gayle.

"Oh, you're the one," he said and was quiet. "Jimmy was a great guy. We did a couple of tours in the Gulf together. Can I do anything?"

"You can stay away from her," said Gayle.

He leaned across the table toward Norris. "Some people are rude, you know what I mean?"

"Realistic, you mean," said Gayle.

"Where does she get that?" asked Drew.

Gayle laughed and headed for the register to take a payment.

"So you've had a few encounters with Alex," Drew said.

"I'm not sure I'd call them encounters. He's questioned me."

"Does he think you had something to do with it?"

"You might say that."

"Did you?"

Norris was quiet.

"Sorry. You shouldn't be too hard on Alex, though. He has to look at all the angles."

"Yes, but there's one angle he won't consider."

"And that is . . . "

"The body wasn't Jimmy Ketah."

Drew took a long look at her. Took a swig of coffee.

"What makes you say that?"

"I saw the photos. It wasn't him."

"You sure?"

"Positive."

94

"What does Alex say about that?"

"Traumatic stress syndrome. I'm so distraught, I can't let the body be Jimmy."

"Sounds reasonable. Maybe he's right."

"Maybe he is. I don't like the feeling that he thinks I'm out of my mind, though. Or somehow involved in drugs. Or a murderer."

"Look at it from his perspective. He doesn't need anyone bent on finding a dead man that's already been identified and dispatched to his tribal relatives for funeral rites. Why should he investigate a missing person that he's pretty certain is a corpse? And he sure as hell doesn't need any good-looking female from the lower forty-eight reminding him he's a lonely man without a woman. It's a whole lot easier for Alex if you are crazy or a criminal. Don't worry about it. Believe me, everything he asks you he already knows."

11

"ANITA'S ON VACATION, would you like to talk to the bank manager?" the teller asked.

"No, I need to talk to Anita," Norris said, then changed her mind. "Sure, I'll talk to the manager."

Norris heard the swish, swish of the woman's nyloned thighs rubbing together as she made her way across the acres of carpeting to a glass-enclosed cubicle where she leaned on the desk talking to a younger woman in a gray suit. Norris swiped her sweaty palms on her jeans and picked up a bank brochure to occupy herself. They had equity loans for everything. Cars and boats and trips and college educations for the children. The smattering of photos depicted happy couples of various ages acquiring things. The cheerful white middle-class family and the happy black couple. The thigh swishing returned.

"Mrs. Jordan will be with you in a moment," the teller said, leaving her to wait.

Norris watched the power-suited Mrs. Jordan talking on the telephone in her cubicle. She picked out another brochure, this one on investing. What was taking so long?

"Doing some banking?" Alex asked.

Norris looked at Mrs. Jordan who stayed in her cubicle, head down, intently searching through papers.

"Busted, huh?" said Norris as she walked out of the bank with Alex.

"You can't walk into a bank and expect them to tell you anything about private accounts."

"I know it was dumb. But I had to try."

"Didn't you believe what I told you?"

"I believed you. I didn't necessarily believe the teller who I think let Smitty and Charlotte walk out with the money but said it was Jimmy."

"Don't you think I questioned her?"

"Sure, but I think you may have wanted an outcome that was consistent with your case."

"What am I going to do with you?"

"Re-open the case, let me see all the files."

"No can do."

"Then you do it."

"Stop, Norris, before you get yourself in trouble."

"You *do* think something's going on."

"I didn't say that."

"But you think it."

"Go back to the boat and let me do my job."

NORRIS WALKED INTO THE RED BEAR and saw Gayle sitting at a table with the petite waitress she'd seen at Percy's. Gayle waved her over.

"You know Mimi, right? Join us. Calvin, bring her a draft."

"I'm not staying. I'm trying to track down where Ole went last night."

"That shouldn't be too hard. Hey, Cal," Gayle yelled across the room, "you see that old fisherman Ole in here last night, always wears the yellow boots?"

"Nope. Those old-timers usually hang over at the

Pine Cone or the Paradise," he said, delivering Norris's beer. "Drowned I hear."

"He was her next door neighbor down at the old marina."

"Whoa, babe, you are one unlucky woman. What are you . . ." he said to Norris.

"Shut up and go tend your bar," said Gayle, cutting him off.

Norris got up from the table.

"Where are you going?"

"I have to find out where Ole went."

"Not before you finish your beer. Right, Mimi? Nothing's going to change in the next few minutes. We'll suck these up and go with you."

A perfectly quaffed man in his thirties sidled up to the women, leaving his three buddies at the pool table. "I'm sorry to hear about Jimmy Ketah," he said to Norris as he handed her his business card. "I'm with Sorenson, Sorenson, and Lambert, Attorneys at Law. I'm Lambert, Tony," he said, "if you need anything," laying a hand on her shoulder.

"Yeah, she'll call you if she needs you," said Gayle. "Now scoot. We have our periods and you don't know when we might go into a rage."

He walked back to his table, red-faced. Gayle asked Mimi if she'd checked him out.

"Ring line," said Mimi.

"You guys don't miss anything. Maybe he's divorced," said Norris.

"And maybe I'm Beyonce," said Gayle. "I like hanging out with you. You're quite the catnip."

"I feel like there's a neon sign flashing: 'Over here, guys, a lonely one, new meat, move on in.' "

"Well, sweet pea, you have been hanging out in the bars alone," said Gayle.

"But I have a reason for doing it and everyone knows it," said Norris. "Nothing seems to be private in this town."

At first Norris was grateful for the offers of help. So many willing men. She thought it'd be easy to track down Jimmy or Smitty or Dix. But she didn't count on Juneau. Juneau and its roads to nowhere. Juneau and its isolation. Juneau and its men. Lots of men. Hungry men, burnt-out men, sweet men, young men, good-looking men, sinewy, burly, skinny-assed, any-way-you-like 'em men coming at you like horseflies. She was tired.

"Sometimes I think none of these helpful guys give a damn about Jimmy. They're glad he's gone," said Norris.

"That's what happens in Alaska where the male-female ratio is about eight to one," said Mimi. "Maybe you shouldn't be so nice."

"To hell with them all," said Gayle raising her glass.

Gayle was jovial and direct with the bartenders, easier and able to get more out of them than Norris. The Pine Cone, a hole with a few barstools, five tables and a battered pool table in the back, was a bust. Ole hadn't been there. Same thing at the Klondike.

On the TV above the Paradise bar, a couple of guys in wife-beater T's were pulling in fat ripe bass from some muddy Arkansas lake. The bartender Vern leaned on the counter doing a crossword puzzle and the other customers—two men retired from the world—sat at separate tables, one slumped over asleep, the other merely in a stupor.

"He was here alright," said Vern. "Sat right there and drank J&B till he couldn't stay on the bar stool."

"Was there somebody named Waco around?" asked Norris.

"Naw, I haven't seen Waco in a while."

"Was Ole drinking with anyone?" asked Gayle.

"Hell, I don't know. These old coots come in, grab a beer or a shot, visit a bit and totter over to the next place. Not that I recall, no. Who cares what the old duffs do? They aren't hurting anybody."

"Ole drowned," said Norris.

He was taken aback. "After he left here?"

"This morning," said Gayle.

"That's good. I mean, it's not good, but I don't need the cops shutting me down. Things are tough enough with the damn no-smoking laws and now making me responsible for the drunks. I don't force 'em to drink. I'm a service, not their mama."

"We just thought maybe he talked to somebody last night that might give us a clue to—"

"Norris was real fond of him," said Gayle, interrupting. "He was like a grandfather to her and she was just wondering who saw him last and if he might of said something, that's all."

"Oh, like what were his last words? Hard to say. Like I said, there were any number of the old-timers in here."

"OK thanks," said Gayle.

They started for the door.

"Hey, that guy Mick was blabbering to him for quite a while, now that I think of it."

"No shit? Actually talking to him?" asked Gayle.

"Yeah, he was giving Ole an earful and Ole acted like he was real interested."

"Who's Mick?" asked Norris.

"The loony you saw the other day," said Gayle.

"Captain Paranoid," added Mimi.

"Did you hear what he was talking about?" asked Norris.

"Hell, Mick's been blabbering about his CIA theories so long, nobody listens anymore. Not that you could decipher it if you did."

"Anything would help," said Norris.

"He's on this 'twenty-bucks' kick and something about the cops. I wouldn't have noticed except he flipped the twenty almost in my face."

"Yeah, the twenty-bucks deal is new," said Mimi. "I guess somebody sent him some money."

"Or bribed him," said Norris.

"YOU ARE ONE CRAZY WOMAN," said Gayle as they walked up the unlit dirt path to Mick's boarding house. "It's midnight and we're paying a social visit to a man who's certifiable."

"At least he's not a psychopath," said Mimi. "At least we don't think so." Reconsidering. "Are you sure we should be doing this? What if he hacks us up into little pieces?"

"Mimi, shut up. He's just confused, PTSD, not a psycho killer," Gayle replied.

"You could say Norman Bates was just a little confused too," said Mimi. "I'm going home. You two can tell me all about it in the morning. That is, if you're not stuffed into garbage cans all over town."

"Come on, Mimi," said Gayle.

"Don't say I didn't warn you," Mimi said heading back down the path.

"Warn you!" yelled Mick, jumping out from behind a laurel hedge.

Amazing how fast half-drunk screaming women can run.

NORRIS STUMBLED DOWN THE PILOTHOUSE STEPS into the galley and found the light switch. She started to fix some coffee and moved the paperback lying near the sink. Funny, she could swear the book had been stowed

101

behind the table. Not again, she thought, suddenly alert, completely sober, sniffing for the scent of Brut. No cologne mingled with the salt air, bilge, varnish. She cautiously made her way to the cabin. Jimmy's sweater was lying on the other bunk. Her skin prickled. She was positive the sweater had been at the foot of the bunk she'd been sleeping in. She liked the other one snug and empty like Jimmy had left it.

She scanned the shelves above the bunks. No doubt about it, the books and papers had been disturbed. She started back for the galley and thought she heard footsteps coming down the dock. She turned out the lights and listened in the dark. All was quiet except for her pounding heart and the clanging of the halyards against aluminum masts. She started to relax and heard it again. The steady rise and fall of footsteps coming down the dock. Coming for her? She wished she knew what was worth dying for.

The footsteps stopped in front of Ole's boat.

Norris knelt on the bunk and looked out the porthole. She could see the shadow of a man lurking near Ole's boat. The shadow lit a cigarette and stood looking at the cordoned police tape. Norris edged off the bed and felt for Jimmy's shotgun under the bunk. She'd laughed when Jimmy had shown her how to use it. Took a couple of seconds. Shotguns were no mystery. Not when she'd grown up in the woods. Not when ducks and pheasant were winter staples. She hadn't used one since she was twelve when she blew the head off a blue jay. Sport with her cousins. The end of shooting animals for her. She watched the shadow through the porthole as she ran her hand along the shelf and located the box of shells.

The shadow moved. No longer a shadow, the man moved toward her boat.

She dumped the shells onto the bed and fumbling, terrified, shoved them in one by one. Her heart raced. She could hear him stepping on board. Feel the boat list under his weight. The man on deck was coming toward the door. She snapped the barrel closed and stepped toward the galley just as the door handle turned.

The door started to open.

She released the safety and swung the shotgun up.

"Freeze! Sucker," Norris yelled.

12

"SUCKER?" A STARTLED VOICE answered.

"Warren?" said Norris, holding the shotgun at his chest as he stood still on threshold to the wheelhouse. "Warren! What are you doing here?"

"Darling, put down that weapon and I'll tell you. You know you could kill someone with a thing like that."

"That's the idea," she said, slipping on the safety, lowering the gun.

"I knew it was a mistake for you coming to this wild place. You've become totally uncivilized in a matter of days."

"It's been a lifetime. Ole, the fisherman next door was drowned yesterday."

"*Was* drowned? Don't you mean drowned?"

"I think he had help."

"What do the police think?"

"An accident. He slipped and fell."

Warren cocked an eyebrow at her. "Aren't we a bit paranoid?"

"Maybe. I don't know. I don't know what to think about anything. What are you doing here?"

"Don't you mean, 'Warren I'm so glad to see you?' And would you mind putting that rifle away?"

"It's a shotgun."

"Whatever. It's beastly."

"I'm sorry. I am glad to see you." She leaned the shotgun against the bulkhead and gave him a hug. "Very glad. Come. Sit. Talk to me."

She stowed the shotgun in the cabin and returned to the galley to fire up the propane stove.

"You handled that wretched machine like a professional, my dear. Since when do you know anything about guns?"

"Since forever. It's no mystery. There were always guns in the house. My father was a hunter. Yours too."

"That doesn't mean I ever touched the things. You are full of revelations. Just like keeping baseball from me."

"I didn't 'keep it from you.' You were never interested."

"That is true. But you could have *told* me. You could have insisted."

Norris laughed. His recurring theme was that she'd kept baseball a secret from him, even though he knew she was always playing ball. Always with her dad who coached. She married a ballplayer, for god's sake. A few years ago, Warren called her up in the middle of the night, accusing, "Why didn't you tell me!" And went on and on explaining to her what a fantastic thing that he'd discovered. One of his friends had taken him to a Mariners game. "It's Zen and ballet and poetry all in one. You kept it from me all these years! Norris, how could you?" She'd laughed at the time too. Warren could be so wonderfully dramatic. He'd discovered what she'd known all her life. What so many already knew. He was newly in love with the game.

"You don't know how good it is to see you. How did you find me?"

Warren lit one of his long, thin, brown Sherman cigarettes. "I went to the police station and asked if anyone knew a lunatic woman who'd lost an Indian. Not only did everyone know, they were kind enough to assign an officer to drive me here who pointed out your parking space or berth or whatever it is you call it. Some odious little man who still uses Brylcreem."

"Farley," Norris said, half-smiling.

"I believe that's what his nametag said. Quite a little brute. He wanted to know all about you, my dear."

"I hope you didn't tell him anything."

"Oh, loads and loads. None of which is true. Nice of him to drive me here but you weren't here, were you? That was hours ago. Leaving me to wander on my own on this island."

"Um, not an island."

"It might as well be. You can't get here except boat or plane. Now tell me that's not an island. And do you always greet a visitor with a loaded gun?"

"Only when I'm scared."

"You have been through it haven't you? You look awful. And that eye. Did someone hit you? I will make someone very sorry they ever laid a hand on you."

It amused her. As if. She was certain he was thinking glove slapping followed by a duel. "I tripped in some rigging and hit my head. It's healing."

"Time to go home."

"I told you on the phone. I can't. This is the only connection, the last link to him. I need to be here."

"I spoke to the detective. You should forget everything and concentrate on him. *Very* nice."

Norris knew he didn't mean Alex was kind. "Very nice" in that particular tone meant get him to bed as soon as possible.

"You talked to Inspector Tanner?"

"Honey, I've been here for hours. I've seen all the shops, talked to the detective, had dinner, listened to a man-and-wife duo sing along with a portable synthesizer in the hotel lounge, traipsed through the bars . . . The only things I haven't done were look at whales, see the glacier, walk through the treetops and ride the tramway. And I don't intend to do so tomorrow because I'm taking you home with me. You can't make a dead man come back. You have to face it, Norris."

"You believe Alex."

"He's convincing. And stress can do terrible things to a mind. Look at all those post office workers.

"I am not stressed."

Arched eyebrow.

"OK, a little. That body was not Jimmy. So where is he?"

"I'm sure I don't know. But if the police are satisfied, his wife and best friend are satisfied, where does that leave you?" asked Warren.

"Nowhere."

"Exactly. You're no detective. You can't just keep asking all these questions. This is a closed society and you are an outsider. People do not want to talk. You've come to town and proceeded to tell everyone they're crazy. Especially that studly detective. He's doing his job. The case is closed. You're coming back home where you belong."

"I don't belong anywhere."

"Well, you certainly don't belong here."

"I think I do."

"Norris. They wear fishing boots to dinner."

That made her smile.

NORRIS DROVE GAYLE'S FORD TAURUS toward Mendenhall Glacier—the one thing Warren wanted to see. The highway wound through patchy suburban settlements and what was left of the marshy wetlands.

"Did it ever occur to you that Jimmy might have wanted to disappear?" Warren asked.

"Of course. What do you think I do at night, sleep? But if he wanted to disappear, why would he bring me to Juneau? Why not disappear when he's already in Seattle?"

"Let's suppose this is an elaborate cover-up. The wife and the best friend and maybe the cops, or a few of them, are in on it. What's the motive?"

"Money," she said. "Love. Fear. Revenge."

"All very attractive in their own way. Let's suppose it's money, since there was that very nice deposit in Jimmy's account," said Warren. "Drugs do you think? Was Jimmy a user?"

"Not that I know of."

"What about his friends? That guy you told me about named Dix and the fishing partner in jail in Seattle?"

"Danny, yes."

"OK, let's assume there was some sort of deal going down. Did Jimmy do anything suspicious in the time that you knew him?"

"No."

"Was he ever out of your sight besides the bar that night?"

"No." She thought about it. "Getting the fish from Ole and at Eden's when he put the fish in her freezer . . . the fish!" she said, making a U-turn in the middle of the highway, partially running off the asphalt onto the shoulder annihilating a good deal of grass.

"I suppose this means we're going to Eden's," said Warren.

THE NOTE WAS STILL TAPED to the window. Norris rang the bell anyway. She was just about to use Jimmy's keys when the door opened. An Asian-looking woman wearing a silk Chinese robe the color of smoke with embroidered white peonies stood in the doorway. Her black shiny hair was caught up on top of her head, twisted into a bun, a little askew, pierced with ivory chopsticks keeping it in place. She was smiling. Wearing sunglasses.

"Welcome," she said, pulling the door open wide.

"I'm Norris Reed and this is Warren . . ."

"You're Jimmy's girl. And the tall one is your friend from Seattle. Juneau is a very small town. News transmits through the air like osmosis."

Norris guessed she was in her fifties. Great-looking fifties. Norris didn't want to think what Jimmy's relationship with her was.

"Jimmy and I were lovers at one time," said Eden, reading her. "No more. So you can put your mind at ease. He was nineteen when I first met him. I was almost thirty." She took a slim cigar out of an ornately carved bentwood box on the coffee table. Offered the open box to Warren and Norris.

"Cohiba," Warren said, "How nice."

She offered a silver lighter subtly etched with a Tlingit wolf. "Now, about Jimmy."

"Do you have any idea where he is?" asked Norris.

"I have an idea, yes. Eden blew a long thin strand of smoke and looked at the ceiling. "You have the same idea. Not with us anymore."

Norris couldn't speak. She put a hand on the windowsill. Steadied herself.

"I'm sorry. It's no use pretending. Whoever did this wanted Jimmy dead. Now he, or they, are playing games. I'm sorry about the fisherman too. I suppose he was in the way."

109

"He knew something," Norris said almost in a whisper.

"Did he tell you?"

"No," said Norris, not entirely telling the truth.

"You're lucky. I'd get the hell as far away from Juneau as you can. This is not a good place for you. The more you dig, the more you stir. It is not healthy for you, stirring."

"See, Norris?" said Warren.

"Listen to your friend. And don't fight Alex. Alex can be formidable. He looks like a pussycat, in fact, he is in many ways, but you are crossing him. I would never cross Alex Tanner."

"You sound as though you have," said Norris.

"Yes. But we've reached an agreement. Alex stays out of my life and I stay out of his. Now, would you like to see Jimmy's room?"

"I already have. I thought he might be here. I have the keys."

"Exactly what I would have done. He made this." She was handling a basket that looked as though it were made of gossamer. Norris touched it. It was taut, transparent, but not rice paper. Not any medium she could think of.

"Salmon skin," said Eden. "Our ancestors used everything. Some made salmon skin rain gear. It's water repellent, of course," she laughed. "They used and wore animal skins, bone, antler . . . wearing the items imbued the wearer with the spirit and the power of the animal. A sacred responsibility."

"Are you Tlingit?" asked Warren. "I suppose your name does not originate in Genesis?"

"Actually, it's Edensaw, meaning glacier. It's gender specific. My parents were expecting a boy. I am alas, not recognized fully by the Tlingit. My father was Russian, my mother Tlingit. In those days it was a disgrace for her not to marry as her lineage dictated but she was in love. Thus, I am an outcast as well. My parents are gone and I've never been ambitious enough to follow my lineage either here or there. I'm basically alone. Jimmy was like a brother to me. My only family."

Norris at the window, motionless.

"Is the Chilkat blanket real?" asked Warren nervously, scanning it intensely, changing the subject.

"My mother's," said Eden. "The only thing my grandmother gave her when my mother was banished."

"It's stunning," said Warren. "What's this fringe?"

"Goat wool and cedar bark entwined. Cedar to keep the fleas and bugs off when draped and dragging on the ground."

"Very ingenious," said Warren. "I should recommend the idea to some of my friends for their domestic beasts . . . Norris is a great admirer of Tlingit art as am I, but she has made a study of it, haven't you, Norris?" Warren said, trying to bring her into the conversation. "You most likely could tell her what the colors in this blanket are derived from. Weren't you and that woman Lydia on Vashon Island experimenting with leaves and things to see if you could replicate the colors? You'd be astonished what secrets the most ordinary homely vegetation harbors. Now, if I were going about it, I would simply pick a blue flower, boil it up and expect to get some sort of blue dye. Not so. Blue probably comes from an onion or ragwort or some such perfectly unblue thing."

"Did you really experiment with these colors?" asked Eden.

"Yes, a couple of years ago," said Norris. "My friend Lydia is a weaver with a farm on Vashon where she raises sheep and goats for wool. She's constantly working with natural dyes. We found an old text on the Tlingit and were ecstatic to find the recipes for the dyes. The black is from iron filings boiled in cedar bark, the pale turquoise is from copper nodules soaked in a slightly acidic solution and the yellow is from wolf moss."

"Wolf moss!" exclaimed Warren. "How delicious! Not from wolves, I presume."

"Yes. Not from wolves. We wove tapestries from our dyed wool."

"I'm afraid I'm only an accumulator of things from others' imaginations, not clever myself," said Eden.

"But with an excellent eye," said Warren, which made her smile.

"What do you do, Warren?" she asked.

"Antiques—a small establishment on Capitol Hill," he replied, fishing out a slim silver cardholder from his overlarge messenger bag, handing her his card. "If you're ever in the city, please call me. I operate by appointment only, of course."

"I'm sorry if this sounds rude, but we actually came here about the fish," said Norris.

"Ah, the fish," said Eden, darkening slightly.

"We thought there might be some clue or . . . I don't know," said Norris.

"You were thinking something was smuggled in the fish and Jimmy was killed over that something. And the fish might hold the answer. I, too, assumed the same thing. That's why I thawed them this morning."

Norris frowned. Warren rolled his cigar in his fingers, waiting.

"The fish were only fish. Nothing in them. I sent one to be smoked and I have the other filleted. Would you like to join me for dinner?"

Norris hesitated.

"We'd love to," said Warren.

"Let us fix our fish," said Eden. "Jimmy would like this," she said putting her arm around Norris, escorting her to the kitchen.

"SHE DIDN'T TAKE OFF HER SUNGLASSES." Norris said, parking the car above the marina. "You think she has a drug habit?"

"Maybe, but they were mostly covering up her black eyes. No doubt she fell in some rigging and hit her head. . . Or perhaps someone persuaded her to lie about the fish."

"What do you mean?"

"Whatever fish she filleted, weren't the fish Jimmy took her. I took the liberty of looking in the freezer on the back porch on my way to the loo while you and Eden were engaged in the living room. The fish, wrapped in newspapers like you said, were still there."

"We have to go back and get them."

"No we don't."

"Oh, yes. We are going back for those fish."

"No we're not."

"Give me one good reason why."

"Because they're in the back seat."

"Warren!"

They grabbed the fish, Warren depositing them in his shoulder bag, and headed down the catwalk to the dock.

"You are something, you know that?" said Norris.

"Yes," he concurred.

Norris slugged him on the shoulder and they trudged arm in arm toward the dock. Norris stopped, grabbed Warren.

"The boat!" she yelled, running down the ramp without him. "Jimmy's boat is gone!"

They stood speechless at the empty slip looking at Norris's few belongings piled neatly on the dock. The mask of Raven on top.

13

FARLEY LEANED BACK IN HIS CHAIR, picking his nose, as he talked to two rookie-uniformed patrolmen about the missing boat.

"Any news on our vanishing trawler?" Farley asked, wiping his finger on the cuff of his pants.

"Whose trawler?" asked Alex, overhearing the conversation.

"The screwy Reed woman. That woman's trouble with a capital T. You can smell it, boys. Once you get seasoned, it's a sixth sense," Farley said, tapping the side of his head for the rookies. "You can feel a bad situation rising." His sixth sense must have been a little off kilter because Alex had already grabbed him by the shirt collar and pulled him straight out of the chair. The rookies didn't move.

"When?" asked Alex.

"Last night about eight, nine," squeaked Farley. "She called and said she wanted to talk to you, but Humboldt . . ."

"Uh, huh," said Alex, releasing him so he thumped hard on the swivel chair.

"I told Humboldt it wasn't a good idea and he said you didn't need to be distracted. He said anything she needed he'd handle. It was Humboldt's idea. I didn't like it and I told him in no uncertain terms." Farley sputtered.

Humboldt came out of the men's room zipping up his pants.

"Since when do you censor my messages?" asked Alex, the veins on his neck pulsating as he stepped toward him.

"Since you've been thinking with your dick," said Humboldt.

"Where is she?" asked Alex.

"At the Baranof Hotel with her queer friend," said Humboldt, brushing at a wet dot of urine on his pants.

"Actually, we're right here," said Warren.

NORRIS AND WARREN waited in Alex's office while he made a trace on the missing boat. Farley entered, carrying two mugs of coffee. "Cream, no sugar. Sugar and cream," he said proudly, handing each the appropriate mug. "At least they left your things," Farley said to Norris. "If someone was out to get you, they'd take your stuff or dump it in the channel. I would."

"He has a point, Norris," said Warren.

"Sure," said Farley, leaning back against the desk exposing his white socks and ugly black crepe-soled shoes. "It's easy to make things bigger than they are. You're like me, Miss Reed, an overactive imagination. Guess I'm just a crazy kind of guy."

"Guess so," said Warren.

Norris kicked Warren on the ankle out of Farley's sight.

Farley straightened and they could see Alex in the hallway being harassed by a tiny withered woman in an immaculate lime housedress. Her hair was a pale apricot lacquered bouffant that could be mistaken for cotton candy. Her face was powdered clown-white, the eyebrows penciled black and startlingly arched with perfect round circles of rouge decorating her cheeks. She'd missed her lips with the lipstick or perhaps she'd gone out of the natural line to make her lips appear poutier. The woman poked Alex in the chest with one of her thin crooked fingers. Her bracelets jangled.

"She lost her dog a couple of days ago and hasn't let up on Tanner. Thinks someone stole it out of her yard. Says it's purebred but it looks like a mop to me," said Farley.

"Lhaso Apso," said Warren.

"That is right," said Farley. "Sounds like a country, don't it?"

"It does indeed," Warren said.

Alex wrested himself from the haranguing woman and entered the room.

"Find the boat?" asked Farley.

"I'd like to discuss this with Miss Reed and her friend," said Alex.

"Sure thing," said Farley pretending not to be hurt. "Need more coffee, just yell. Cream, no sugar. Sugar and cream," he said, cocking his finger like a pistol, shooting air and winking.

Alex gazed at his desk for a moment. It looked as though he might like to punch Farley. Norris wanted to punch him too. He was so damned puppy dog nice in a completely sleazy way.

"A very helpful individual," said Warren.

"Yeah," said Alex. "About the boat . . . It's on its way to Angoon."

For a fleeting moment, Norris let herself believe Jimmy had taken it. Alex read her.

"Jimmy's wife Charlotte had someone get it."

"Oh," was all Norris could say.

"It's legal, I suppose," said Warren, trying to be helpful.

"Perfectly," said Alex.

"If she wanted it that bad, she could have had Smitty

tell me and I could have gotten my things. She didn't have to wait until I was gone and steal it out from under me."

"They didn't steal it. And Smitty is the one who took it," said Alex.

"They killed him," she blurted, "And Ole."

"You're making the situation worse than it is," said Alex. "There's nothing unusual about anything that's happened. Wives claim property. Old fishermen step off docks . . ."

"And Indians get bludgeoned to death in alleys behind bars," offered Warren.

The room went quiet.

"I'm sorry," Norris said. "I don't know why I said it except for just a moment it made sense. I think all they did was take advantage of the situation. I suppose Jimmy had life insurance and they had nothing to lose by saying the body was his. I don't know if I blame them."

"We checked. No life insurance," said Alex. "No strong motives that we've found."

"Except the money in the bank," added Warren cheerfully.

"I'm checking that. No reason to think they knew about it."

"What about Waco?" Norris asked.

"Waco hasn't been seen for a week or so. Ole couldn't have talked to him. I've known Jimmy Ketah a long time and couldn't swear that body was his. Couldn't swear it wasn't. I've gone through all the files and the photos and there's nothing that points to it not being him."

"What about his clothes?"

"Anybody could have taken the vest," Alex said, "And the only explanation for the socks is you're wrong."

"You see, Norris," said Warren. She gave him a stare.

"What's up?" asked Drew, appearing in the doorway, taking off his aviator sunglasses and stowing them in his shirt pocket.

"Can you give us a few minutes? We're trying to solve a little problem."

"I heard about the boat. Can I help?" asked Drew.

"I think we can handle it," said Alex.

"There's nothing to handle. Jimmy's wife took his boat," said Norris.

"No shit. Left you with no home."

"Drew, I'll meet you at Percy's in thirty minutes," said Alex.

"I'm cool. Sure you don't want me to stay? I'm a decent problem solver. Hey, you could share my place, Norris. I'd be out of your way. I'm hardly ever there. It's only a trailer over at Winston's but it's bigger than Jimmy's boat."

"It'd be better if she went back to Seattle. She needs to get some rest, regroup, get a perspective," said Alex.

"I'm not some mental patient," said Norris.

"Getting there," said Warren. "Officer Tanner is right. You need to step away and get a perspective on things."

"Why are you siding with him?"

"Because you know me. A sucker for a man in authority."

Alex blushed and Drew laughed.

"Drew Murdock," said Drew holding out a hand to Warren.

"Warren Bartholomew. She's an old friend, that's why I can talk to her that way."

Warren was enjoying himself. "She was even strong-willed as a child. Remember how you would hide from your mother, not come in from playing outside until she called the right name—which you changed according to any whim? If anyone ever told you what to do, you would do the opposite. You hate being told what to do."

"This isn't funny, Warren," said Norris.

"Lighten up, dear," Warren said.

"Two people have been murdered and you want me to lighten up?"

Warren sing-songed between his teeth, "We're getting strident, darling . . ."

"Go to hell, Warren."

"She seems fine to me," said Drew. "Why don't you listen to her, Alex? You got your skinheads and the knife with their prints and case solved, all in one day. A little too convenient, isn't it?"

"Stay out of it, Drew," said Alex.

"I'm out. Just saying if the lady wants to be in Juneau, I don't think the law should pressure her to leave."

"I'm not pressuring her."

"Whatever you say, bud. Norris, you say the word, you can stay with me."

Alex exasperated. Warren amused.

"At least in Juneau I have a purpose."

"Purpose? You mean obsession. You don't want to mess things up for the detective, do you?" said Warren.

"He's perfectly capable of screwing up on his own," said Drew.

Alex shot Drew a look.

"This is making you crazy, Norris," said Alex, his eyes catching hers.

Norris and Warren got up to leave.

As they left, Drew called out after her, "View of the channel. Satellite dish."

14

THE BARANOF WAS THE BEST HOTEL in Juneau—stately, nine-storied. Historic, handsome and perfunctory, a Bauhaus of hotels, nothing excessive, some mahogany and marble, catering to visiting government types, conventioneers and visitors arriving by ship, ferry or yacht.

Warren had been lucky to get a room. It was still spring, early in the tourist season, but there were a couple of important bills on the legislative docket that kept otherwise out-of-town state lobbyists and legislators in Juneau for the duration. The desk clerks said they were full. Warren had straightened them out. Or, rather, he had acquired the Presidential Suite.

He opened the double mahogany doors and pounced on an envelope that lay at their feet, holding it to the light as though examining it for a hidden cipher. From Eden. A thanks for returning the fish, which they hadn't intended to do. They'd smuggled the fish into the presidential bathroom, Norris at the ready with her Swiss Army knife, only to find that the fish were not Jimmy's Coho, but smaller Jacks. The newspaper wraps dated after Jimmy's disappearance. Chagrined and foolish, they had returned the still icy fish to Eden with apologies. "We seem to have walked off with your fish," Warren had said, standing on her doorstep. She hadn't missed the fish, amused.

WARREN ORDERED LOBSTER BISQUE, rib eyes medium rare, Caesar salads and a bottle of Cabernet, California was fine. He then switched on the TV and cruised the channels, the remote held away from him as though it might detonate. "Let's see if we can find some entertainment. No. No. Awful. Worse," he said surfing like a pro.

"Since when do you watch TV?" asked Norris, settling in on the opposite end of the overstuffed couch, feet up, pillows plumped.

"Since . . . 'House Hunters International!'" Norris, you have to watch. I discovered it last night. Americans travel the world over to relocate and then complain that there's no oven in places like Singapore or Brazil that you could probably bake bread on a sidewalk and grumble that bathrooms and bedrooms are too small. It's a fascinating look at our countrymen abroad. Oh, Paris! Let's see what horrors the nice couple from Atlanta find."

After dinner, swathed in the oversized hotel robe, Norris swallowed the Oxycontin Warren gave her to help sleep. She padded to her massive bed, already turned down, Godiva chocolate in place on the pillow. She pulled a clean white T-shirt out of her bag that she'd never unpacked. She slipped the T-shirt on and for an instant felt homesick for Jimmy and the boat. Her clothes were saturated with the smells of the marina, the sea, the trawler—everything she associated with him. She got into bed and pulled the comforter over her head.

THE CLOCK SAID 12:30. It must be wrong. How could she have slept for fourteen hours? And no dreams. She went to her door and waited, listening. No movement.

She opened the door to the living room and called for Warren. No answer. Tapped on his bedroom door.

"Enter," he said. She found him lounging like a pasha in his silk burgundy and gold striped pajamas, doing a crossword, traces of breakfast on a tray alongside a disarray of newspapers.

He reached for the phone and ordered her breakfast. "What an attractive nightgown."

The T-shirt covered her enough but she helped herself to his overlarge hotel robe.

"Much better," he said, making a face. "The *Juneau Empire* is there," he said, pointing to the newspaper. "Nothing much. Tide tables. A school board wrangle of some sort. City Hall run amok. A policeman drove a couple of runaway juveniles home. An illegal fishing arrest. Oh, and a new show at an art gallery downtown owned by none other than Edensaw Michaelov. Our Eden. She called and invited us but alas we can't since we have to make our three o' clock flight."

"I've booked us. We're leaving," he said before Norris could protest. "You're exhausted and even though you're still under suspicion about the money business, they can't keep you here." Then as though she had given him undying gratitude he said, "You're welcome."

Norris stood at the window overlooking the rooftops of the motley, scrambled town, its buildings trickling down to the spectacular channel while Warren babbled about the plans he'd made. Norris spied a ramshackle hut on the top of the roof of the building across the street. Just like an artist's garret—an atelier in Paris, maybe a little less romantic—blue-chipped window trim and torn curtains, a couple of dried geraniums in the rotted window box. A broken catwalk crossed the tarred roof to a stairwell. Access from the bookstore below.

She could almost smell the moldy room, see the stained porcelain sink and the two-plate burner, the cupboards with faded flowered curtains instead of doors. She could live there in that awful little apartment. She could live anywhere. Norris considered. Maybe she should leave everything behind and contact "House Hunters International."

"I've promised Alex you won't run away and gave him your Seattle address and Rita's phone number, along with mine, of course."

She leaned her forehead against the windowpane.

15

WHAT *ARE* YOU DOING?" asked Warren as Norris scrolled through her cell phone as their taxi sat in traffic on I-5 headed to Seattle from Sea-Tac airport.

"Looking for the number to King County Jail."

"Oh, no you don't," said Warren grabbing for the phone. "You little bitch. I thought you were awfully complacent, coming back without kicking and screaming. It's that person, the one who was thrown in jail. Jimmy's friend."

"Danny. He must know something."

"Don't do this."

She found what she wanted and punched in the numbers on the phone. An electronic voice guided her from department to department.

"It's after six and do you even know his last name?"

Alex had mentioned it when he questioned her at the café but she was so upset with him . . . and then the money surprise. What was Danny's last name? Damn, what was it?

"What are you going to do? Ask the operator if there's a Tlingit Indian named Danny in jail, picked up maybe two weeks ago but you're not sure what day? And why would they tell you anyway?"

She disconnected. Warren was right.

Warren let her be quiet, staring out the window, the phone sitting in her lap.

"Oh, all, right," he said. "Give me the phone." He left a message for a friend to call him back.

"You have a friend who's a vice cop?"

"Why not? Besides, Trixie owes me."

TRIXIE AKA CAPTAIN TERRANCE R. REDDICK JR., of King County Sheriff's Department Vice Squad, met them five days later in front of the King County Jail, a white sprawling 1980s mega-structure downtown only a few blocks from the Tick Tock. He was blond, beefy, and looked like he could bench press a Volkswagen.

"Warren," he said, "Long time." They shook hands and he turned his perfect smile on Norris. "You must be Norris," he said.

"Nice to meet you," she said.

"Call me Terry," he said, "everybody else does."

"Not everybody," said Warren.

"Watch it," said Terry.

They walked through a metal detector manned by a deputy with a flabby gut who nodded respectfully to Terry. An elevator took them to the fifth floor where it opened onto an empty glassed-in waiting room—a mid-size room with cafeteria-like tables and benches, vending machines lining one wall.

"I thought it would be more convenient off-hours so you don't have to wait in line and jostle your way through the great unwashed. Maybe you'll have better luck than the Juneau investigator who was here."

"From Juneau? Alex Tanner?" said Norris, startled.

"Yeah, maybe. Sounds right. When I located your guy, Danny Jenkins, they said he'd had a visitor. "I got his sheet. He's been an oxy regular, recently graduated to heroin. Class C felony possession. Five years but he'll be out before then." Terry approached the glassed-in room and beckoned a guard on the other side to let them in. Norris and Warren waited with Terry at one of the tables for the guard to return with Danny. Danny was lean and muscled, nervous, strung out, his black hair a fuzzy buzz cut, a Tlingit frog tattoo on his right forearm.

Danny hadn't a clue what had happened to Jimmy. The news hit him hard.

"Fucking Alex," he wailed. "He coulda told me. He fucking coulda told me." Anger mixed with jerking sobs, he demanded to be taken back to his cell.

Norris declined dinner with Warren and Terry and walked the few blocks downhill to the hotel and through the tawdry entrance, slipping by the Tick Tock unseen.

She cringed every time she went through the lobby with its high ceilings and marble floors. The handsome mahogany paneling, brass fixtures and white oak reception counter had been ripped out years ago in the name of remodeling. The cafe fared better. Whoever had done the makeover had run out of cash. The 1940s red vinyl booths and the Formica tables remained intact even though some of the cushioned booth seats had cracks handily repaired by Joe with duct tape. The heavy stoneware dishes had been spared as well. All in all, the Tick Tock Café was a good, honest place and her life was not a complete disaster. She wasn't one of the old men. She wasn't Rita. She wasn't Danny going through withdrawal in jail. She wasn't dead.

She let herself into her room and wondered what Alex might have asked Danny.

Or said to him.

She put Jimmy's Raven mask to her face and looked out across the sound.

16

EACH MORNING NORRIS WOKE TO BLUE SKIES. Each morning breathless and stale. If there was one moment she could get back it would be that last. The way he held her in the starlit night. The way his chin rested on the top of her head. Not moving. Not talking. The utter peace of it. She held Jimmy's navy blue sweater to her face and breathed deeply. She made herself put it down. Put it away.

Now that Rita had help in the cafe, Norris didn't have to do breakfast, lunch and dinner but she did. It kept her occupied. Warren kept her occupied too, going out of his way to include her, ignoring her protests. The only thing she wanted to do was paint.

The city was noisy. In the ten days she'd been gone, she'd already become accustomed to the sounds of Juneau. By eleven p.m. the harbor transits, the hum of traffic on the bridge and the expressway, all the extraneous sounds would end. Seattle seemed not to sleep these days. When she'd first arrived those years ago after Bailey and her terrifying river run, Rita and Joe had given her a choice of rooms away from the highway but Norris wanted the corner and its northwestern exposure, the sweeping view of Puget Sound, Bainbridge Island and the Olympic Mountains.

NORRIS SET HER PAINTBRUSHES ASIDE. She'd worked and reworked the painting of Raven all night. It was better. Not perfect. The ethereal predawn blue was fading, the tips of the Olympics caught in sunrise gold. She stretched at her open window, kissed by the cool breeze off the bay, and watched a lonesome ferry ply the silken water.

Norris showered, slipped on a white shirt and clean jeans, and walked the five blocks to Pike Place Market. Saturday. Bustling with the frantic jockeying for parking places, the ebb and flow of the locals and vacationers, the voices of the vendors hawking fish and fruit and vegetables. Francesco Morani tossed her an orange as she passed. He loved to do it across the crowd and she'd catch it. Hold it up and smile.

"Perfecto!" he yelled. The crowd clapped. He juggled oranges and "accidentally" lost a few to onlookers. It wasn't as dramatic as the guys up the row who lobbed the king salmon back and forth over the crowd but it was fun. Their routine.

Norris tossed the orange in her hand as she walked—hellos to those she knew by name, nodding to those she didn't. She did her own shopping during the week. This was her Saturday stroll for fresh bread.

Norris had tried to talk Rita and Joe into letting her do the shopping for the restaurant, but no. They preferred to buy in bulk from their vendors. Almost sinful with the market so close. Norris wondered where the Tick Tock's supply originated. Florida? California? Norris tried to bring fresh produce for Joe to try, but he grumbled: what were they supposed to do with beets and chard and kale and what the hell was arugula?

Norris bought a baguette and threaded her way back through the throng. It was easy to spot the pickpockets, especially the gypsy mama sending off her three kids and waiting in the park to praise or slap them, depending on their success. In a way, Norris wished she could step out of herself and wear clothes like that—the colorful flowing skirts and shawls, the necklaces, bracelets and extravagant earrings down to her shoulders. She did dress up sometimes for special occasions like the play the other night with Warren but felt like a fraud. She was basically a jeans and T-shirt girl.

The tall Jamaican with the long overcoat and the striped woven hat caught her attention. He was so obvious, eyeing the purse sitting on the counter.

"Lady, you're about to be taken," said Norris, startling a hefty, sixty-ish woman in a mint green jogging suit.

The woman stared at her.

"Your purse. See that guy over there? You're open season."

The woman snatched her purse, clutched it to her bosom, gave Norris a nasty look. A bulky woman buying dried flowers two paces away gave Norris a dirty look too. It must have been her sister. Overstuffed twins. The Jamaican was gone. Norris could see his striped cap bobbing along through the crowd. She thought about explaining the perils of the market to them but walked on, secretly hoping the guy sitting nearby on a Mexican rug strumming a guitar pretending to be blind would snatch the woman's purse. The guy's hand on the fret subtly pointed behind her, still appearing to stare straight ahead behind his sunglasses. She looked at him. He wobbled his head ever so slightly in the direction behind her. What the? Norris took a dollar from her pocket and leaned down to put it in his open guitar case. "Behind you," he whispered. She stole a glance. Big guy, ball cap. Ducked behind a pillar when she looked.

Norris quickened her pace, weaving her way, stopping every once in awhile to try to spot the guy. Saw him again. He abruptly changed his pace, lingering casually over a pile of hazelnuts. She was being tailed. She rounded a corner, almost out of the market now, home stretch, where should she go? Catch a cab or bus to throw him off? She was sweating now even though shivering, goosebumps on her arms.

"Norris!"

She jumped. It was Warren banging against The Bistro window as she passed, sharing morning coffee and croissants inside with Bud Tanninger, the *Seattle Arts* theater critic. Relieved, she walked in and joined them.

The owner, rotund Jacques, greeted her effusively. She was glad to see him, feel the bear hug, but kept an eye on the window. No sign of the man. Silly, she thought. Nothing to worry about. She relaxed in his hug.

"Where you been, chicky? You love me no more?" he said, kissing her on both cheeks then suddenly distracted, knocking on the window and making shooing gestures at a trio of young women settling down against his wall. Teens bleak as winter, faces pale, frames thin, wearing dark hoodies, black jeans, zirconium nose studs and rings on every finger. Hair dyed as black as coal. Only a splash of color, the deep red lipstick. Stunning rather. Dramatic, like some sort of netherworld vultures. They paid Jacques no mind. Comfortable, cross-legged, they rolled joints. Jacques gave up in disgust.

"It's nothing new," said Warren. "Although the indigent seem to have gotten younger. Remember when it used to be bums drinking from paper bags? Same thing. New drugs. My god, you can buy heroin on the street."

Norris flinched at the thought of it. Danny. Her suspicions of Eden. Jimmy. Was there really a man following her?

"Warren tells me you're an artist," Bud said, jarring her out of her trance. "Sorry we didn't get to talk the other night."

"Oh, uh, me too, Bud," Norris able to answer, letting the foolish fear go. The other night, she and Warren had gotten to a play just in time, Warren a flying haphazard as usual, late, taking a taxi at the last minute. Norris thought he did it intentionally in order to make an entrance. It seemed to work. It had apparently gotten Bud Tanninger's attention.

The morning went on—small talk about her paintings, how Bud had seen one last night at Warren's, the one over the mantel. Warren interjected that she was leaving her abstract landscapes, moving into her Raven period, couldn't decide if he liked it or not.

"Her raving period?" asked Bud.

"Yes! Yes! Perfect!" exclaimed Warren. "Actually, it's Raven, as in big black bird, although raving might be more appropriate."

Candace and Merilee were making their way through the door. Norris didn't particularly want to see them. They had her slated for a November show at their gallery and she wouldn't be ready. Couldn't be. She'd been working on the one painting for more than two weeks and couldn't get it right.

Warren waved them over. "Hello darlings. You know Bud Tanninger, don't you? Merilee Fast and Candace Shank."

"Shank & Fast. Great gallery. Wonderful to meet you."

"We were just discussing the new work Norris is agonizing over," said Warren.

"Haunting," said Candace.

"Unfinished," said Norris.

"What a show when you've got the series done, though," said Merilee.

Norris sipped her coffee. Warren commandeered two more chairs.

"So what's the problem with the work?" Candace asked Norris.

"I've hit a wall," said Norris.

"You'll muddle through. You've never let us down," said Merilee almost chirping.

"Can we do anything?" asked Candace seriously.

Warren sat back, watching Norris. Norris didn't want to tell them. Not here. Not now. Candace and Merilee weren't exactly bosom buddies.

"Oh, it's a man. Weren't you going fishing in Juneau for the summer?" said Candace, turning to the others, "It's always a man."

"Candace," said Merilee.

What the hell, thought Norris. It wouldn't hurt to tell them. It was useless slogging through it, over and over alone. And Warren, her sounding board, was deaf to it now.

"It's complicated. I don't think you want to hear it," said Norris.

"Of course we want to hear it," said Candace. "Is it your fisherman? Did you leave him?"

"In a way," said Norris, her heart sinking, her face burning.

"You don't have to tell us, Norris," said Merilee. "Candace, you beast. It's too personal. God, you're incorrigible."

"Actually, he's missing," said Warren.

"How awful. No wonder you can't work. You're insane with worry. Where is he?" asked Candace.

"God, Candace, didn't you hear? He's missing. If she knew where he was he wouldn't be missing, would he?" said Merilee.

"I meant, where is he missing from? How does one go missing?" asked Candace.

"That's the question, isn't it?" said Norris.

"Tell them," said Warren.

She might as well. She knew Warren would as soon as she left.

"They found his body," Norris started.

"Oh, god!" said Candace.

"But it wasn't him."

"Norris is convinced it wasn't him," interjected Warren.

"Well, was it?" asked Bud.

"Everyone says it was," said Norris.

She told them everything: Charlotte and Smitty and Dix and Eden, Alex, Ole and even Danny. They listened carefully and attentively. Merilee fingered the chunky amber stones on her bracelets. Candace folded and refolded a sugar packet into accordion pleats. No one said a word until she was done.

"It's a cover-up," said Merilee. "The cops know the body's not Jimmy. And how come they haven't interrogated the wife and that best friend, Smitty? Those two are up to their ears in this. If I were you, Norris, I'd harass the bejesus out of them until they confessed."

"Or got rid of her," said Bud.

"Well, there is that," said Merilee thoughtfully.

"Isn't there anyone you trust up there, Norris? Someone who can help you? What about that Eden or the investigator?" asked Candace.

"Too risky," said Merilee. "He's too close to it. If there's a conspiracy he's in on it."

"I doubt it," said Norris.

"You are so naive," said Merilee. "Don't you read any thrillers? The good guy is always the bad guy."

"This isn't fiction," said Norris.

"Truth is always stranger than fiction," said Warren.

"Everything you see, is not necessarily what is," added Bud.

"That fisherman Ole talked to someone," said Candace.

"You find that someone and you find out everything," said Bud.

"Except that someone he talked to is not all there," Warren said, tapping his temple. "He's delusional, raving and paranoid."

"What if it's not a conspiracy at all, but a serial killer?" asked Merilee.

"And what's the connection?" asked Candace.

"Fishermen," said Warren.

"Priceless!" laughed Bud.

"A good Samaritan helping a dying breed out of their misery," said Merilee.

"Like the Green River killer getting rid of prostitutes," said Candace.

"They never found out how many he killed, did they?" asked Warren.

"No. Remember Ted Bundy? Now, there was a great serial killer," said Bud.

"Ooh, with the fake casts luring innocent coeds to help him," cried Merilee.

"He was so smart. And good-looking too," said Candace. "And working with, of all people Ann Rule, who trusted him completely, and who wrote nonfiction about serial killers! I still get chills when I think about it. Who wouldn't help out some clean-cut charming guy? I mean in broad daylight no less."

"Skillful murderers are always smart and charming,"

said Merilee. "That's why they're so convincing. Psychopaths understand human weakness. They prey on the gullible. They come off as sincere but are totally detached."

"If I were a serial killer I'd do nothing in common. You could get away with it forever," said Warren.

"Clever boy," said Bud.

"But serial killers murder by instinct and obsession, not simply to see if they can get away with it. There's always some perversion that slips them up," said Merilee.

They were suddenly a coven, a secret society infected with their own hypotheses that no longer included Norris. She watched them as they spun it out. Warren was caught up in it too, throwing in bits of colorful intelligence. It wasn't real to them. Only stories. A party game. The crescendo of their voices and the clatter of the Bistro, the jostling of dishes, the whoosh of the espresso machine, descended upon her. Norris excused herself.

"Don't go," said Merilee.

"I've got to get to work," Norris lied.

"Bye, love," Warren said, half-hugging her from his chair. "I'll call you later and tell you how we solved the disappearance of Jimmy Ketah."

They all laughed.

If only, thought Norris, starting to leave.

"Wait. Who did you say? Jimmy Ketah?" asked Merilee. "Norris, that's your man? Really?"

"Oh, my god, Norris," said Candace. "Jimmy Ketah is amazing. He was here in Seattle last month. The buzz was he was selling something fabulous to, well guesses were Bill Gates, Phil Knight, the Bullitts, Amazon."

"Oh, my god. Norris, the money is no mystery," said Merilee. "They all use a broker like Gordon Pierce. Not a word ever gets out how much they pay for original art. A hundred and fifty thousand is not unfeasible. Gordon always uses cashier's checks to protect his clients. Untraceable."

FROM HER HIGH WINDOW, Norris watched the ferries heading out like plump green and white layer cakes lumbering across the sound. They were loaded with summer fares, the cars stacked, the crowds crammed on the decks. Below her on the waterfront the cars sat sectioned off in rows waiting. Those were the lucky ones with only an hour or so to wait. The others, lined up as far as she could see down Alaskan Way, might be there three hours or four. The visitors were biding their time, some reading books or newspapers, some standing in the sun visiting, some lined up for Ivar's fish and chips. Kids in back seats hot and sweaty, yelling are we there yet, fighting, the frazzled look of parents coping. The hot dogs, the popcorn, the candy, Cokes, and ice cream, the sticky hands and spun out screaming squirming of children on sugar highs. How did parents do it?

A gull keened past across the blue blue sky. A wave of loneliness hit her.

A month gone. She'd called and told Alex about the money and he'd thanked her. She asked if there was any news and he'd said no, as though he wondered: news about what? She was back in her routines but removed. A fugitive. Opera and theater and lunch or happy hours with Warren and his friends. Gallery openings. Sailing with friends. Playing poker with the old men. A Mariners game or two thanks to Bailey's old teammate Roger Cooke who was now an announcer. Small lonesome pleasures. At least Rita and Joe weren't tiptoeing around her anymore.

Something caught her eye. A bright flash from the sidewalk below. A tourist taking flash photos in daylight? No. The flash of sunlight on a lens. A camera pointed in her direction. Or a rifle scope. She leapt back. Ridiculous, she thought, catching her breath. Utterly ridiculous. She'd let all that serial killer blather at The Bistro warp her thinking. She peeked again. No one. Nothing.

THE NEXT DAY SHE CHECKED out the spot where she thought she saw the person with the camera. Walking, looking at the building, trying to triangulate where he or she was standing. She thought she found the place, surprised that her window was so visible, although, didn't she love that she could see for miles unobstructed? Visibility works both ways. She looked down for clues. Nothing stood out. The usual detritus of a city street. Her cell phone rang in her pocket, startling her. Number unknown on the screen. She answered it tentatively, a weak hello, mouse voice.

"Norris Reed?"

It was Terry Reddick, Warren's friend from the vice squad.

"I don't know how to tell you this. Thought I should let you know," he said.

"Is Warren all right?" she asked, anxious.

"Not about Warren. Danny Jenkins is deceased."

Silence. Not even a breath.

"Norris?"

"How?" she asked, a whisper.

"Heroin overdose."

"In jail?"

"We don't know how it came in. It happens."

"Did anyone visit him?"

"Apparently a girlfriend from Juneau. Do you know a Shari Strand?"

Norris didn't.

"We've worked with the investigator up there, Alex Tanner. Sent her address and picture we got off our cameras. He recognized her, a sometimes dealer in the area. The Anchorage address on her ID was nonexistent. Trouble is, Shari Strand is a floater, picked up by a fishing boat two days ago off Sitka, wherever that is. Friends, roommates, family? No one knows her, right? No one ever knows anything. I doubt if we'll ever find out what happened. I talked to Danny a couple of times. He was an OK guy, wanted to get clean, wanted to find out what happened to his friend. I'm sorry it turned out this way."

"Me too," said Norris quietly. A connection to Jimmy gone. Two more people dead. Conveniently untraceable. She thought about telling Terry about the man at the market and the possible camera aimed at her window. "Terry?"

"Yeah?"

A pause, rethinking. "Nothing. Thanks . . . Terry?"

"You trying to tell me something?"

"What happened to Danny's body?"

"Retrieved by a friend. Flown home. Guy named Owen Dalton, goes by Smitty."

No surprise.

"YOO HOO, NORRIS." Warren at the door. "I've brought Bud to see your newest work," said Warren, opening the door to let him in. She stowed her paintbrush on her palette and pulled back a strand of

139

hair, smearing vermilion paint along the way. She wiped her hands on her cutoffs.

"Wonderful!" said Bud, staring at the raven on her easel, the bird dominating the forty-by sixty-inch canvas. He examined three other large paintings leaning against the wall, nearly identical. "You've connected with an intangible. It's like they're alive, watching, but endowed with something mystical." Bud was beside himself with pleasure and Warren, having brought him, was pleased with himself.

"Norris has raven dreams," said Warren.

"Beer?" said Norris heading to her small fridge and handing them bottles.

"I love your studio," said Bud. "What a view! Who owns this place? I can't believe they haven't fixed it up. Do you know how many people would kill to have a place like this? They're sitting on an absolute fortune."

"My sister and brother-in-law own it but they can't afford to renovate," said Norris.

"They'd sell or remodel if they could find their partner," said Warren.

"He's a Vietnam buddy of my brother-in-law Joe," said Norris. "The last they heard, he'd bought a sheep ranch in Australia. Trouble is, they're not certain where. It's been nine years."

"They don't even know if he's dead or alive," added Warren.

"What a windfall if he's dead," said Bud.

17

EDEN HANDED NORRIS a cup of hot tea.

"So Charlotte inherits everything? Even this house?" Norris asked.

"No, that goes to me," said Eden.

Norris was back in Juneau. Danny's death and Bud's comment had worked like an acidic tonic. Woke her up. The weight of grief no longer pinned her down, no longer shrouded every waking moment, leaving her helpless and dazed, bewildered. This time she was not helpless and lost. This time she would not leave Juneau until she settled it. One way or another she would find out what happened to Jimmy.

"What else does Jimmy have that someone would kill for?" asked Norris.

"That's rather blunt, isn't it?"

"Eden, I lost him for something."

"Jimmy bought the Seattle place sixteen years ago with his first totem commission," said Eden. "Next came the trawler and his auntie's house on the island besides financing my galleries in Anchorage and Juneau. This place he bought two years ago."

"Wow," said Norris.

"I know what you're thinking. We all had motives. It looks bad. I can't tell you how much I miss him and I wish I could make it right."

"You could tell me about the fish."

Eden picked up the teapot, refilled their cups. "The Coho were just Coho. I'm sorry if you read something into it."

"Did you know Danny died of a heroin overdose in jail?"

Eden nodded.

"What about your black eyes—the sunglasses—when Warren and I were here?"

"I fell. This is not going away for you, is it?"

GAYLE, NORRIS, AND DREW MURDOCK climbed the wide staircase to the porch. A handsome, sturdy home, four stories, built in the 1890s with timber logged from the hill it sat on overlooking Juneau. A tidily tended lawn in front with rhododendrons as big as trees. Norris had walked by many times and thought it was part of a small public park. Now it would be her yard. Carmen Taylor had renovated the house into apartments after her husband Walt died. Kept the bottom floors and the basement—laundry room and storage to share. Stanley Morton, owner of Klondike Krafts, had the third floor. Norris would rent the top.

On the walk up the hill, Drew told her about Walt. They used to fly together for Winston Helicopters. Three years ago Walt took a client to Barton Ridge to hunt Dahl sheep. They landed on a slope and the hunter stepped out into the rotor blades. Walt panicked, went to his aid, and stepped into the blades too. Drew and State Trooper Gifford flew up a day later and cleaned up the remains. Garbage bags full of body parts. Drew took a long vacation in Cabo. Trooper Gifford took a leave of absence and never returned. And that's what happened to Carmen's husband Walt.

Carmen was waiting at the front door, a redhead in her late seventies, an Ann-Margret look-a-like wearing sling-back turquoise mules with kitten heels, black Capri pants and a puce silk tunic with hand-painted fluorescent hummingbirds darting crazily across the front. Carmen ushered them into her immaculate apartment, a mid-century museum that looked as though no one had occupied the living room since 1967—Danish modern ash furniture, coral and turquoise accents. Norris guessed Carmen had nothing to do but clean house. And drink. Her lethal dose of Chanel No. 5 did not cover the reek of gin.

Carmen offered them drinks which they declined. She refreshed her highball and they took the stairs to the top floor. She called it a studio apartment but it was fairly large—a good-sized living room with a hide-a-bed, a separate kitchen and a short hallway to the bathroom.

"It used to have fabulous views until they built that government monstrosity in front of us. You can still see part of the channel through there," said Carmen, pointing with her glass at the bay windows.

The room was practically all windows. The only area unexposed was the door to the stairwell and the hall to the bathroom. Otherwise, windows all around.

"This is fantastic," Norris said, thinking she might even set up an easel. All that light.

"No shower," said Drew as they inspected the bathroom. Norris noticed the same thing, looking at the freestanding iron-clawed tub. Carmen OK'd the idea of setting up a shower and Drew said he could do it no sweat.

"Drew will do right by you. Don't know what I'd do without him," said Carmen giving his bicep a squeeze. She handed Norris the keys and headed out but turned back with a word of warning about Stanley on the second floor:, "Careful, he can talk you to death."

"Welcome to Juneau," said Gayle.

"In celebration of your new home, dinner tonight?" Drew asked Norris.

Gayle nodded vigorously at Norris behind his back.

"I need to get settled," said Norris.

Gayle rolled her eyes.

"How about some help? I could bring takeout," said Drew.

Gayle stared at Norris.

"I guess so," said Norris, not convinced.

"Hey, I don't want to pressure you," said Drew.

"I'm sorry. I'm not up to dating or anything," said Norris.

"Not a date. Nowhere near a date. You're moving in. I'm helping. And if I happen to bring food along with the hardware to fix the shower, that's because I'm hungry. No way I'm thinking of you."

"You are such a pain in the behind," whispered Gayle as Drew left. "What a ball-buster. Drew isn't used to women refusing him."

Norris couldn't help it if other women fell all over themselves for Drew Murdock. Gayle thought she was being dumb and blind, couldn't see what a catch he'd be. Shoot, a pilot and all. Norris could see the attraction from Gayle's point of view. But she still had unexpected paralyzing moments—a trawler powering into the bay, a red pickup, a voice, the back of someone's head, resemblances, reminders—the sudden whump, the intense ache.

"You didn't tell me you were back," Alex said, leaning against the lunch counter at Percy's.

"Was I on probation?" asked Norris, a smart-assed answer that made his eyes go flat. In a way, she was sorry but didn't apologize.

He was cold now, a no-nonsense cop. And she was just another waitress. "Coffee. Black," he said.

She poured it.

Gayle had talked Percy's dragon lady manager Mrs. Pinchot into hiring her for the summer.

"You could have told me she was back," Alex said, to Gayle who was perched on the stool at the counter next to him in her shorts and halter-top having a Coke on her day off.

"You too?" said Gayle. "Hey Norris, what kind of perfume are you wearing? Whatever it is, I want a gallon."

"I'm sorry I was flip," Norris said refilling his coffee. "I would have called you, except I didn't want another lecture on why I should stay in Seattle."

"Still obsessed with Jimmy Ketah, huh?"

"I wouldn't say obsessed. That sounds so psychotic."

Alex looked at her, shook his head, smiled.

"I'm not psycho-obsessed. Every waking hour is not consumed with finding him."

"Just every other hour," he said.

"Uh, huh."

She left him to wait on the moose of a man in bib overalls at the far end of the counter, put the order up, then slipped a piece of blackberry pie ala mode in front of Alex.

"What's this?"

"Blackberry pie. You look like a berry pie sort of guy."

"I am," he said, looking at her quizzically.

"Gee, that was nice of you Norris," Gayle said, slurping the last of her Coke.

Norris and Alex looking at each other, truce.

"Now it's going to get good," Gayle said as Drew walked in.

Drew sat next to Alex. "You look forlorn, bud. Aren't you happy Norris is back in town?"

"Thrilled," said Alex.

Norris nervously waited on customers, conscious of the two men sitting at the counter watching her every move. It was like she was on exhibit. Go away, she thought. Please, go away.

"She has nice hands, doesn't she Alex?" said Drew. "Sort of reminds me of Maya."

Alex wiped his mouth with his napkin, threw it on the counter. "Fuck you, Drew," he said and left.

"Who's Maya?" asked Norris.

"I'm going home now," Gayle announced as she swiveled off the counter stool.

MAYA WAS ALEX'S WIFE," Eden said to Norris. "They'd been married less than three months when she died."

They were sitting on Eden's back porch drinking Margaritas in the sun.

"Drew and Alex met in the Gulf War. They took a trip to Bali on leave and both met Maya. Drew brought her back to the states after his tour and they lived together in Seattle for almost a year before she dumped him to move in with Alex. After a month, they got married in Vegas. Apparently, no hard feelings.

"Things got sticky after about a month. A lot of arguments. Maya was temperamental, liked to play the guys against each other. She was incredibly exotic, lovely, and who could blame them? One night Alex and Maya had a yelling blowout on the dock in front of their apartment and Maya somehow ended up in the water. Alex hit the lake, diving. The water dark, winter cold. After several attempts he finally snagged her, dragged her back onto the dock. Tried to resuscitate her. It was too late. She had gouged her head on a cleat as she fell into the water. Some of her scalp and strands of hair were still on it.

Drew blamed Alex, said he murdered her. It came out later that Maya wasn't only playing the flirt: she was actually involved with Drew. She told him Alex had threatened to kill her and was afraid for her life. Drew tried to convince the police. They didn't buy it. It was officially an accident."

"Maya was seeing Drew when she was married to Alex?"

"Yes."

"How did Drew and Alex end up in Juneau?"

"Jimmy."

"My Jimmy?" said Norris.

"They were all in the Gulf together. Alex went through a bad time after the war and losing Maya. He fell into a crowd in San Francisco. Women, drugs, you name it. Jimmy went after him and brought him back to Seattle."

"So Alex lived in Seattle with Jimmy?"

"Danny and me too. We all lived in this falling down grand old former whorehouse on Lake Washington, The Casa de Lago. It was three stories high, built part on land and part on piers into the lake and all of the apartments opened onto huge full-length seventy-foot porches. They say the loggers would row across the lake to the whorehouse before Mercer Island Bridge was built. The porches wide for dancing. I don't know if it was true or not. But it certainly was a romantic place. Drew built a heliport on the dock so he could land whenever he was flying through."

"Drew was there?"

"He roomed with Dix when he wasn't flying on assignment somewhere. Alex went through his rehab living with me."

Norris was stunned to silence, took a long swallow of her margarita and suffered brain freeze. Hands to her temples. These people had a whole lifetime together that she knew nothing about. They were nearly a decade older and had managed to live completely distinct other-lives. Except for Drew who was still flying.

"Are you all right?" asked Eden.

"It's amazing, that's all. You were all there when Maya died."

"We lived there, yes. It was a horrible time. I blame Maya. I think she wanted a skirmish where eventually Drew would kill Alex. She started it. Her drama backfired. Karma, huh?"

They drank in silence and watched a heron alight at the end of her dock.

"Refill time," Eden said, getting to her feet and going into the kitchen. Norris followed.

Eden placed fresh ice cubes in their glasses, poured tequila, Cointreau and lime juice.

"What did you all do in Seattle?"

"Smoked dope and pretended we were artists. Well, actually we were but only Jimmy took it seriously and I realized right away that I had a good eye but couldn't stick with anything long enough to finish it. I dabbled. Photography, watercolors, some writing."

"What about Alex?"

"Alex got well. He helped Jimmy with a couple of stressed steel sculptures—you can see two in the Arboretum, one at the Frick museum on Capitol Hill. I don't know why he gave it up. Once we were into our thirties the lifestyle didn't suit us anymore. I suppose we grew up. We each wanted to make a decent living. And funny thing is, for Jimmy and me at least: we wanted to come home. Jimmy bought his boat and I started a gallery, thanks to him. A gallery was difficult to sustain in Juneau when the government was much smaller. Most of the town used to close up in winter. The airport was in the boonies. I migrated to Anchorage and opened a gallery there, which did fairly well. Now, I have the one in Juneau too. Drew tells me you're a painter."

"Drew?"

"Norris, we all know each other. You think we don't talk?

Duh. Of course they talk to each other, thought Norris.

"I'd like to see some of your work," said Eden. "Why are you waitressing instead of working on your art?"

"Because it's good, honest work and it's mindless."

"And takes no heart," added Eden handing her the glass. "It's hard to be creative when you're bereft. You'll heal. All this will dissipate. In the meantime, you could work for me. I'm having trouble manning the gallery. I want an artist in there who can carry on an intelligent informed conversation with customers. However, artists, as you know, tend to be a little flaky."

"Thanks, I'm happy where I am now, besides at Percy's I . . ."

"At Percy's you can keep an eye on nearly everyone in town."

Norris smiled.

They took their refills and went back out into the sun.

"I can't get over that you all knew Jimmy really well and nobody has a clue why or how he disappeared," said Norris.

"Believe me, I wish I did. I know in my heart that Jimmy is gone, whether the body they found is his or not. Jimmy was my best friend on this earth."

"I didn't mean to accuse. But it's so entangled."

"I guess I'd feel the same way if I were you and realized that we all knew each for eons. One of us must hold the key, huh?"

19

THE TRAWLER HADN'T BEEN TOUCHED. Jimmy's books still lined the shelves and the bunks were made, just as she'd left them. Drew was talking to Smitty in the galley. The whole island had opened up since Norris arrived with Drew. The opposite of her trip with Ole. No one hid behind curtains or ignored them. Mel at the grocery store gave them beer and sat out on the porch for a visit. Drew treated everyone like his best friend and everyone treated him in kind. It was nice. He made people feel good.

They jumped off the boat onto the dock and the girl with the bike and the purple tennis shoes was there hanging over the rail with the one-eyed dog.

"This is Lauren," said Smitty. She wiggled her fingers in a wave to Norris.

"We've met," said Norris, smiled back.

"Hey, Lauren, how'd you get so big? You're turning into a real beauty," Drew said.

She made a face.

"Don't you act like that. Tell Drew you're sorry," said Smitty.

"Sorr-y," said Lauren quietly.

"*Not*," said Drew whispering in her ear, which made her giggle.

"She really looks like Jimmy, doesn't she?" Drew said to Norris.

Norris stared at him. It hadn't dawned on her that this girl was Jimmy's daughter. It hadn't crossed her mind. But yes, she did. There was something in the eyes—a playfulness and a seriousness that reflected her father.

"Aren't you using the boat?" asked Norris.

Smitty shrugged, and said, "Charlotte."

"She won't even let us kids on it," said Lauren. "It'd make the coolest clubhouse."

"It's a working boat," said Smitty.

"That's not working," said Lauren.

"You want to go out to Grandpa Jack's or not?" asked Smitty.

"Yessir," she said.

They walked down the dock and got in a shiny sixteen-foot aluminum boat with a sixty horsepower Yamaha.

"New boat?" asked Drew.

"Yeah, my other one got dry rot," said Smitty.

"My dad's money bought it," said Lauren. "He died so you could have it."

There was no answer to that. Smitty fired up the outboard and they were off. They flew past fishing shacks and private docks. The one-eyed dog sat bracing forward, face to the wind, ears flapping, a trip he was used to taking. After twenty minutes, they passed Grandpa Jack's dock, long out of use, covered with moss, seaweed, mussels and barnacles. Smitty gunned the boat into a sandy inlet on the otherwise rocky shore. He jerked the motor up out of contact with the bottom and they drifted in until it was shallow enough for Drew to leap out and pull the boat on shore. Norris and Lauren jumped out onto the sand. At the high tide line, half on sand and half on patchy grass, sat a well-worn wooden skiff without its motor. They could hear the whine of an outboard coming from behind the fishing shack that was Grandpa Jack's summer home.

Grandpa Jack, with his long gray and black hair streaming down his back, was revving an Evinrude clipped to the side of a barrel of water. He turned the handle, upping the revs. He turned it down and shut it off. He shook his head in disgust, his hands on his hips.

"Hey," said Smitty, in his soft monotone as they approached.

"Hey!" yelled Lauren, running to his open arms.

"I told you I'd get you a new one," said Smitty.

"Nothing wrong with this," said Grandpa Jack, a little more sour than he needed.

"This here's Drew and Norris, friends of Jimmy's," said Smitty.

"Seems like I met you," he said to Drew.

"Yes sir. We went fishing out over Whistler's Point years ago, caught some Chinook," said Drew.

"That's right, that's right," said Grandpa Jack. "What brings you out this way?"

"Remember you told me you had something urgent to tell Jimmy that night?" Smitty said.

The man's face went dark.

"Nope. But that doesn't mean anything. Probably needed some cigarettes," he said, patting the one-eyed dog.

"Or Doritos," said Lauren.

"That's right," he said, looking at Lauren fondly. "Gotta have my Doritos."

"Just like Jimmy said," confirmed Smitty.

"C'mere, I'll show you something," said Lauren tugging at the Norris's sleeve.

She led her down a grassy path into the near woods to a large flat rock about the size of a Fiat. Lauren climbed up and looked to the other side.

Norris followed. Water bubbled up from the ground forming a crystal clear pond, the surrounding area lush

153

with sword fern, salmonberry and mosses. Maidenhair fern sprouted from the rock's underside.

"Look, trout lilies," said Lauren pointing at the delicate flowers hidden in the foliage.

"Nice," said Norris.

"You loved my dad, didn't you?" Lauren said abruptly.

"Yes, I did," said Norris, starting to fog up.

"Good," said Lauren. "He needed someone."

They stood side by side and watched the clear water. A school of minnows darted by.

"It's artesian water," said Lauren. "It sounds better than just an old spring."

Norris agreed and asked where she'd learned about artesian water. From the Internet of course, Lauren told her like, duh, and looked at Norris like she was an alien when she said didn't even have a computer.

"I got a new iPad at home. The whole school is wired."

"Wired, huh?" This remote village on the western edge of civilization. Wired.

They were quiet for awhile, watching water-skippers glide across the water, salamanders in the mud. Lauren took her hand and they walked through the woods to the shore. No one in sight for miles. Just beach and rocks and driftwood against the tree line. Ocean vast to the horizon. Norris got the nerve to ask, "Do you have any idea what happened to your dad?"

Lauren stiffened, said nothing. They stood holding hands staring out to sea for a long moment.

"He left me standing on the beach," Lauren said quietly.

"What do you mean?"

"Abandoned. It's like nothing. I'm here but nothing."

Norris drew her in, holding her tight."

"I know," she said.

20

THE ISLAND MAY HAVE BEEN MORE FRIENDLY but Norris and Drew didn't learn a thing. Jimmy was dead to the island. Smitty offered to take them where Jimmy's burial ceremonies had taken place. Norris thanked him, no.

Smitty opened the door of the blue house with yellow trim, welcoming them. The only hitch in the village was Charlotte. She could have been pretty, petite as she was, but Charlotte was nervous and hidden, her face veiled in her long black hair, concealed behind a curtain. The old woman with the long gray braids who had come to the door on the visit with Ole was at the kitchen stove stirring tomato sauce.

Charlotte picked up a fussy baby with an orange-smeared mouth and deposited it with the four- and six-year-olds lying on the living room carpet watching cartoons on a new flat-screen TV. Norris, Smitty and Drew stood awkwardly near the door while Charlotte remained inside, unwelcoming, wiping up the mess the baby had made on its highchair.

Norris spotted a two-foot-tall plaster Madonna standing on a shelf with some shells, a picture of a potlatch, a half-empty baby bottle, a small totem and a carved wooden box in Raven's motif, clearly Jimmy's hand.

Norris asked if Charlotte and Smitty were certain the body was Jimmy's. The old woman muttered and

Charlotte whispered, almost hissing, "Don't start, auntie." The woman put down the wooden spoon and walked to her bedroom and shut the door. One of the kids looked in Charlotte's direction and promptly turned back to the TV. Smitty said no doubt about it, that body was Jimmy's right, Charlotte?

"That's right," snapped Charlotte. "I guess I should know." Challenging Norris with fiery black eyes.

THE SHIPS MADE THEIR WAY into the channel, luminous white against the stupendous mountain backdrop.

"They're magnificent, aren't they," said Norris.

"Yeah. If only they'd stay out there," said Gayle.

Gayle, Mimi and Norris sat in an empty booth on a break. Two hours until the *Nordic Princess* arrived with fifteen hundred on board.

"Here's your boyfriend, Norris," Gayle said, nodding toward Mick coming through the door. He cased the café as usual, scanning like a dutiful spy. He planted himself at the counter and looked to both sides suspiciously then pulled a newspaper out of his shirt, a secret document. He unfolded it just enough to read and laid it flat on the counter, his arms surrounding it so no one could see. He read intently, jamming an angry finger at the newsprint every once in a while.

Gayle and Mimi stared at Norris.

"Oh, no," Norris protested, "I had him yesterday." Mick had been in the restaurant two and sometimes three times a day in the few weeks since she'd been back. She tried to find out if he had spoken to Ole, but he was skittish. And incoherent. She stared at Gayle.

"I had him at lunch," said Gayle.

"Yesterday, twice," said Mimi.

"All right," said Norris, giving in, moving to the counter.

"Orange juice?" Norris asked, knowing full well he wouldn't answer and it was orange juice he always had. Norris wondered if he had once ordered it and no one ever bothered to ask again. What had Gayle said? Seven years he'd been coming in, sitting at the counter drinking his orange juice and reading his secret documents, always the same *New York Times*, at least that's what they thought, nobody knew what date. She wondered how long he'd been this way. If the Delta Force pin on his beret was real, if he'd once been in the elite Army special ops. No one had been working there long enough to tell her except Percy himself, and he was retired at a leisure village in Palm Springs.

Norris brought Mick the orange juice and set it in front of him. He eyed her, quickly smothering the paper with his arms, head down. Not until she'd moved to the end of the counter did he uncover the newspaper and continue reading.

Norris wiped the already clean Formica counter and watched him. He wasn't that old. Maybe late fifties, sixties. He was simply weathered, his face and hands tanned like rawhide. But his eyes were bright. Quick blue.

He drank the juice without interrupting his reading. When he was finished, he fished in his pocket and put his quarter on the counter. He folded the paper neatly and stuck it back under his shirt. In a startling motion, he thrust the twenty-dollar bill toward Norris.

"Twenty bucks!" he said, flapping it toward her. "No cops." He shoved the bill back in his pocket and hurried out the door.

"The twenty bucks again?" asked Gayle.

"I wonder what happened," said Norris.

157

"Stuck in Juneau," said Gayle, in a whinnying laugh.

Norris finished her shift and started for home. As she crossed the street and started up the hill, she saw the black Crown Vic take the corner and slowly pull up beside her. The driver's window was open and Alex had his tanned arm resting on it.

"I know what you're going to say," Norris said.

"Then I guess we don't have to have this conversation," Alex said.

"OK, I'm sorry. I thought Drew could help me find Smitty and make some sense of everything. You know how people talk to Drew."

Alex adjusted his sunglasses. She could see her own reflection in them.

"Did they?" asked Alex.

"No."

"We've had an open-ended murder case on the books for five years in Angoon and no one will say a thing. They're tight out on the island. It gives new meaning to community spirit."

"Did we get you in trouble?"

"The village officer reported Auntie Menah and Tilly Jackson were upset. I think because you and Drew didn't stop to talk to them. I told him you were free to go wherever you wanted. So, how are you and Drew getting along? Tight, I hear."

"People don't have enough to do, do they?"

"Nope. Can't get away with anything."

"He believes me."

"At least he wants you to think he does," said Alex. "I appreciate your loyalty and tenacity, Norris. I wish I had you to work with. Want a lift up the hill?" he asked, putting the car in gear.

"You know where I live." A statement.

"Doesn't everybody?" he smiled.

NORRIS BOUNDED UP THE STEPS, skipping the second, reminding herself that she really needed to get it fixed. Maybe Drew would do it. She carefully opened the front door and tried to sneak through the hallway past Carmen's door and get upstairs without being discovered. Funny that Carmen had warned her about Stanley liking to talk. She'd learned that Carmen liked to chat too. And chat and chat. Lightly now. She got by the ten paces to the stairway. Now, if she could get past the next floor and Stanley, she'd be home free.

Norris quickly crossed the landing. Stanley's door was half open. Norris dashed by holding her breath. One step, two. Four more stairs and she'd be safe. Norris didn't want to hear about his hard-luck life. Or Carmen's. Or the lives of the people she worked with. Norris thought she should be more sympathetic but Juneau was full of lonely people who'd lost somebody and were left behind. She was already one of them.

GAYLE DROVE THE WAY SHE WAS—casual and careless, chatty and bordering on crude. Norris liked her no-nonsense tell-it-like-it is persona but the driving? It wasn't the one hand on the wheel with the opposite hand gesticulating with the cigarette out the window or the reckless passing with a horn blast and a friendly finger as much as the talking and the looking at everything except the road.

"I wish I had a muumuu," Gayle said, commenting on a woman at her roadside mailbox.

They were headed out of town to the UPS shipping center to send Gayle's son a care package. Twenty-three years old, his fourth tour in Afghanistan. Norris walked to the end of the parking lot to watch the planes while

Gayle went inside. A couple of trucks loading oversized cargo from the UPS plane across the tarmac caught her eye. One of the trucks she recognized as the Mexican pottery guy, the one at the Fred Meyer parking lot. He was signing a cargo slip on a clipboard held by a woman—a woman Norris recognized. Eden. They shook hands and he drove off. A couple of men finished loading a van that apparently belonged to Eden.

"There you are," said Gayle, approaching the fence where Norris was standing. "What's so interesting?"

"You know that Mexican guy who sells tapestries and statues at Fred Meyer's?"

"Yeah. I sent my kid one of those wall hangings to decorate his tent to remind him of home—a real nice whale breaching. So?"

"He seems to be in business with Eden."

"Wow. Covering the high-end and low-end markets. Smart woman. I wonder what else she's into."

Exactly what Norris was thinking.

21

THIS FAR NORTH IN THE HEIGHT OF SUMMER the sun barely set. Norris worked days, roamed nights. She did her job, was friendly on the surface, declined picnics, softball, tennis, bingo.

She spent some time with Eden, dropping in at the gallery or visiting on her porch. Eden, who cheerfully told Norris that, sure, she hedged her bets by importing the Mexican goods as well as selling exclusive art and artifacts. And no, she wasn't aware that Smitty was selling on his own. She didn't know if he had a place on the mainland or where he might stow the pickup.

She took long walks along the high perimeters of town at midnight, one a.m., two . . . Like Norris, Father Davidovitch appreciated the twilight midnight hours with the city asleep below and the cruise ships berthed. He had seen her in his church that morning in April, saw her leave and understood what it was that made her run. Norris was grateful for his serene company. A man with few burdens except those of others. A man who knew absolutely his purpose in this life. She envied him that comfort.

Most nights, they ended their walks with a cup of chai in his office. He kept a teakettle on the pot-bellied stove and always had to shove away mounds of papers, books and notes on his desk to make room for their mugs, never apologizing, wondering every time how the things accumulated. Admiring the icons on his walls, Norris asked if many of the Tlingit were Catholic. He said not many early on, those being mostly Russian Orthodox and Presbyterian but perhaps twenty percent today, with a vague certainty there wasn't a Catholic church in Angoon. She could ask at the Diocese Center or the cathedral downtown.

She told him about Smitty and the Madonnas in his pickup. Odd, he wasn't aware of Smitty Dalton selling religious objects. The big guy, right? Right.

She tried to paint, tried to capture the elusive light of the northern nights. She did a decent painting of the church and another of Father Davidovitch in his office clutter. She probably wouldn't have done either if Eden hadn't arrived one evening with an easel and supplies. Norris had brought a few of her favorite brushes with her, brushes rolled in a piece of turquoise silk her mother gave her from China before she died. Norris tried to work on the current canvas, a row of ravens on her windowsill—at turns, Edgar-Allan-Poe-macabre or comic. She wanted to get them right. They were always there, single or a pair, curious, watching her, cocking their heads like spaniel puppies waiting for a treat, always with keen eyes for shiny items they could take.

She was missing one earring from a pair left on the kitchen table and foolishly hoped they would bring it back or maybe bring her a prize, a ring, a trinket in return. She was used to them now, their constant presence, their incessant chatter, which sometimes seemed not merely squawking, but talking. Somehow they connected her to Jimmy. She began to imagine that she should understand them. Somewhere in the back of her mind a consciousness. They were talking. To her. It happened when she was distracted painting or mindlessly preoccupied—washing dishes, folding laundry. A language specific and clear, if only she could decipher it.

She spent some time with Drew when he wasn't flying which was rare. In summertime Alaska everybody takes advantage of the long daylight hours. Flights to remote villages and construction sites, wilderness rivers and lakes, forests ravaged by wildfires to be reseeded. Engineers, geologists, biologists, vulcanologists, trekkers, fishermen and State Troopers—everyone had to have a helicopter.

Drew was easygoing, nonintrusive. A friend. He amused her. Drew had that disarming charm. He could strike up a conversation with anyone instantly. Norris was amazed how people responded to him, would tell him intimate details of their lives. Norris knew most everyone tolerated her tireless inquiries because of Drew. Norris knew, too, that Drew was interested in more than helping her find out what happened to Jimmy Ketah. How could she not know with Gayle and Mimi reminding her every day?

Finally he encouraged her to stop hanging out in the bars hunting for implausible links. It was no use asking about Jimmy anymore. Or about Waco who hadn't shown up again. Sometimes Norris wondered if it were all an act. Drew Murdock, the cool, friendly, smooth-talking, ageless boy-wonder pilot.

Father Davidovitch, Eden and Drew were all welcome diversions and painting helped but there were still too many hours of light with no relief, leaving her off-center, sleepless, longing. She thought she could handle anything alone, she'd been alone for so long. She didn't count on twenty hours of daylight keeping her awake, the constant sun wearing her down. Like sleepwalking. Drifting, unfocused, removed. Over and over she'd do the scenarios, every detail again. There had to be something she'd overlooked.

"CHICKS REALLY DIG A GUY IN A UNIFORM," Farley was telling Mimi. "See that one over there with the tits?"

"I see four women sitting at the booth," said Mimi.

"The one with the tits, in the pink thing."

One of the women wore a fuchsia spandex tube top that stretched across her ample bosom.

"Watch this," Farley said, winking at the young woman and licking his coffee mug seductively. She stared right through him. "See," he said.

Mimi and Norris laughed. "Oh, yeah. She's hot for you," said Mimi.

"How's it goin'?" Farley asked Norris when Mimi went into the kitchen.

"Fine," said Norris, wondering why Farley was being friendly.

She'd been cool at one of his first suggestive encounters and he'd snubbed her ever since. Today here he was asking her to go to a movie, out for Chinese on Friday. Sorry, she was busy.

"C'mon, try me, you'll like me," Farley whispered, wiggling his tongue.

"Excuse me?" said Norris.

"You heard me."

"I may have heard you. I just can't believe you," said Norris.

"Wrong color of skin?" he said. "A white man not good enough for you?"

Norris turned her back on him, walked away.

"What you gonna do? Call the cops?" snorted Farley, who headed for the drugstore's rack of magazines where he made a point of looking at bare-assed women in *Maxim*.

"What a jackass," said Gayle.

"The first time he came on to me," said Mimi, "he asked me to go on a picnic. He said, 'I'll bring the wine, wear a skirt.' "

"Eeeeew," Gayle and Norris said in unison.

Mick made his usual reconnaissance landing on the stool at the counter and spread out his newspaper. He seemed especially agitated today. Mimi put his orange juice in front of him and he jumped, frightened. Mimi and Norris exchanged a shrug and went on to their customers.

He was talking rapid-fire nonsense. It was almost like the ravens on Norris' windowsills, jabbering a language at the edge of her understanding.

"Hospital for observation. Hah!" he said, "Don't trust the cops. Twenty dollars! Don't tell. Waco? Wake up. Wake up! Everything fine he says. Waco, look out!! Rock! He smashed it! Everything fine, he says. Everything fine. He smashed it. Skull pops and him cool. Everything fine. Waco! Noooo, No." Mick put his hands over his ears, shaking his head back and forth. "No reason no reason no reason smash his head like that. Twenty bucks! No cops."

Norris jerked to look at Mick. She was taking an order at the booth behind him and heard him . . . heard him like the ravens chattering, then an explosion of understanding.

"What did you say?" she said, and he was up and out of his seat in a flash, grabbed his newspaper and was off.

"Twenty bucks! No cops!" he shouted back at her.

"Wait!" she yelled after him, running.

As she cleared the door she ran straight into Alex.

"Alex. Get him. He knows. He saw it, Alex!" Norris said, pushing him down the sidewalk.

Alex took off after Mick who was already a block away. Alex gained on him and Norris watched them disappear around a corner.

MOST OF THE CUSTOMERS WERE OUTSIDE on the sidewalk next to Norris.

"What'd he steal?" asked Farley, his hand on his holstered gun.

"Nothing," said Norris.

"What the hell is going on?" Mrs. Pinchot said, coming out of her inner office, her half glasses still on her pointy nose, a pile of order slips clenched in her scrawny chicken hand, the claws painted bright red.

"Norris thinks Mick saw the murder. He was the one who talked to Ole," said Gayle.

"OK, the party's over. Everyone back to work," Mrs. Pinchot said. Customers and staff shuffled back inside.

"Are you sure?" said Gayle.

"I heard him," said Norris. "He said someone smashed Waco's head with a rock."

"G-i-r-l-s," Mrs. Pinchot glared as she clicked on her four-inch spiked heels back to her den and shut the door.

"DID YOU GET HIM?" asked Norris when Alex returned.

"He locked the door on me. He was scared to death."

"No wonder. His refrain *is* 'no cops,'" said Gayle.

"What did he say to you?" Alex asked Norris.

"It was all garbled, but it seemed like another man was there. Someone crushed Waco's skull with a rock and gave Mick twenty dollars and said no cops," said Norris.

"He said Waco? And someone gave him twenty dollars not to tell the police?"

"As far as I could make out."

"Maybe the mystery man was a cop," said Dooley, a longtime Juneau fixture sitting in one of the booths.

"Anything else?" said Alex, ignoring him.

"Not that I can remember. He knows something, Alex."

"I don't see how we can get anything out of him. This is a guy who thinks the CIA has him wiretapped," said Alex.

"This is a guy who thinks the gumball machine is a person," said Gayle.

22

NORRIS OPENED THE DOOR to her apartment and jumped back. The windowsills were covered with ravens. There must have been twenty of them. "Hey, come on in, guys, make yourselves at home, tell me everything you know. I'll put the teakettle on. Cookies? You'd like some cookies, wouldn't you?" she said.

The ravens cocked their heads watching her go to the kitchen. More stood on the kitchen sill.

"Who are you talking to?" asked Drew behind her.

"Drew!" she yelled, jolted.

"Jumpy, aren't we? Who were you talking to?"

"The ravens."

"Uh, huh. You can tell me while we fix dinner," said Drew.

"I don't have any food."

"I do," he said. Drew took her hand and led her to the bathroom.

"How'd you get in?"

"Carmen," he said.

"Oh, my god," Norris said, staring at the bathtub. There were two Dungeness crabs and a rangy bumpy-legged king crab, crawling over a small tuna, a Coho and a pile of shrimp along with a six-pack of beer spread out on ice. "Where did you get them?"

"I have a lot of spare time when I take people out, so I make use of it."

"You caught them?"

"Yeah, with a couple of cases of beer."

"With beer, huh."

"I leave a few cases on an island about twenty miles out and my fishing friends leave what they feel like in exchange. I hadn't checked the island in four days. Bonanza. Tonight we'll have the Dungeness and tomorrow we'll have a feast. We'll invite everyone we know."

While fixing salad and setting water to boil, Norris told Drew about Mick who hadn't shown up in days. Lying low, scared by the chase no doubt.

"I think I have a better chance to talk to him than Alex, even though Alex said not to. Mick's more scared than dangerous," said Norris.

"Yeah, but whatever he knows may lead to someone who is." Drew said as he picked up the crabs, pincers waving, and plopped them into the boiling water.

They carried their meal to living room and settled on the couch. Norris took a bite of an open-faced crab cracker sandwich. "If I'm ever on death row, this is what I'll order: Dungeness, soda crackers and mayo," she said.

"I'll remember that," said Drew, leaning back and watching her. He swigged on his beer and kept his eyes on her.

"What?" she asked.

"Nothing," he said, smiling. "Just looking."

"Well, stop. You make me nervous."

She fixed him a crab sandwich and shoved it toward his face. He ate it all in one bite and grabbed her wrists. They looked at each other until Norris broke away.

"Do you think Alex is covering up?" asked Drew.

"Do you?"

"I don't know."

169

"But you don't trust him."

"We have a history."

"Eden told me."

"We were best buds until Maya." said Drew, taking a swig.

"You loved her," said Norris.

Drew blushed. Odd seeing him vulnerable. He, the confident one, the sanguine. "Yeah," he said.

"And you blame Alex."

"Alex was responsible for losing her."

Norris took a deep breath. "Am I responsible for losing Jimmy?"

He was quiet for a long moment, then pulled her toward him and kissed her. Their mouths were salty.

Norris could have succumbed. She wanted to forget. To be surrounded. Overwhelmed and taken. For a moment she let herself be in another place. He was too much. She shoved him away. He didn't leave though, asked to stay. And she didn't feel like saying no. Now, with him sleeping in her bed, she wanted him gone.

She sat in the armchair at the window in her T-shirt, her bare legs pulled up, knees to chin, her arms wrapped around her shins. As far back as she could remember, she thought life would be simple. Marry a ballplayer, live happily ever after. She started out right, but it was the ever after she was having trouble with. The isolation in this far corner of the continent came crashing down and pinned her in its sheer mountain enormity. Pressed her right to the icy core. She shut her eyes and listened to the noisy clatter of Drew's intense sleep. She'd never known anyone to fall asleep as quickly as he did, talking one moment, a sudden intake of breath, a quick gulp like he was drowning. Sleep captured.

She'd fallen asleep too, but not before tossing and turning, she under the covers, Drew on top with a

170

throw, unable to move his heavy arm from across her chest. She couldn't find a comfortable position. He was thick with upper body muscle. Dense. The heat radiated off him. She'd gone to sleep, falling finally into the rhythm of his breathing until he woke her shouting, "Look out!" Her heart exploded in terror and she pressed against him, hiding her head in his armpit, trembling.

He said it was nothing, only a dream. Sometimes flashbacks from the Gulf. And then he was swallowed in sleep again. She slept fitfully, her dreams ominous and tormented. Her recurring shadow dream was back. She was freefalling and blind. Every time it started with a rush . . . of what? All around her the sound swift and delicate and she couldn't see. The air getting colder and colder, then the scream again. Every night she heard it. She woke sweating.

She extricated herself and slipped out of bed. She went to the kitchen for a glass of water. She stood watching him. Rather than go back to bed she sat in the chair. In a couple of hours he would go, flying out with dawn's first light. There was a semblance of night now in the summer dimming twilight—a few scant hours of dark then dawn before four. A couple of hours of dark and she could usually sleep. Not now, though. She wanted him gone.

23

NORRIS STOOD ON A HIGH CLIFF overlooking the
channel. No. Not the channel. Open sea. She had a vista
for miles. She was above the mists and fog hiding the
whole of Gastineau Channel and shrouding the islands.
She heard the dreaded sound, the whoosh and the wind,
but this time she could see and she wasn't on a cliff, she
was flying.

She thought she was riding a bird then knew she
wasn't. She felt the wind in the wings, felt the wings
resisting, the wings flapping, cutting through the air. She
was strong, the wind in her face, no longer terrifying. She
could feel her powerful wings catching an updraft and
sailed with it. Wings! She'd had flying dreams before, and
falling dreams, but never wings. She soared along the
coastal mountain ranges and islands, gliding. She was
Raven. She had inhabited Raven's body but she didn't
have Raven's mind. Raven was hunting. For food?

They scanned the high meadows alit with morning and
she saw the Dahl sheep grazing in patches of green and
snow, wildflowers profuse, gently lilting in the morning
breeze. They cruised and cruised and then headed toward
the glacier. They flew above the ice and she felt the cold.
They flew and flew, dread mounting. She suddenly felt a
warm presence. The sun coming up? She started falling
then awoke. Drew was touching her arm. He was dressed
and ready to go.

"I hated to wake you from dreaming," he said.

"It was strange. I was flying," she said.

"Speaking of which, I have to go." He kissed her on the forehead and left her to shake off the dream, still curled in the chair.

"WHAT'S WITH YOU, GIRL? You're a zombie today," said Gayle, delivering the French toast piled with whipped cream and strawberries to the table of regulars. She rang up a bill at the cash register. "You look terrible. You look like you haven't slept all night."

"She hasn't," said Katherine Paget, who owned the Whale of a Buy gift shop a block away, "I happened to see Drew Murdock's pickup leave this morning when I was up getting the newspaper." She plopped a strawberry slathered in whipped cream into her mouth.

"Norris, you bitch! I'm so jealous, I could kill you," said Gayle. "Tell us every detail. He's good, isn't he? Tell me he's fantastic."

"I don't know," said Norris.

"Miss, where's our order?" It was the tourists in the booth by the window.

"Coming right up," Norris said, searching her pockets to see if she still had the order ticket. For the life of her, she didn't know what they were having. She went in the kitchen to see if she had an order up.

"Doesn't know," Gayle said, shaking her head.

THE NIGHT WAS BALMY, THE AIR SWEET and cool after a hot day, a perfect night for baseball. That is, if you played baseball at midnight. Father Davidovitch and Norris descended the long stairway from the hillside and turned the corner to the church. It looked as though someone had left a dark piece of cloth on the gatepost. When they got nearer, Father Davidovitch picked it up. A black beret.

"Looks like Mick's," he said.

"Where's the pin? He always had that Delta pin on it," said Norris. "Maybe it's not his."

"Have you seen anyone else wearing a beret in summer in Juneau? At least we know he's still in town," Father Davidovitch said as they headed downhill to Mick's boarding house. They knocked and called until someone in an adjacent room yelled at them to shut the fuck up. Norris was momentarily embarrassed for Father Davidovitch. Then remembered he'd been in the Russian Navy.

Norris had never had a close relationship to anyone in the clergy because most of them she'd ever met had seemed such prigs. Isolated and out of touch. Weak, pasty men. But here was a robust man of the world. He'd earned the privilege to counsel and guide. Maybe even to preach. You could confide in and admire such a man in spite of his religion.

They conjectured where Mick might be hiding, wondered why he'd left his hat. It had been a sweltering day and too hot to wear a wool cap, even though no one had ever seen him without it. Father Davidovitch said he missed their walk last night—didn't exactly ask where she was. Norris told him Drew stayed over which brought a wry smile. A questioning twinkle in his eye.

"He just slept. I didn't," she said.

"Still having the dream?"

She told him how it changed.

FARLEY LEANED ACROSS THE CASHIER'S COUNTER talking to Gayle. She was listening closely, rapt. Gayle would never be interested in the weasel, thought Norris.

Look at those stubby little fingers—Gayle's conviction about the correlation of finger and foot dimensions to dick size.

"Oh, god!" Gayle said, flapping her hands like she'd stuck them into a pile of fish guts, had to get the smelly clingy bits off. "Norris! They found crazy Mick stuffed in a trunk."

"A kid and his dog found him," said Farley. "Maggots and flies everywhere."

"Eew, eew, eew" said Gayle.

"Mick?" asked Norris, her stomach lurching. "Where did they find him?"

"That old Russian church up on the hill," said Farley.

"Hey, Norris, don't you know the priest there?" asked Gayle.

But Norris was already in the bathroom retching.

Alex walked in and motioned to Norris as she exited the bathroom. She met him at the door.

"Who did it?" yelled Gayle across the room.

"Don't know," said Alex.

"Oh, sure you do, Alex. You were the last person to see him alive," said Gayle, teasing.

Farley enjoyed it, sucked an obnoxious laugh through his teeth.

24

"DO YOU HAVE TIME FOR A DRINK, DARLING?" asked
Carmen, poking her head out of her apartment door as
Norris came in.

"Do I," said Norris.

Carmen in orange Capri pants, a lime green tunic and
bobbing orange "Sputnik" earrings. Carmen was so
neatly put together that none of her crazy outfits looked
ludicrous. She expertly refilled her highball glass
decorated with hand-painted palm trees and handed
Norris a gin and tonic in its twin. Norris took it gladly,
sitting on the immaculate orange vinyl couch.

"This came for you dear," said Carmen, handing her
an envelope. It was unaddressed, unstamped. "It was
left in the mailbox this afternoon. I happened to see
who delivered it."

"Norris" was hand-printed on the front and
"private" underlined three times. She opened the
envelope and retrieved a single sheet of paper, on which
was scrawled, "Watch your back." Enclosed was a
yellow and red striped Delta Force pin.

"You saw who delivered it?" asked Norris, trying to
be calm, keep her hands from shaking.

"He was a young man wearing a black t-shirt with
the sleeves ripped off and faded blue jeans with holes
unraveling at the knees. He didn't appear very well

kept—shoulder length, unwashed blond hair and a rather ratty goatee—you know blonds really shouldn't try to grow facial hair. Does he sound familiar?"

"Oh, sure," Norris faking. "Uh, it's an invitation to a party."

Carmen seemed to buy it. "We used to go to parties," she said, swirling the drink in her glass, a moment of wistfulness.

"Refill?"

"Thanks, I've got to go."

"I hope it's a nice party, dear."

"Sounds like Quentin Graves," said Alex.

"The guy's a junkie," said Humboldt. "Besides, we're not sure he left it."

"The description fits," said Alex.

"So what if it's him?" said Farley. "Practical joke, if you ask me."

"Nobody did," said Humboldt.

"We'll put out feelers for him. There aren't too many places Quentin can be," said Alex.

"I still say it's a waste of our valuable time," said Farley as Alex escorted Norris out.

"Shut up," said Humboldt. "If Tanner wants to search for a low-life junkie, that's his business."

"The killer chose the church because I go there," Norris said to Alex as they walked outside.

"Not necessarily. Anyway, I don't like it. Low profile now, no harassing anyone."

"Go home. Be a good little girl?" Norris said.

"Something like that."

NORRIS LEANED OVER the rail at the wharf watching the channel, a subdued gray in the afternoon cloud cover. A summer storm, precursor to things to come. She supposed winter would be bleak.

It started to rain and the sweeping squalls patterned the surface of the water. The intense desire and despair was softening. Norris didn't know what Jimmy looked like any more. He was memory hidden in the shadows, an echo of some fleeting thing she'd grasped in one fine moment. Norris could make herself crazy trying to remember, yearning to get him back. Jimmy Ketah was hers in a heartbeat. Etched in her being. Then gone. Jimmy was like a childhood story, now faded, whose essence you feel but can barely recall. You simply remember that you loved it.

THE CROWN VIC CAME to a halt beside her.

"We got lucky. Get in," said Alex, then drove toward the bridge. "A patrol saw Quentin walking near Sandy Beach headed toward the bridge."

"So everybody's pretty familiar with Quentin," Norris said.

"Quentin is a twenty-five-year-old addict who's in and out of trouble all the time. He's likely to OD before he's thirty. Last week a couple of our boys picked him up off the old Glacier Highway passed out in the middle of the road. He'd taken a handful of pills. Didn't know what they were, was just hoping to get high. They took him in and got him a burger. He sat there, ate, barfed and started eating again, picking up the bigger chunks and chowing down. The officers were grossed out. He's famous. Everybody knows him."

They crossed the bridge and cruised the waterfront. A squall scurried across the channel and rain fell in fat blobs onto the windshield.

"A lot of my time is spent chasing the trail of drugs that users and small-time dealers like Quentin get. It's as bad here as big cities in the lower forty-eight, maybe worse. Especially Anchorage and the Mat-Su Valley—Palmer,

Wasilla. Weed's a given. Cocaine and Oxy aren't as bad as they were but it's 'hello meth and heroin' . . . and alcohol abuse is just as bad. It's outlawed in the villages so they smuggle it in or make homebrew. Substance abuse is a never-ending cycle. It's like mercury, you know? You think you can catch it and it shoots off in another direction.

Norris hadn't thought of mercury in years. She and Rita used to love it when a thermometer broke and they could play with it, scooting it across the kitchen table like a game of mini hockey.

"There he is," said Alex, making a U-turn.

Quentin trudged barefoot along the side of the road in his razor cut raveling jeans and black sleeveless T-shirt, just like Carmen said.

"He's a nice kid. He might make something of himself if he could get clean." Alex got out of the car and walked toward him.

"Quentin. How's it goin'?"

"Hey, man," said Quentin. "What's happening?"

They walked toward the car. Quentin made his way unsteadily.

"What're you on, buddy?"

"Nothin'."

"You're a little unstable."

"Yeah. I hurt my foot."

He showed Alex an open cut on the bottom of his left foot.

"How'd you do that?"

Quentin thought long and hard. "I guess I lost my Tevas out on the tailings," he said finally.

They approached Norris standing by the car.

"This is Norris," said Alex. "You delivered a note to her this afternoon."

"I did?"

"Big house on the hill by the museum."

179

A glimmer of recognition flickered in his eyes.

"We need to know who gave you the note."

"I can't remember."

"You know I'm patient to a point and then I get unhappy. You don't want to get me unhappy," said Alex.

"No, man. I can't."

Alex patted him down and retrieved a lighter, a cigarette pack and eight dollars—three ones and a five, crumpled—all of which he put on the trunk of the car. He examined a small wad of tinfoil.

"Uh, oh," said Alex.

"I don't know how that got there. It's not mine."

"Yup. Amazing how things magically appear in pockets." He unrolled the foil and found only burnt residue, hard to determine what it was without testing. Meth? Coke? Or heroin. "You know you're on parole for using, right?"

"I don't know nothin' about nothin'."

"OK," Alex said as he started to cuff Quentin. "I'm detaining you while I call your parole officer and one of two things will happen: I suggest you go back to jail or I suggest you go to rehab. Right now I'm leaning toward jail."

"Dude, you can't do this," pleaded Quentin as Alex cuffed him and placed him in the back seat. He grabbed the hand-held mic. "Your choice," to Quentin.

"Dude, dude! Wait. You have to swear I never told you."

"You never told me," said Alex, releasing the mic button, still holding it.

"This older dude. Name of Dix."

"Dix," repeated Norris, almost inaudibly.

"You know where Dix is?"

"He hangs out. Lives across the street above the Gold Rush. Or he could be at the college."

"School's out. Any other bright ideas?"

"I don't keep track of him."

Alex held the mic to his mouth, pressed the button to contact dispatch.

"OK! Far's I know, he's in Cabo," blurted Quentin. "Man, I wish I was there with them."

"Them?" asked Alex, disconnecting.

"Fuck," said Quentin scrunching down uncomfortably in the back seat.

"Who, them?" said Alex looking in the rearview mirror at him.

"Smitty and Charlotte," said Quentin almost whispering.

"They're in Mexico?" said Norris as Alex put the car in gear and sped away.

He made the call to Quentin's parole officer and they dropped Quentin at the hospital detox clinic then headed back to town.

"Funny they're all in Cabo. I'd understand it if it was winter. But summer?" said Norris.

"God damn it."

Dispatch crackled over the radio.

"What." Alex answered irritably.

"Trooper Lopez wants you to call him," said LuAnn, the female dispatcher.

"I'll call him later," said Alex.

"He said it's important," LuAnn said. "Something about Sarah and Tom Flynn finding a severed hand?"

25

"LOOKS LIKE IT'S A FIT," said Humboldt.

"It gives you the creeps, don't it?" said Farley, staring at the hand lying on Alex's desk. The fingers on the hand drawn up claw-like, the skin patchy with deteriorated spots of flaking gray. The hand sat on a sheet of plastic wrap the Flynns had wrapped it in. Next to it, spread across the desk, the photos of the body that was supposed to be Jimmy Ketah.

Alex poked at the fingers with a pencil.

"That's not Jimmy's hand," said Norris.

Humboldt glanced at Alex, a "who-invited-her?" look.

"I'm afraid I agree," said Alex.

"What do you mean you agree?" said Humboldt.

"I knew Jimmy and this doesn't look like his hand," Alex said.

"Remember that old movie about the guy that gets his hand cut off in a car wreck and it comes back to haunt him?" said Farley. "Who was that? He wore those dumb black-rimmed glasses. A British guy. Oh yeah, Michael Caine. Don't understand the appeal of that guy. I'll never forget that hand crawling around." Farley demonstrated, his hand crawling across the desk and up his arm toward his throat. "It was headed for his wife I guess, or to strangle someone else, I forget," said Farley.

"Who gives a shit about Michael fucking Caine. Don't you have to be somewhere?" snapped Humboldt.

Farley, reddened, scooted out.

"I don't know why we keep that asshole around," said Humboldt.

"Watch it," said Alex with Farley still in earshot.

"Who cares if he heard me? Farley's got no self-respect, the worse you treat him the more he jumps to please. You could curse Farley up one side and down the other and it'd blow over like it never happened. Funny how some people just ask for it."

Norris wondered about Humboldt's wife. If she ever just asked for it.

A young guy in crisp blue jeans and a sleeveless white sweatshirt emblazoned with a red "Michigan" across the front stuck his head in the office. A small medical cooler was swung across his shoulder. "I'm here to pick up a delivery for the 501 flight to Anchorage. They didn't tell me what."

"Come on in," said Alex, slipping the hand into a baggie.

"Whoa, a hand," said the kid. "Cool."

"What the fuck? You're sending it to Anchorage?" asked Humboldt.

"Yeah. See if forensics can get us some fingerprints," said Alex.

"It's pretty deteriorated. Why bother? The amputation's clear it belongs to the body. A perfect match, I'd say," said Humboldt, agitated.

Alex didn't respond and let the kid pack the hand in his dry-ice cooler and depart.

"There's no point," said Humboldt.

"I'd like to get a positive ID," said Alex.

"We've got a fucking positive ID," said Humboldt. "From Ketah's wife. How much more positive can we get? That damn woman's got you by the short hairs. Since the day she came in here she's got you wondering, when it's cut and clear. You want to re-open this case so you can show off. Show her what a concerned, sensitive kind of guy you are. I don't see why you don't just fuck her and get it over with. She don't look like some ice queen to me," looking at Norris.

Norris blushed crimson.

"I'm following procedure," Alex said, clenching his fists so hard the knuckles went white.

"Procedure my ass. Chief Corso's going to put our balls in the wringer if that bitch is right. A god-damned perfect case down the shitter because Alex fucking Tanner wants in her pants."

"You're way out of line," said Alex.

Humboldt stormed out of the office, his face red with rage.

Alex was embarrassed, flustered. "I don't know what to say," he said.

"You don't have to say anything." Norris said, at a loss herself.

"Humboldt better watch his blood pressure," said Farley leaning in the doorway. "What happened?"

Neither spoke.

"The doc warned him about stress. He's on beta-blockers. One of these days he's going to explode, kablam!" said Farley barely able to contain his glee.

Humboldt exited the men's room and passed Alex's office, still red with anger. Farley sniggered to himself. Then went after him, "How about some lunch, boss? I'll run down to Big Boy's for a cheeseburger, fries and a shake."

Norris and Alex exchanged a look.

"Is it that bad if the body's not Jimmy?" she asked.

"Complicated. Humboldt's aching to make lieutenant ahead of me. Only one slot and a tight, orderly case looks good. Murders are pretty rare here and he's been commended for a job well done. And his lap dog Farley's bragged about it all over town, how Humboldt solved it clean and quick, intercepted the punks at the airport, doesn't mention only because he happened to be there sending his mother-in-law off on vacation. If anyone else had been in the vicinity, it would have been a different collar. And if the dimwits hadn't shoplifted some magazines and Snickers at the airport gift shop, they'd have gotten out of town without being missed. Luckily, most criminals aren't playing with a full deck."

"Except this one," said Norris.

"We'll see," said Alex.

26

THE DREAMS WERE INTENSIFYING. Raven was taking her someplace specific. Norris finished her shift and walked up the hill. Things were falling in place. Alex agreed the body was not Jimmy and Drew was taking her to the glacier to trace her nightly flight. Today felt like a new day. It was about time.

Norris saw the purple tennis shoes at the top of the stairs.

"Auntie wants to see you," she said.

"Will it cost me?" said Norris, making Lauren grin.

"Nope."

"Where is she?"

"In there." Lauren shrugged toward Norris' door.

Norris fumbled with her keys.

"It's open," Lauren said and turned the knob. "You just have a dumb old lock. Any skeleton key in the world will open it," matter-of-factly without the slightest hint of unease, let alone apology.

The woman with the long gray braids sat in a chair looking out the window.

"Nice view, huh," she said. "I bet it was better before they put up that government building."

"Can I get you something to drink? Water. Iced tea? Coffee?" Norris asked.

"Coke," said Lauren leaning on the door as though she were guarding it against Norris's sudden desire to escape.

Norris took a Pepsi from the refrigerator.

"I only have Pepsi," said Norris, handing Lauren a bottle.

"Coke's better," said Lauren but took the Pepsi and started to sit down on the couch.

The woman spoke to Lauren in what Norris assumed was Tlingit. Lauren made a face and went out into the hall closing the door behind her.

"Did she leave or is it a trick?" the woman asked. The woman was looking at the door and it took Norris a moment to realize she was blind.

"She's out in the hall and the door is closed," said Norris. "How did you. . . you said . . . about the view."

"I remember the hills and this house. I saw the construction going up."

"But on Angoon . . ."

"I'm good at seeming sighted."

She lightly stroked the arms of the chair.

"Jimmy had a gift," she said with no introduction. "Jimmy was an artist. He could have been an Ixht like his great-grandfather."

Norris nodded. It didn't surprise her to find that Jimmy Ketah was considered gifted in shaman skills, a healer, a seer.

"You understand Ixht?"

"Yes," said Norris.

"Jimmy wasn't satisfied. None of the children are anymore. Village life does not suit them. It's the city they're after. And money. What they don't know is that everything they need, everything they could ever want is right in front of them. They have an addiction to things." She turned and stared out the window.

"Are you sure I can't get you something?" asked Norris, uncertain, nervous.

"No. I don't have much time. We left the rest at

Costco. We ducked out, took the bus to town. If we get back to the airport by four everything will be fine."

"Won't they worry?"

"We always ditch them. They yell at us," she said mischievously. "It's only a problem if we miss the plane back to the island. So tell me who you are and why you're hunting for my Jimmy."

Norris stammered.

The woman laughed. "You were lovers. He met you in Seattle and brought you to Juneau to fish with him but before you got your bearings or even got to know him he was gone."

"Yes."

"Have you been dreaming?"

"Dreaming?" The question staggered her.

"Nightmares. Hauntings. Dreams."

"I've been plagued by ravens. They sit on the sills all day and all night, they talk, they . . ."

"Enter your dreams."

"Only one."

"I thought so. If Raven has called, you must listen. We are Raven, you understand?" Norris did. The Tlingit had two main kin groups, Raven and Eagle/Wolf. You belonged to one or the other. "If Raven has chosen you, who are you to fight him?"

"But Raven is a trickster too," said Norris.

"So you know about Raven."

"I know Raven can become anything he wants. I know Raven is part of the creation myth. Raven stole the box of light and hid it under his black wings until he opened it and illuminated the world. Raven can be quicksilver and trickery."

"Raven is playful. But Raven is all knowing. Where does Raven take you?"

"Rooftops, the channel, treetops, mountains . . ."

She didn't let Norris finish.

"Not the route. *Where* does Raven take you?"

"The glacier," said Norris, shaking.

"Yes. And you know why."

"No," said Norris, frightened.

"You do."

"Because Jimmy's there," said Norris, confirming what she already knew, the haunted nightly journeys with Raven, the soaring, the rush of wings, the fear, not being able to look at the glacier, the swoop and sweep, the banking, the flight back.

"Because Jimmy's on the glacier and we have to get him back. He must be cremated and set free." With that, the woman rose.

Norris was cold. She didn't want to hear it.

"You'll know what to do. No one believes an old woman. But you can convince someone."

"It's only a dream," said Norris.

"Is it?"

The woman walked to the door and felt for the knob. Norris opened it for her.

Lauren was sitting on the top step.

The woman took Norris's hands in both of hers feeling them, reading them. Took her face in her hands. "The only thing you must think about and think about very carefully. Your life depends on it. If Jimmy is on the glacier, and we know he is, how did he get there?"

Lauren led the woman down the stairs. Norris watched them go but didn't see.

Helicopter, she thought, paralyzed.

27

"I THOUGHT I SAW LAUREN and Jimmy's auntie leaving," said Drew appearing at the lower landing.

Norris, still at the top of the stairs, couldn't speak, her throat constricting at the sight of him.

"What'd they want?" He was already bounding up, now at the door.

Norris hesitated. "She wanted to visit, get to know me."

"Did she say anything about Jimmy?"

"Very little. She was curious about me."

"Does she think Jimmy's dead like Smitty and Charlotte?"

"Yes." It wasn't exactly a lie. She did think he was dead. She just didn't think the body cremated in Angoon was Jimmy. But Drew didn't need to know that. He was satisfied with the answer. Norris was relieved.

"Let's go find your Raven trail," said Drew.

Say no, she thought. Do anything. Say you've got a headache. The flu. She wished she hadn't told him about the Raven dream. Or Mick or Dix or the hand . . . This is stupid, thought Norris, bolstering herself. If Drew had anything to do with the disappearance of Jimmy he wouldn't be so willing to take her up on the glacier. Unless he was going to dump her there too. She hadn't told anyone she was going. Her throat went dry.

Calm down, she told herself. Breathe.

"You OK?" he asked.

"Sure. I'm fine. I forgot. I have to call Alex."

"Call him later."

"I really should call now." She punched in the numbers on her cell, heart pounding.

Drew watched her. She couldn't tell if he was scrutinizing or not. He shooed a couple of ravens off the windowsill.

Not in. She left a message. She was relieved. If Drew had any questionable intentions, he wouldn't have let her phone. It would have been easy enough to stop her. He was strong enough to throw her across the room or out the window, easy toss.

"You ready?"

Norris felt foolish. A little ashamed. He seemed completely guileless.

They climbed into the company pickup. In the cab, the mingled smells of tobacco, oil and fuel reminded Norris how much she liked men and machinery, how her childhood was surrounded by logging and trucks and loaders and dozers and mills and hunting and fishing and baseball. How familiar men were. And how the ways of most women were a mystery to her. Rita changed in high school, forgetting about playing cowboys and Indians and becoming obsessed with hair and makeup and conniving about men, endlessly reading the romances she piled by her bed, swooning to the radio with her girlfriends, tying up the telephone for hours. Rita tried to persuade Norris to wear dresses. Norris liked her jeans.

Then the family fallout, the screaming battle when Rita confessed she was pregnant her senior year in high school. Nothing had happened like the magazines or television promised and now Joe Jr. was grown, living in

Florida, estranged from his folks, no family of his own. Rita wanted Norris to fulfill her aborted dream of the suburban life as though a fifties myth could be recreated, much less sustained. Or ever existed.

All of the baseball wives were infected with it. Getting their man, getting their house, getting their life. And it was the same with Gayle and Mimi. It seemed like these days everyone lived on the fringes of hope. When I win the lottery my life will begin. When so and so loves me my life will begin. When I get my man and the house and all the stuff my life will begin. Wanting material things made life frenzied and cheap, like Jimmy's auntie said.

Norris was an outcast, did not conform, did not particularly care for the trappings of so-called success, but she wanted something too. Wanted it with all her being. One very small impossible thing. That Jimmy was still alive.

"SO HE'S BEDDED YOU," said Drew. "That's why you put me off."

"Can't men have female friends without sleeping with them?"

"Possible. Not likely."

"It's just better if we're friends and it has nothing to do with Alex."

"Sure," he said, unbelieving, a little perturbed. "Be careful. You don't know him."

"Alex says the same thing about you."

"Yeah? Well . . ."

They pulled into the Food World parking lot just short of the channel bridge.

"Need some smokes," he said and bounded out. She

watched him enter the store, passing a bagboy who shoved a loaded shopping cart for a bleached blond in black tights and a pink see-through top. Drew must have been amusing because the woman and the bagboy both laughed.

She smiled and thought about the conversation in The Bistro that morning with Merilee, Candace, Warren and Bud Tanninger. Psychopaths are generally more charming than the rest of the population. Great. The description fit both of them. Charming, cunning, subtle, jealous, dangerous. Her friends in Juneau: Drew and Alex. Psychopaths. Get real, she told herself.

They drove across the bridge and into the parking lot of Winston Helicopters. Farley sat on the trunk of his squad car tossing rocks at ravens perched on the power lines. It looked like the ravens were daring him. As soon as he heard the pickup, he jumped down. The ravens flew.

They got out and Norris asked to use the bathroom. Drew told her to use his trailer, the door's open, and headed toward Farley. "What's up?" Drew asked.

When Norris returned, Farley still looked jittery and was smiling too much. But Drew acted like they were chums, leaning casually against the squad car. Farley was shaking his head and then both he and Drew were laughing. Drew clapped Farley on the back and Farley gave Drew the old shoot 'em finger routine and left in his squad car.

"What was that all about?" asked Norris.

"Nothing. Farley was on a break."

"He seemed nervous."

"He wasn't supposed to be on a break," said Drew smiling. "There she is," he said, pointing to the green and white Jet Ranger helicopter straddling a yellow "H" stenciled in the center of the concrete helipad.

Norris wondered if Farley was really on a break or if Alex had sent Farley to stop them. What if Farley was supposed to detain Drew? Norris put the notion out of her head. If Alex wanted to stop them he would not have sent Farley.

Drew strapped Norris in—double shoulder straps and a lap strap—and showed her how to adjust her headset.

"Once we're in the air, do what I say," he said, talking to her through the headset. "If we get in trouble and I tell you to jump, unbuckle and do it. Don't take the time to ask why. A split second could mean the difference between survival and death if we're going to crash. Don't hesitate. React. You'll have to trust my judgment."

Norris nodded. Could she do it?

Drew went through his preflight routine flipping switches, checking gauges. The warm-up whine of the jet engines took hold and Norris wondered if she might be playing Russian roulette.

The Ranger's engines reached a high deafening rev and they were off with a forward exhilarating thrust. Drew glanced over at her.

"Like it?" he said, through the headset. No earplugs or shouting in this state-of-the-art machine.

Did she. What a rush. The gentle wavering lift and then the forward propulsion swooping down for a moment then up and away. Wow, she thought, jet pilots must really get a dose of adrenaline. This could be addictive.

They cut across the channel toward the glacier tucked in its mountain crib. The glacier didn't appear as blue or as translucent as before and Drew explained it needed cloud cover to absorb itself, to emanate the intense humming turquoise. In the bright summer sun it seemed less ethereal.

She hadn't believed it when Drew told her that the ice from the glacier didn't melt like other ice. Laughed when he said it was so compact it was actually blue. He'd brought her a slab. Vodka on the rocks—blue rocks—twist of lemon.

Now they were heading directly toward it, sliding over the suburbs, marshlands, trees and cul-de-sacs, now flying low on the path Norris had tried to describe, sweeping up the streaming glacier runoff, the gurgling rocky beginnings of Mendenhall River. Over the parking lot, skirting across the tour buses packed tight in the parking lot, the paths and viewpoints crammed with sightseers, over the lodge, the lake and the last of the trees and onto the ice.

This close, the glacier held no mystery. It was immense but the ice was dirty and pockmarked with stones and debris, the blue showing only in the crevices. Norris searched for any clue to her dreamscape and saw nothing resembling it. Drew would be stupid to fly where he dumped the body, she thought for a fleeting second. She remained wary for a while then let it go and succumbed to the thrill of the flight, skimming across the great expanse of ice that seemed to have no end. She was beginning to think the ice went on forever when they reached a far edge and the world dropped away. Norris gasped as her stomach dropped. Drew laughed.

She loved it. She no longer considered where Drew might dump her on the glacier. She was above the ice. Swooping. Foolish. Smiling. Endorphins pumping. They were only dreams, she told herself. Dreams and a superstitious old woman.

28

THE GLACIER HADN'T GIVEN UP any secrets and she was back safe. Silly to suspect him. On their approach back to Winston's Norris thought she saw Smitty's red pickup parked in a yard near the airport.

Now she was looking for the pickup in Gayle's Taurus. She'd been curious where Smitty kept the truck for his excursions in town and no one knew where or even if he had a place on the mainland. Or at least wouldn't tell her.

After a few attempts on dead-end streets she found the dirt lane leading to Smitty's truck sitting in a weedy yard next to a lean-to shed. The yard was strewn with piles of crab pots, a tangle of netting and orange floats, a deteriorating tarp over a stack of tires, an engine, a few indiscernible car or boat parts and a corroded washing machine. Moss-laden moose antlers hung above the shed's padlocked front door.

She carefully climbed the rotten steps and knocked on the door. Nothing. The windows reflected glare so she couldn't see in, even with her hands cupped over her eyes. Or were the windows blacked out? She walked around back and saw where someone had been splitting wood on a fir round. No, not splitting wood. Smashing figurines. Splintered shards—Madonna heads, moose legs, pieces of Bambi—the yard ornaments she'd seen in the bed of his truck.

"WHO KNOWS WHAT GETS IN SMITTY'S HEAD?" said Eden laughing into the phone. "He probably had no luck reselling them and got mad. Honestly, I wouldn't worry about it."

Norris wouldn't. It was just plain weird.

She disconnected the call and stared in the fridge. What to eat? Not much choice—half a carton of spoiled milk. Pomegranate juice. Last week's fish. A lump of Havarti cheese, moldy at one end. And three huge tomatoes next to the wilted lettuce. Mimi's homegrown tomatoes, each one bigger than a grapefruit. Nice and firm and gorgeous red, not the rock hard waxy pink hothouse tomatoes Rita would buy by the bushel. Mimi had begged her to take more. She had so many they were rotting on the vine. That's what happens when the growing season is short and robust saturated with sunlight. Giant vegetables and lots of them. Norris slapped at a mosquito dive-bombing her neck. Unfortunately, the growing season was robust for insects too.

She took a tomato and the cheese out of the fridge, tossed the lettuce in the trash, poured the milk down the sink, put the fish on the windowsill for the ravens and decided on a broiled cheese sandwich on sourdough. The one slice in the loaf still soft. She threw out the rest of the bread and pulled a butcher knife out of the drawer to slice off the veiny gray cheese end.

A raven on the kitchen windowsill snacking on the fish startled. It squawked and flew. Before Norris could discover what alarmed it, there was a knock at the door. Norris listened. She wasn't expecting anyone. Shoot, it was probably Carmen. The knocking stopped and she started to move back to the kitchen, not wanting company. A slight noise caught her attention. The doorknob was turning. Norris was transfixed. She couldn't move if she wanted to.

She stared at the doorknob as though she were welded to it. She was certain neither Carmen nor Stanley would try to enter. She wished she'd listened to Alex about installing better locks. And remembered Lauren saying how easy it was to get in. She wondered if Drew really had left for the Kenai Peninsula like he said. Her brain said run! Rooted, she couldn't take her eyes off the knob.

"Norris, are you in there? It's me, Alex."

"Alex," she said, almost croaking it out. His voice released her. She opened the door and he pushed by her without a hello.

"You alone?" he asked, weapon drawn. He didn't wait for her answer. He was already in, checking the kitchen, the hallway, the bathroom. Norris followed him.

"Come on in. Make yourself at home."

He didn't respond. He pulled back the shower curtain with a quick snap that made her jump then checked the hall closet.

"Are you looking for someone?" she asked.

"Yeah. You," he said, putting his weapon back in his holster.

"Is that for me?" he asked.

Norris blinked. Oh, the knife. She still had the butcher knife in her hand.

"No. Dinner."

He didn't relax. "You're coming with me."

"What's going on?"

"I'll tell you later. Come on."

"You're kidnapping me?"

"Yeah," he said.

"You're serious."

"Deadly. Let's go."

Norris went to the closet and started gathering a few things. Alex tossed back the clothes.

"Don't take anything. No toothbrush, nothing. It's better if it looks like you've vanished."

"I should leave a note for Drew."

"No."

"But what'll he do if he comes back and I'm gone?"

"Exactly what we want to find out."

Norris stared at him. He was at the door, waiting.

"The body was Waco's and Jimmy's down vest was in Drew's Jet Ranger. There are dark stains soaked through that could be blood."

Norris dropped the butcher knife, grabbed her bag and they started for the door. Alex jerked her purse out of her hand and threw it back into the apartment, the contents spilling across the floor.

ALEX DROVE ONTO THE EXPRESSWAY and punched the accelerator, headed south toward the airport.

"You're shipping me out," she said.

"Until I get Drew."

"Are you certain the vest was Jimmy's?"

"I'm not certain of a damned thing but it matched your description. The stains could be anything—sheep, elk, grease, mud."

"When did you find it?"

"This afternoon."

"I was in the Jet Ranger this afternoon," said Norris.

"And Drew talked Farley out of detaining him."

"Yes." She suspected it. "How did you find it?"

"One of the mechanics at Winston's found it stuffed under the passenger's seat, saw it covered with what looked like blood—fit the description we'd put in the paper. I radioed Humboldt to get some cars out to Winston's to stall Drew until I got a search warrant.

Humboldt sent Farley instead with no backup and Judge Viceroy didn't think I had enough probable cause to issue a warrant."

"Why would Drew leave it under the seat and not get rid of it? Why would he risk having me there?"

"Drew is a gamesman. Having you in the helo would heighten the charge he gets out of playing. The higher the risk, the more fun."

"If I vanish you have to investigate my disappearance and Drew was the last person to see me alive."

"You got it. We'd have to hold him for questioning."

"Sounds like Drew isn't the only gamesman."

He rounded the entrance to the airport, cruised by the terminal and kept going. Slammed his fist on the steering wheel. "Idiot! What was I doing, thinking I could sneak you safely out of town without anyone noticing. The point is to have Drew as the last person to see you. I'm not thinking clearly."

Alex drove into the library's parking garage. Two stories of covered municipal parking with the library floors on top overlooking the bay.

"Wait here. Do not get out," Alex said, flipping the door lock. "Back in twenty minutes."

She waited. All she had was what she was wearing: white jeans, a sleeveless red and white checked cotton blouse, moccasins she'd bought downtown. She watched people coming and going, but knew they couldn't see her behind the dark tinted windows of the Crown Vic. After about fifteen minutes, a fairly new white diesel Ford F150 pickup parked beside her. Alex. He got out, looked around, said, "Now." No one to see him smuggle her into his pickup, he tossed her a gray sweatshirt and told her to hide on the floorboard, cover her head.

"Really?" she said.

"If it's not Drew, someone else has been watching you and knows your habits."

Finally he really believed her. She didn't know whether to feel elated or sick. Jimmy's vest was in Drew's possession. She wanted to throw up.

Alex left her hiding while he turned in the Crown Vic at the station. More than twenty minutes passed. It was hot and claustrophobic, the sweatshirt over her head stifling. It was getting late and she could hear people getting into their cars and leaving. It got so quiet that she imagined no one was in the garage any more. All had gone home to their dinners, their husbands and wives, their children, their dogs, their lives. She was so far from it now. All she'd ever wanted when she was little. It made her think of Bailey and their imagined life back then. They were so young. So naive.

She thought of Seattle and Rita and Joe and the old men and the star-struck fateful night. Her room. The trawler. Jimmy. Norris wiped a tear on the sleeve of the sweatshirt and saw "Property OSU Baseball" stenciled in orange, now faded, across the front. She buried her face in it and cried.

Voices so close, it startled her. An instinct to flee. Why not run, hail a taxi, go to the airport and leave it all behind? Nothing she could do would bring Jimmy back. She had just about made a decision, thinking how could she do it: run home, get her purse—too chancy; run to Eden's, borrow money, have her take her to the airport—when she heard the footsteps. Yes, definitely footsteps coming toward the pickup. Please let it be Alex, she thought and held still, not moving a muscle. The key turned in the lock.

She pulled the sweatshirt off her face.

"Sorry it took so long," he said, starting the engine. "If you can hang in there a few minutes we'll be home."

"Home?"

"My place."

They drove south out of town along the channel. She couldn't see much from the floor—the tops of buildings and the stacks of two cruise ships giving way to sky and a steady stream of telephone wires, treetops of alder and cottonwood, a few second-growth firs. Juneau had been logged off more than a century ago. Gold Rush days. She'd seen photographs at the museum of the scraggly new town, the patchy clear-cut mountains in the background. Frame buildings, mud-rutted streets, boardwalks. Men posing on stumps of giant old-growth fir and cedar and hemlock, axes resting on shoulders, smoking pipes for the picture. Women in dresses filthy and caked in mud at the hem, aprons stained, their strong rough hands at their sides.

Alex turned off the asphalt and she heard the crunch of gravel. The pickup stopped.

"You can get up now," he said, getting out.

Norris watched him unchain a metal gate of welded recycled machinery parts. Cowbells tinkled as he opened it. He motioned for her to drive through and she rolled the truck forward through the gate. He shoved the gate shut then scooted her over and drove down a curved sloping drive toward the channel. In the center of the lane, the weeds were mowed. Through the saplings Norris saw a mobile home. A doublewide with a cedar porch and wood window frames, not the original aluminum prefab. More like a cabin than trailer. They wound down to the flat piece of land where it stood completely surrounded by trees. No neighbors visible in any direction. Through the alders in front, he had waterfront access to the channel and a view of the mountains on Douglas Island. She stepped out of the truck into the happy leaping lunges of his dog.

The malamute ran from side to side trying to decide which to leap on first. It was odd seeing Alex as a domesticated man at home—the cabin with its hand-hewn porch, the cord of wood stacked neatly next to the back door, his leaping dog. The dog nearly knocked her over. She dug her fingers into his deep fur and took hold of his laughing intelligent face.

"Oh, you beautiful boy," she said.

"Not that beautiful. Down, Ishi," he said.

Ishi jumped and clamored while Alex changed his water, retrieved a cup of dog food from the bag on the porch and poured it into a huge ceramic dish. Ishi pounced on his dinner. Norris followed Alex onto the back porch and into the house.

It was like walking into an oven.

"The house sits and bakes all day," said Alex, apologizing. "The tin roof doesn't help. Some day I'm going to build a real house."

Alex left her in the kitchen and began opening windows. It wasn't like any mobile home she'd ever seen. It was completely remodeled with wood paneling and alder cabinets. Aren't you the clever one, thought Norris, certain he'd done the work himself. Nice work too, smoothing her hand across the oak counter, the curved edge. Open plan, the kitchen separated from the living room by a polished uneven slab of what looked like madrone driftwood. The only things left of its innate trailer-ness were the low ceilings and the dimensions. It was nice. Homey and woodsy.

Alex disappeared down a hall and she heard a fan start up. A huge fan. A cross-breeze was already blowing through and it immediately started to cool. He returned to the kitchen with a semi-automatic and laid it on the counter.

"Know how to use one?" he asked.

"No," said Norris, almost recoiling. Handguns were not in her repertoire. She accepted shotguns or rifles to kill animals for food, but handguns? Handguns were used only on people.

"You do know what this is," he said, unloading a magazine and holding it out to her.

"Sure, a magazine clip," she said. "I go to movies."

"OK, what we're going to do is have a lesson in firearms."

"Why would we do that?" asked Norris.

"Because I don't want to come home from work some day and find you dead."

THE AUTOMATIC WAS HEAVY IN HER HAND. Cool, lethal black steel. If a thing can feel dangerous, this certainly did.

"It's my favorite, a Sig Sauer .45," said Alex. "Some consider it the Cadillac of semi-automatics, although some prefer a 9mm for the larger magazine capacity." Alex took the Sig from her and laid it on the counter.

He plopped a small gym bag on the counter and pulled out a .38 Smith & Wesson special revolver, a .357 magnum Colt Python, a 9mm Glock 17, and a 9mm Browning semi-automatic.

He lined up bullets along the counter, making her match them to each weapon. They practiced sighting, gripping, loading, safety and maintenance. He demonstrated taking them apart and reassembling and they were ready to shoot. That is, after he made her load the clips, which made her fingers ache.

Handling the weapons took the edge off. Norris began to appreciate their finely crafted precision, each a work of art. Alex thought she could use the Sig .45 but the stock was too wide for her palm and she had to use both hands, rather than just her thumb, to flip the safety off.

"No good," he said. "You don't want to be fumbling around if you need to fire. You want minimum reaction time."

She tried the Browning and it was better but she still had to stretch her thumb uncomfortably to reach the safety.

"I didn't know my thumbs were so weak," she said.

"It's awkward at first. You'll get used to it. Try this one."

She took the Glock 17 and slid the safety off. She sighted it out the window.

"Use both hands, always. Feel comfortable?"

Relatively.

They walked across his driveway and through the alder toward the channel until they reached his shooting gallery. He said he had targets set up and Norris expected to see beer cans on a fence. Instead, it was an outdoor sculpture garden with metal targets resembling avant-garde mobiles. And lurking behind almost hidden, a steel human torso. The grass was long with dandelions speckled through.

"Wow, Alex. Eden told me you were talented but I had no idea."

He gave her a curious look and handed her the Glock.

"Keep your finger at the side off the trigger at all times until you're ready to shoot. And keep your hands away from the slide action. It'll rip you up. Go ahead aim at the big one, the torso," he said. "Just sight your eye down the barrel and align the "V" at the end of the barrel. Safety off. Fire."

And she did, hitting the cutout steel human torso right in the chest, the bullet singing off the steel.

"Great," he said. "Fire away."

She had seventeen rounds but by the ninth, her arm ached and began to shake. Norris handed the gun to Alex and he finished it off, hitting each target in a row.

He made her load and fire each gun in turn and she gladly returned to the Glock. Barely a kick. It took a while for her to get used to controlling the weight at the end of her arm but when she did, she hit her targets, large and small, fourteen out of the seventeen.

"You sure you've never done this before?"

"I guess I've always had pretty good hand-eye coordination. It's a baseball thing."

He looked at her curiously.

It felt good. Being familiar with the weapon made it feel like it was hers and that, she supposed, was the point. They picked up the shell casings and headed back to the house. He took the bag of weapons down the hall except for the Glock and left her standing.

"I'm going to take a shower. Make yourself at home," he called from the hall.

Interesting, thought Norris. Kidnapped. Taught to shoot. Left on her own with the loaded gun. Trusting, isn't he?

The living room was full of plants. A dwarf citrus with tiny green lemons, jade plants in two large oriental vases and a philodendron as big as a tree. The air blew through rustling leaves. His TV sat in the middle. Jungle viewing. The shelves underneath held DVD and CD players and to the right was a floor-to-ceiling bookcase filled with mysteries mostly. One shelf of books was from the police academy maybe—poisons, criminal psychology, criminal and forensic investigations, abnormal psych, *The Anatomy of Motive*.

Interspersed were a few glass floats, a huge bullet from what? A machine gun? A bee encased in amber, an ornate brass hookah from Iraq she guessed, and a framed black and white photo of a young couple in their twenties taken sometime in the 1950s, judging by the cut of the cotton dress and the make of the Chevrolet they were leaning on. The woman wore what appeared to be bright red lipstick. You could see a barn in the near distance, a bough of an apple tree in the foreground. The man wore rolled cuff jeans and a crisp long-sleeved white shirt. Maybe they were dressed up for the picture. Maybe they were heading off on a date. Or church. Whatever, they were happy and touchingly innocent. His parents, Norris thought.

On the opposite wall above the window hung a wood carving of a salmon. Signed JJK in the corner. Intake of breath. She shut her eyes.

"WANT A BEER?" Alex called from the kitchen.

He stood at the refrigerator door in jeans and a T-shirt, barefoot, his hair still wet from the shower. He looked like those innocent people in the photo. Oregon farm fresh. Still a boy. Even though she knew he had to be in his forties.

"I've got Heineken, unless you want hard stuff."

"Heineken's fine," she said, astonished to see his refrigerator full. She wondered if it was full because she was there. Had he stocked up to keep her a long time? She took the beer he handed her, then put it down and asked for the bathroom.

"Down the hall past the bedroom on the right," he said. "Excuse the mess and wash your face, hands and arms. You'll have lead residue from shooting."

"You're joking."

"Nope."

There wasn't a hall really, just a short space beyond

the kitchen that opened up into the bedroom, a large room that must have been two bedrooms with the wall taken out to accommodate a king-size bed, unmade. So it wasn't planned, his bringing her here. She relaxed a little.

In the bathroom, a pile of clothes lay next to the toilet. The mess he apologized for? Everything was tidy. Even the sink was clean. He kept his house in order. But thank heavens not too neat. She was glad for the unmade bed and the breakfast dishes still in the sink. She wouldn't be comfortable if he were completely anal-retentive, then again, wouldn't be comfortable if he were a slob. No bachelor glamour for her—the food-caked dishes, the takeout cartons, piles of dirty clothes, bathroom sinks with soap residue and shavings. No, this is a man who takes care of himself. A good man, she thought. You're in good hands.

She looked in the mirror and wished she hadn't—hair disheveled from her impromptu sweatshirt cloak, the jeans filthy from the floorboards, the now crumpled sweaty top. She washed like Alex told her, plus her pits, fixed her hair and wandered back to the kitchen where Alex was trimming the fat off a couple of steaks.

"Steak OK?"

She was going to have a toasted moldy cheese sandwich on stale bread and he's fixing steak. She retrieved her beer.

"So do we just wait until Drew returns?" she asked.

"That's about it."

"You're certain about the vest?"

"You described it. And so did the mechanic. Unfortunately, it's probably been dumped by now. I doubt if it will ever reappear. Especially now. He'll guess why Farley's was there and know that I know he had the vest in the chopper. First we eat. Can you make a salad?"

He put the steaks on the grill outside and she tore lettuce and chopped green onions and carrots. She wished she had one of Mimi's tomatoes and then saw he had homegrown ones of his own lining the windowsill.

"We need to talk," Alex said, returning inside.

"Uh, oh. That's what they say in soap operas or bad movies when someone has something unpleasant to say."

He pulled a chair out for her at the table.

"This looks like an interrogation. Who dreamed this up? Humboldt? Chief Whatshisname? Hey, Tanner, she trusts you. Scare her, take her home, make her feel safe, and then ambush her?" she said, anger rising, taking a long pull on her beer.

"Nobody knows you're here. This is not a trap. Nobody told me to do anything. I just thought you could give me some insight."

"After all this time?"

"I'm sorry I didn't believe you from the first. Norris, look at it from our point of view. This stranger comes in, says her boyfriend's missing. We have a body except she says it's not him. Now why would she say that? Kinda confusing since his wife and his best friend sure say it's him. We have it cut and dried—case closed. Then, Ole takes a walk in the channel. An accident. Tough luck. Odd coincidence. No connection. The boat taken legitimately by the victim's wife. Still, case closed. So we have to consider: maybe she's yanking our chain; maybe she's more involved than she's letting on. We have some unaccounted for homicides here—Ole looks like, Mick and let's not forget Danny—all of whom were connected to her. Interesting Danny was fine until she went back to Seattle. Maybe she's in on this whole thing with Drew, keeping a step ahead playing the innocent, helping to cover tracks. Maybe she's a user and major supplier. Got in over her head.

"Or maybe she's nuts," Norris contributed cheerfully, taking a deep swig.

"Yeah. Humboldt and Chief Corso have had a great time teasing me. I believe you're not mixed up in anything. You were legitimately distraught about Jimmy. I've seen no indication of drugs."

"That's why you kept showing up everywhere. Keeping an eye on me, huh?"

"I wanted to know what you knew. Danny and his girlfriend Shari's demise was suspicious but it was Mick that changed everything. See, there's Drew. We . . ."

"Have a history."

"Drew told you no doubt."

"And Eden too. I tend toward Eden's version."

"About—?"

"Your wife's . . . accident." Norris peeled at the label on her beer, slippery with condensation.

"Drew would like to see me crash and burn."

"You think Drew murdered Jimmy and Ole and Mick to get back at you?"

"It's not that far-fetched if you knew Drew. I've never figured out why he came up here anyway, so I've always been wary. I can't get over the feeling that someday, somehow, he's going to frame me."

"You think he will kill me next. To somehow even the score for Maya?"

"Guessing."

The steaks were done. Neither was hungry.

They spent the night mapping the past days, Alex wanting to know everything—coincidences, people, every detail, every insignificant thing.

She told him everything except Jimmy's auntie and her dreams. Too strange, she thought.

"You don't think Smitty and Charlotte killed Jimmy, even though they profited from it?"

"No way. Smitty is as docile and as kind a man you'd ever want to meet, and Charlotte," he said, "She can be exasperating, but she's no mastermind and certainly no killer. Besides, they've got a parcel of kids to worry about."

WHILE NORRIS DID THE DISHES, Alex changed the sheets. Norris wondered what the sleeping arrangements would be. She didn't have to think about it long because Alex told her the bed was hers and took a sleeping bag from the closet. He grabbed his blue terrycloth bathrobe from a hook along the wall and showed her where the towels were, gave her a new toothbrush. He said she should feel free to borrow any of his clothes if she wanted and headed for the living room.

"Thanks, Alex," she called after him.

"We'll see," he said.

He left her alone. She took a shower, found one of his T-shirts and hopped into the cool sheets. Through the windows above her head she watched the evening light turn a pale pink. Twilight. Must be about midnight, she thought. Maybe she could sleep tonight. Sleep here safe. She watched the softening sky and started to drift. It's nice here, she thought, and out of the corner of her eye glimpsed a raven flit from the tallest fir out of sight. So they've followed me, she thought. She didn't want to believe Drew was a threat to her. Hoped Alex was wrong. We shall see soon enough she thought, wondering how it would play itself out. She shoved the Glock under her pillow.

Sleep came swift and heavy and before she went under she thought, ah, yes, sleep. Maybe no dreams tonight. She was wrong. She was gliding towards the glacier, panic mounting. Over the lodge, beyond the fringe of trees onto the ice, up crevices, the route blazing with new clarity and she saw a monolith jutting out of the ice and the horrible dread overtaking her then the blackout and the unearthly scream. She awoke in a sweat, heart racing. She opened her eyes and Alex was leaning over her.

Norris jumped. "You scared me," she said.

"You scared *me*. You screamed."

"I did?"

"Yeah. It was real eerie, like you were real far away. Jesus, I didn't know what to make of it."

All this time, all these nights, it wasn't Raven screaming. It was Norris.

29

THE SOUND OF THE SHOWER WOKE HER. She'd gone back to sleep after the dream. The sun was up and so was Alex. She could smell coffee. She wondered what time it was.

She had gotten used to her apartment, able to tell the time of day by the sun revolving around the windows. Sunlight in the bay windows meant morning and it worked its way around to the kitchen and back to the front again. She couldn't tell tucked here in the woods.

She hadn't heard the shower shut off but there he was beside the bed getting clothes for work from the open shelves above the closet. He smelled like soap. He grabbed a clean pair of jeans and put them on, his back to her, dropping the robe to the floor.

"So you don't believe in underwear, huh?" she said.

It startled him.

"I thought you were asleep."

"The shower woke me. Well?"

"Oh, yeah. Habit, I guess. No way to wash underwear let alone ourselves in the desert. Army didn't issue enough. Got used to it."

He picked up his robe, put on a shirt and walked to the kitchen. Apparently he wasn't the modest sort. Well, it was his room. And Norris didn't care. He wasn't an exhibitionist or showing off, he was simply getting dressed. He had a remarkably taut body for forty what?

Forty-one, forty-three years old? Not pumped up or muscle-bound the way some men overdeveloped themselves, just lean and strong.

"Orange juice?" he called from the kitchen.

"Yes. Please," she called back, wondering if she should get up. She didn't have time to anyway because he was there handing it to her. She drank as he sat on the bed to put his socks on.

A pang of longing seared through her, that last morning with Jimmy putting on his socks. Norris watched. It was casual, unaffected, comfortable, as though they'd been married for years. As though it wasn't unusual to have a woman in his bed. Well, maybe it wasn't. He was single, good looking. Yes, but this was Juneau. There weren't that many single women around. One for every six men? Eight? What had Gayle and Mimi said? She put the glass on the headboard behind her and sank back into the pillows. Safe.

For the first time in months she felt safe. She closed her eyes. His movement getting off the bed made her open them.

"Where's your weapon?" he asked.

She reached under her pillow and held it out to him in the palm of her hand.

"Let's see if you remember how to use it," he said opening the sliding glass doors to a deck at the end of the room.

"Hit that longest branch on that alder to the right."

"This is ridiculous. I'm not even awake. I'm in bed."

"Do it."

Norris sat up and aimed, fired. She hit the limb.

"You sure you never handled a handgun?"

Norris slid back onto the pillow, the gun still in her hand. She didn't tell him she didn't hit exactly where she was aiming, but it was close.

"There are two extra clips in the drawer. You're not to leave the property. Don't let anyone see you. And I want you to keep the gun with you at all times. Even if you take a shower. Understood?"

"If Drew came here, I couldn't shoot him."

"If you had to, you would." He took her orange juice glass and headed to the kitchen. "My office and mobile number are next to the telephone. Don't phone unless it's an emergency. I should be back around seven. Keep your wits about you. Ishi's here and coffee's on."

Norris lay back and looked at the gun, passing it from hand to hand, trying to keep it familiar. It wasn't. But it was warming up.

She helped herself to a plaid flannel robe hanging on a nail next to the blue one he'd been wearing, still damp from his shower. She headed to the kitchen. She considered calling Percy's to tell them she wouldn't be in. No calls, he'd said, and she wondered what they'd do when she didn't show up, sorry to make it harder on Gayle.

The day moved slowly and Norris did his laundry and hers. She did the dishes and even carefully dusted all his plants, leaf by leaf with Kleenex. Then she sifted through his closet. He sure had a lot of shirts. Plaid flannel shirts and white cotton shirts and a row of polo shirts, mostly white or black. She took one of the white shirts and tried on a pair of his clean jeans, neatly stacked on the top shelf of his closet. More than a dozen pair. Probably wears them only once like underwear.

She pulled on his jeans. Pretty tight and too long. She sucked in her stomach and rolled up the cuffs. And what about makeup? She was tan and didn't need much but did wish she had just a bit of mascara. Blond eyelashes made her look so wan. Oh, screw it, she thought. I'm here to survive. She wondered where Drew was.

Norris sifted through the bookshelf again and almost picked up *Notorious Crimes of the Decade* but decided instead on Cormac McCarthy's *All the Pretty Horses*.

She went outside to sit among the rocks by the channel. Ishi was happy to have a companion and made a nuisance of himself slobbering all over her while she tried to read. She took him back to the house and clipped him to his chain. He ran after her and when he came to the end of his lead sat whimpering, looking forlorn, emitting sporadic yelps to get her attention. She almost felt sorry for him. She wondered if malamutes swam and thought of Cosmo, her Brittany spaniel, left with one of Bailey's teammates at Lake Chelan.

Now *there* was a water dog. Chasing ducks for hours, swimming so far out after mama ducks he'd be returned by worried water skiers. "He was way out in the middle of the lake," the rescuers would say incredulously. "We were afraid he'd drown." Norris and Bailey always thanked them and offered them a beer. But they never felt anxious about Cosmo.

She wished Cosmo was with her now swimming in the channel. He was her constant companion at their Lake Chelan cabin where she spent most of her time when Bailey was on the road. Cosmo, slobbery Cosmo, would make her mad when he'd come back to the cabin as a two-tone dog—half white, half mud. She'd lure him back to the dock and shove him into the lake. He'd swim in a circle then climb out clean and stand next to her to shake it out. She always tried to run but he'd catch up. He thought this was an excellent game. He was wonderful when he was clean, the silky white coat, the rich brown spots. One brown patch over an eye, those big floppy ears, burrs and flowers tangled in them. How she missed that big happy dope. At least she knew he was in loving hands.

Norris looked back at Ishi sitting watching her. He cocked his head to one side and then the other. She walked back and hugged him, sinking her face into the thick fur at his neck. He licked her and she pulled away, wiping her face with the tail of her shirt. She unclipped him and returned to the rocky beach.

"Sit, Ishi," she told him and he did. "Good boy. What a good dog," she said, patting him. Ishi seemed happy to obey. How wonderful to have the parameters of your existence explicit. Sit. Stay. Guard. Oh, no! She'd left the Glock in the kitchen. A quick stab of panic gripped her but she reasoned it out. If anybody came near, Ishi would bark. Ishi wasn't anxious in the least. It was simply a lazy summer day, the sky a brilliant blue, a slight breeze riffling the alders, making the leaves glisten like jewels. And the quiet. There's no quiet like an Alaskan quiet. Well, probably a Siberian quiet. And the Arctic, Antarctic . . . Anyway, it was still. Serene.

Too quiet.

Norris ran to get the gun.

SHE'D BEEN TRYING TO READ and had fallen asleep on the beach. She could tell it was evening by the cool breeze springing off the water. The sun was nowhere near setting, but it was a bit to her right, so she guessed it must be near seven.

Ishi barked and she sat up, alert. She heard nothing but Ishi was running toward the house, barking. She heard the scrape of the gate and the tinkle of the cowbells as it opened. She hid behind a mound of blackberry vines and put her thumb on the safety. She heard the approaching crunch of tires on gravel and the rumble of a diesel engine and finally saw the white pickup. She hung back until she was certain it was Alex. He was out and Ishi was getting hugs and she felt a little arc of pain. Nice life. Man and dog. She was just a voyeur. A moment in their lives. She wasn't really here, just passing through. She stepped into sight.

"There you are," he said, shoving Ishi down. "Any visitors? Phone calls?"

"Nada."

She helped him carry in bags of groceries. Good grief, the fridge was already full. There were bags of canned goods. Was he expecting a siege? Or does he always keep his cupboards stocked? She didn't ask. She had a moment's guilt about not having dinner ready. Why hadn't she thought of that? Well, she wasn't here to be his wife. Still . . .

"Did anybody miss me at work?" she asked.

"Yeah, they asked me to check up on you. Your boss lady Mrs. Pinchot was not a happy woman. Neither Gayle nor Mimi had a clue where you'd gone. I let Farley blab his opinion that you'd probably skipped town with Drew. I made a show of checking your apartment. You weren't there. And your purse was on the floor, all its contents spilled. Disturbing."

"I bet," she said, passing him the cans of food that he stacked neatly, beans and vegetables on the left, soups on the right.

"What about Drew?"

"Still on Kenai. Should be back tomorrow."

"What if Drew doesn't know about the vest?" asked Norris.

"He knows. But to make things interesting he might claim it was planted."

"Well, it could have been."

"Uh, huh."

Norris and Alex finished last night's steak, stir-fried with fresh veggies. Then Alex washed the dishes and she wiped. She could see the television through the pass-through. It must have been National Geographic or Nova, scorpions crawling around making nests and devouring other insects. When they'd stacked the dishes away and cleaned the kitchen, they headed outside for more target practice.

"You're a fast learner," he said.

"I like it. My family's always been competitive."

"Women are often better with small firearms than men. Better concentration when they put their mind to it, better fine motor skills. But don't tell anyone I told you that," he said.

In the dwindling light, they walked down the shoreline, Ishi trotting in front of them, sniffing at shells and rocks. He climbed over a downed tree and as they approached, Norris could see a skiff pulled onto shore.

"Is that yours?" she asked.

"Yeah."

"Could I take it out sometime?"

"I don't know, you'd be pretty easy to spot."

As she got closer to the boat, something registered. She walked around it.

"I've seen this boat before."

"There are a lot of skiffs around."

"No. I'm sure of it. I just can't remember where." It hit her. It was the boat she'd seen at Eden's when she went over alone. When Jimmy first disappeared. That whiff of Brut. She stood still.

"What's wrong?"

She raised her Glock and pointed at him, "Drop your weapon," she said.

Alex shifted uncomfortably.

"Now!" She racked the slide.

30

ALEX GENTLY PLACED his Sig on the ground, holding his hands out in front of him.

"Easy," he said, rising slowly.

"And get rid of the .38 on your ankle strap."

"I don't have it on."

"Show me!"

He lifted both his pants legs up and she was satisfied.

"I saw the skiff at Eden's. Did you follow me there?"

"It could be a different boat."

"It isn't. This one's hunter green with a yellow tag on the stern and a maroon and silver Mercury outboard motor, exactly like the one I saw."

"You have an eye for detail . . . ever consider law enforcement?" he said, trying to make it light.

"Tell me about the skiff," she said, holding the Glock on him, trying not to shake.

"Norris. It wasn't me. I had an off-duty checking you out."

"Why?"

"I was interested to see how you spent your time. You were raising a lot of flak at the time, in case you don't recall. Now slowly put the safety back on."

She did.

"Did he follow me in Seattle?"

"Yep."

She lowered the gun and slugged him on the

shoulder. "You tricky bastard! I wish you'd told me."

"It wouldn't have been effective surveillance if I'd told you. You weren't supposed to see him. I'll have to tell him he was spotted . . . and smelled. Careless. Very careless. You would have done the same thing if you were in my position. And by the way, I'm proud of the way you went for your weapon just now. Good girl."

"I don't know whether to thank you or still be upset. And some women don't like to be called girls."

"Geez, gimme a break. It's an affectionate term. Don't get feminazi on me."

"I didn't say me, I said *some* women. Just pointing it out."

"Right. Are we OK about the skiff business now?"

"I suppose."

"Good girl," he said, flipping her French braid.

"Jerk."

HE WAS IN THE KITCHEN FIXING POPCORN. Norris was channel surfing on TV and stopped at a National Geographic special on King Tut's tomb. Alex handed her a bowl of popcorn then sat in his recliner while Norris stretched out on the couch. They watched rapt and silent as Egyptologists discussed the treasures. Alex told her about Kuwait City and Desert Storm. How attractive and exotic parts were but how foreign and terrifying too. He'd hardly slept. The unknowing. The kids playing soccer in the streets? The women at the market? The men in the cafés? Who could you trust? Any moment you might land on an IED. The constant taste and grit of dust. Mornings you shook your shoes for scorpions. She let his voice drift over her. She fell asleep on the couch and barely felt it when he placed a blanket over her. She could smell the sea breeze and the sunshine mingled in her hair and snuggled in like a kid as he tucked the blanket around her shoulders. He watched her.

She slept.

SHE FLEW ABOVE THE CHANNEL and could see Alex's house and the pickup below. Ishi curled sleeping in his bed on the porch. A few lights twinkled in the twilight of the city as Raven caught the channel breeze and glided effortlessly over town. She saw the cruise ship *Scandia* at the pier, drifted over the library and federal buildings, past the courthouse, down the street past the Red Bear, up the alley where the body was found and on up the hill past her apartment where she saw Father Davidovitch taking his stroll on the old boardwalk. Raven headed up and over Mt. Juneau, leaving the town behind. She swept up the riverbed and the lupine meadows, the cottonwoods, past the car park and over the lodge and the lake toward their regular route. Tonight Norris didn't want to go any farther. Her heart beat rapidly and Raven flew on with an urgency she hadn't felt before.

She could see the crag of a monolith approaching and didn't want to go on. She tried to fight her way back but Raven was driven. The ice glowed white in the scant moonlight. Crevices loomed and disappeared as they beat their way east across the vast ice field as it crawled and crept away from the bay. Creaking, snapping, a living thing. Raven zigzagged back and forth and swooped near a crevasse, which made Norris' stomach lurch in the swiftness of Raven's descent. It was a deep chasm and Raven slowed, gliding, alert. Raven swooped and screamed a scream that Norris thought would end the world. She did not black out. She could see. And what she saw was Jimmy. Naked. Encased in the blue ice. Raven screamed again and Norris shot out of the sky, the screaming muffled, far away.

Alex had her pinned down. A hand over her mouth.

"Norris. Stop. Please." He looked besieged. She was breathing hard, her body clammy and damp with sweat.

"It was just a dream. It's all right," he said calming her.

"Alex," she said and clung to him.

He tried to lean her back on the pillow.

"Jimmy . . . " She fought to get the words out right. "I know where Jimmy is," she said.

"Tell me," he said.

She told him the dream and he listened silently.

"It was only a nightmare."

"It wasn't."

"OK. Can you draw me a map of the glacier."

"I can show you. I know it backwards and forwards."

"No. You're staying here. I'm sure it's a nightmare, but I'll check it out anyway. You relax. You going to be all right?"

"I guess I have to be, don't I?"

He hugged her. Norris relaxed a little. She was so tired. Her wings ached. Her wings! She wanted to sleep. Nothing but sleep. Forever.

IT WAS LATE AFTERNOON WHEN NORRIS AWOKE. Even though she must have slept all day, she was exhausted. Her hair stuck to her neck. Her T-shirt clung wet to her back. She forced herself to get up, moving heavily as though crawling from a boggy quagmire. She called for Alex. He wasn't there. Already six. He should be back soon. She went outside and fed Ishi, hugging him tight. The thought of food made her stomach turn. She forced herself to eat an apple and didn't taste a thing.

She took her gun and went to the shower. The water felt good. She wanted everything washed away. She stepped out of the shower and combed her hair, the Glock next to her at the basin. Still wet, she threw on his blue terry robe, just wanting the smell of him around her. Something human. Something kind. She walked into the living room and saw that the pickup was back. But Alex wasn't in the house. She gripped the gun and looked out the window. Through the trees she could see him at the water's edge, his hand on Ishi's head. Ishi sat still too.

Norris walked softly to his side. He was watching the golden light on the mountains. She was afraid, but had to stand near him. She hoped he wouldn't tell her what he had found on the glacier. In some remote part of her brain, she was hoping it had been a dream.

Quiet. They stood still. The far mountain shoreline was washed in fog, tinged pink, too delicate for a watercolor. She wanted him to touch her, wake her up.

"You have to tell me," she said.

His didn't look at her. She knew. She knew what he'd found. She could read through him. "Alex," she said lifelessly, her voice weak as though she were leaving this earth.

"Yes," he said, reaching for her. "It was exactly as you said."

THEY WERE SILENT IN THE PICKUP. They were heading to the airport to identify Jimmy's body before it was sent to Anchorage. Alex told her Drew had flown on from the Kenai Peninsula to the Brooks Range, some 1200 miles away. Not a threat now. He had it handled. With the body, a good chance for evidence linking to Drew. He told her, too, about Humboldt's leering smile as he'd explained to Chief Corso how he'd found the body. An anonymous tip. Fishy as hell. They passed the newest cruise liner docked at the pier with its mass of visitors surging into town or queuing for tour buses.

Alex reached over and touched her arm. "We'll get through this," he said.

She didn't respond and he stopped the truck by the side of the road.

"Look, you don't have to do this. I'll take you home."

A tour bus passed.

"No, I have to do it," she said.

"Sure?"

"Positive," she said.

"I hate to let you see him like this."

"You forget. I *have* seen him." Then, "Did you identify the bullet wound?"

"I didn't say anything about a bullet wound," he said, putting the pickup in gear.

"But Alex, it's so obvious. Almost dead center in the forehead." Norris could see the black dot, right where Jimmy's third eye would be.

Alex was quiet.

"Wasn't it?"

"Jesus," he said, whispering to himself.

Then, "Yeah," he said. He put his hand on her knee. "Listen. Don't say anything about the dream, OK? I said I got an anonymous tip."

"Alex," she said, scaring herself, "What if it wasn't a dream but a memory? What if I was there and I can't remember. Or maybe I was out of it."

"High, drugged?"

"I don't know. Horrified. Traumatized. Maybe my mind put it away and it only came out in a dream. The only way I could deal with it. And don't tell me it hasn't crossed your mind."

"There's only one problem with your scenario. Why would anyone let a witness go?"

"Because they thought I was unconscious?"

"Weren't you on Jimmy's boat all night?"

"I guess I'm trying to make sense of it. A dream seems so fantastic."

"No kidding," he said.

"You do believe me?"

"I had Winston take me up there."

"No, I mean you believe me that it was a dream."

"I want to. Let's leave it at that," he said.

They were already at the airport. Alex drove to the back of the terminal where they were loading cargo into a 707. A man who she supposed was Chief Corso, along with Humboldt, a lieutenant she'd never met, Farley and a couple of other uniformed officers stood around a pallet with an orange body bag laid on top. Grandpa Jack was nearby with Jimmy's auntie. And Lauren.

Alex brought Norris forward. An attendant unzipped the bag. Everything moved in slow motion. The sound of the zipper cut through her. At last the bag was open. She took a breath.

And looked.

Jimmy was still encased in the blue ice. They'd chopped a rough block out around him. The ice had started to melt and had a glassy sheen rather than the frosted glaze up on the glacier. There was something beautiful about him lying there encased, perfect except for the purple-black hole in his forehead.

Tears blinded her and she stepped away.

Alex motioned for them to zip him back up.

Norris started towards the pickup while Alex supervised the loading of the body into a refrigerated compartment in the plane. Lauren ran to her and buried her face under Norris's arm.

"Grandpa Jack wants to talk to you," she said, muffled through sobs.

He solemnly walked toward her.

"We knew that other body was not Jimmy but thought it best to let it be. Let our own people deal with it. Now Jimmy is found and he can be at peace. We would like you to come to the potlatches when they send him back to us," he said.

Norris looked over his shoulder to Jimmy's auntie who stood alone, nodding.

"I'd like that very much," she said.

"I'm sorry about your visits to Angoon. We are very private and do not like outsider inquiries. Especially over our boy."

"I understand."

He kissed her on the forehead.

"You have to come. My father would want it," Lauren said. She ran for the waiting taxi. Lauren pressed her hand flat against the window as a goodbye. Norris waved and leaned back against the pickup. She could see Alex talking earnestly with Chief Corso. A raven winged past, high, going east. She almost smiled. She wasn't horrified at seeing Jimmy. She was released.

FARLEY APPEARED OUT OF NOWHERE and leaned on the pickup next to her.

"So we got the right Indian this time, huh?"

She didn't answer.

"You know, Lieutenant Robinson and Chief Corso are mighty curious about how Alex found him."

"Get lost, Farley," Alex said, arriving at the pickup.

"Just telling her how it is," said Farley.

"Yeah? How is it?" asked Alex, moving him aside and getting in the truck.

"Well, I'd watch my ass if I were you. Mighty peculiar you finding your missing person in time to ID the Indian," yelled Farley, jumping back as Alex tore out of the parking lot.

"That sounded like a threat," she said.

"Yeah. I'm going to drop you off at my place then I have to face the chief when I get back. Any suggestions?"

"Tell him the truth."

"The truth is you told me where to find the body."

31

ALEX DROVE, CONCENTRATED.

"From my point of view, is there any reason why I shouldn't arrest you?"

"No."

"Try to convince me."

"Alex, the raven took me there. I can't explain it."

She was a prime suspect, that is, a prime accessory. She could tell he wanted to believe her but the raven stuff was difficult to swallow. He was protecting her. He was out of line.

They were on the expressway almost to Juneau when the squad car approached fast from behind, light bars flashing. Alex pulled over to let it pass and it fishtailed to a stop in front of him. In the rearview mirrors, they could see Humboldt's vehicle pull up and stop. Farley got out and so did Humboldt.

"What the hell's going on?" Alex yelled as they approached.

Farley sneered, his hand on his holster. Humboldt ignored Alex and proceeded to Norris' window.

"Norris Reed," said Humboldt, "You are under arrest for the murder of Jimmy Jack Ketah. You have the right to . . ."

Alex slammed his fist on the steering wheel and accidentally hit the horn.

Farley couldn't help but snigger.

NORRIS WAS ALONE IN THE HOLDING CELL sitting on the bunk, her knees drawn up under her chin. She could hear angry voices above her, upstairs.

"You got a so-called anonymous tip, Alex. What do ya know, we got an anonymous tip too: your girlfriend told you where to find the body."

The cell door opened and a female uniformed officer brought a tray covered with a paper towel and slid it onto the bed next to Norris. The officer relocked the door from the outside and departed out of sight. Norris picked up the paper towel and there on the tray was a boiled Dungeness crab, a carton of soda crackers, and a small jar of mayonnaise. Norris jumped up fast. The tray hit the floor and in a split second she was banging on the door yelling for Alex.

Several uniformed officers gathered in a hurry but none of them opened the door until Alex arrived. He had them open the door, grabbed her and looked at the mess on the floor.

"What's this?"

"It's Drew! Did I tell you what I'd want my last meal to be if I were ever on death row?"

Alex squinted at her, confused.

"I told Drew. It was a joke. And now . . ." She couldn't stop shaking.

"Who brought this?" Alex demanded. Staff and officers huddled gawking at the door shrugging, looking at each other.

Norris told him it was a policewoman. She was tracked down in the kitchenette and brought to Norris to identify. The policewoman said she'd had a note from Alex to deliver the tray.

"Where's this note?" said Alex.

She'd thrown it out, she guessed. Alex hadn't sent any note, blew up and went straight to Chief Corso demanding that Norris be protected while in custody. Nothing like that had better come close to happening again.

It wouldn't happen again because Norris was released within the hour.

"They didn't believe me, did they?" said Norris as she and Alex walked to his Crown Vic.

"Doesn't matter; they had nothing on you."

"I thought Humboldt was going to erupt."

"Yeah. At least he didn't manufacture any evidence."

"Would he?"

"I don't know. He's obvious, not sly. But you never know. I'm beginning to doubt my own judgment these days."

"What about Drew?" she asked, still standing at the car.

"He's still on the North Slope. Everybody's asking about you," he said, changing the subject and unlocking the Crown Vic door for her to get in. "Gayle. Mimi. Your sister called. And Warren called to see if he could post bail and so did Eden. And someone named anonymous."

"Drew?" she said, still standing by the car.

"Could be. But I doubt it. The call came from Angoon."

"Since I've been 'found' I should go back to my own apartment."

"I'd rather you stayed with me. I have gates and Ishi."

"You said you have Drew handled so he's not a threat to me."

"Yeah. Winston says he's scheduled to be back in a three days. I guess I'd feel more comfortable if you weren't alone."

"What did Chief Corso say to when you demanded I be let free?"

"He said you were ruining a good officer."

"Am I?" she said.

"Yes," he said and kissed her quickly.

She kissed him back and he pulled her toward him, his mouth hot on her. She felt like she was falling. The rush of wings reverberated in her ears and she buried her face in his neck.

"I better stay at Eden's until this is over," she said into his collar.

"Right," he said.

NORRIS SLEPT ALL NIGHT and most of the next day. No dreams. No Raven. When she awoke, Warren was sitting in an armchair, quietly smoking, watching her.

"Hiya, ducks."

"Warren! What are you doing here?"

"I heard about a couple of garage sales this weekend and thought I'd check them out."

She hugged him around the neck. "You've never been to a garage sale in your life."

"Eden was nice enough to call and tell me about Jimmy. I thought you might need some company. Um, you need a bath, dearie," he said.

She'd been sleeping in Jimmy's upstairs room at Eden's with the partial ceiling, the sun glaring in all the long day.

"I'm sort of sweaty, huh?" she said, sniffing her armpits, recoiling.

"Don't be vulgar," he said chiding her. "You know what Grandmother Bartholomew used to say: "Horses sweat. Men perspire. Women glow.""

"I'm glowing, huh?" said Norris, happy to see him. "You know what's strange?" she said, sitting on the bed cross-legged. "I've slept all night and all day but I feel exhausted, like there's not enough sleep in the world to catch up."

"No wonder. It's not every day you get to identify a lover's body and then get arrested for his murder."

TWO PEROXIDE PLATINUM BLONDS in pink uniforms from the Cut 'n Curl beauty shop sat in a high-backed booth at the bakery behind Norris and Warren. The women were in the middle of a conversation.

"We thought maybe we could bolster his image after the Jimmy Ketah fiasco and he kept saying it wasn't a fiasco."

Warren raised his eyebrows at Norris as the woman continued.

" . . . and I said, if you say so. They let her off and made you look like a fool. He said he didn't want me meddling and I said we were trying to help and he said, you and 'shit for brains'—he calls Farley that all the time—there's a team. And I said and you're so damn fine arresting that woman without a shred of evidence, it's a wonder Chief Corso didn't have your badge. And he said thanks for standing by your man. And I said this isn't a fucking country and western song and hurled the pan of sausages at him. All over his favorite blue shirt. He started to hit me and stopped to look down at his shirt."

"What'd you do?" asked the friend.

"I said those sausage stains will never come out."

The women roared in laughter.

"Who?" mouthed Warren.

"Vince Humboldt's wife, Sandy," whispered Norris.

"I think it's too dark," said Sandy Humboldt, looking at her fingernails, a deep metallic plum, flashing them away from her into the aisle so anyone could see. Even Norris.

"Oh, no, hon. Dramatic and sexy," said her friend.

"That's me," laughed Sandy. "It's called Plum Crazy."

They lowered their voices. Norris and Warren strained to hear.

"You still seeing John?"

"Not after Vince found out. I'd like to know who told him. Probably the little shit-for-brains," she said and they reeled laughing again.

"So who are we seeing now?"

"Uh, uh." said Sandy coyly.

"But you never keep anything from me."

"This time's different."

"Girl, what are you up to? It's not Chief Corso, is it?"

"God, no. Let's just say I'm going on one amazing vacation when Vince makes lieutenant."

"I wouldn't count on him getting it, Sandy. Everybody knows Alex is a shoo-in."

"Is that right?" said Sandy. "Well, everybody is in for a big surprise."

NORRIS DROPPED WARREN off at the museum and parked Eden's BMW in back of the State Office Building. LuAnn from dispatch had called with a message from Alex for her to meet him in the archives at noon. Norris had told him about Sandy Humboldt's conversation, warned him to watch his back. He'd thanked her, laughed a little, said now you're worried about me?

Maybe Alex had news and didn't want to be seen with her in public—the archives had few visitors, as private a place in town as you could practically get. And far away from Farley and Humboldt.

The government building sprawled up the hill covering almost three blocks. She was halfway tempted to go up the hill and check on her apartment but she was running late.

Up close, the building wasn't as ugly as it seemed. It had some nice features, the stairs spilling out like cataracts and wide brick esplanades surrounding the whole building. There was plenty of space for office workers to eat their brown-bag lunches on the benches overlooking the channel or enclosed in little courtyards against the walls of the glassed-in two-story atrium lobby.

Norris climbed the brick stairway to the lobby where a group of ten- and twelve-year-old girls in spangled red and black sequined costumes were tap dancing. She skirted the performance and entered the library archives through the glass doors and metal detector. She didn't see Alex.

She headed to the counter to ask the librarian if she'd seen him when a bespectacled young man stopped her. He blinked nervously as he tried to spit out his message in an awkward stutter. A-A-Alex needed her to m-m-meet him in the conference room on the first floor.

Norris had to navigate around the dancing girls to get to the elevators at the far side of the atrium lobby. A few government workers stood around the edges of the atrium watching, snacking on apples or chips, bits of lunch. The only people enormously engaged in the spectacle were the moms at the periphery, proud and smiling, mouthing the words to "Hello, Dolly" as their darlings flounced and pranced, ribboned ponytails and pigtails flying. Norris loved ballet classes and performances when she was eight or ten. Loved the satin tops and net tutus her mother used to make, the particular smell of new leather ballet slippers. By twelve though she felt on display with too-tight tops on newly developing breasts, the nipples hardening in spandex tops, her legs white and cold and goose-bumped and exposed. There were a couple of girls in that embarrassed state dancing now. Too old and self-conscious, mortified in public. She wished she could rescue them.

She reached the elevators and descended. On the second floor, a stop. The doors opened.

"Hello, Norris," said Drew.

32

Ta da!" Drew said, like he'd just performed a magic trick.

"I thought you were still up north," she said, hoping not to show her alarm.

"I left the helicopter there and hitched a ride with the mail plane. Didn't want Winston upset about wasting jet fuel. Where have you been? I went to your apartment. Carmen says you haven't been there for almost a week. You haven't been to work either. And Father Davidovitch is getting worried."

"I'm staying with a friend," she said, trying to be cool, carefully sliding her hand into Eden's borrowed shoulder bag.

"Sleeping with him?" Drew asked more hurt than challenging. He pushed the "stop" button on the elevator panel.

"What do you want?" she asked, fingering the Glock in the bag.

"I want to tell you you're making a mistake. I know Alex has you thinking I killed Jimmy. If you really want to know what happened, ask Alex."

"I will. In fact, I'm on my way to meet him now."

"Actually, you're not."

She stepped back.

"I had LuAnn call Alex and tell him you needed to see him ASAP at Eden's. Then LuAnn gave you the message to meet Alex here. Simple." He was so cavalier it was unnerving.

Be cool, she thought, her hand on the Glock.

"And she organized my death row delivery, huh?"

"I thought you might need some cheering up."

Norris held the Glock tight, the steel heavy, smooth, cold to the touch. She could shoot him right through the leather.

"Relax. This was the only way I could talk to you alone. I don't like it when friends of mine turn someone against me. Alex is covering for himself."

"I don't believe you."

"Alex is clever. I'll give him that. Did he tell you about the times he and Jimmy got into it over drugs? No, huh. There's so much you don't know. I only want you to be safe. Did I ever do anything to make you afraid of me? Anything to make you doubt me?"

He hadn't. Still, she didn't know if it was an act.

"I've had plenty of women but you and Maya were the only ones who ever touched the real me. And Alex is going to take you too. You just don't know it yet." He leaned in as though he wanted to kiss her. She arched back. He didn't force it. He punched the "open door" button and the doors slid open. Drew stepped out into a waiting group of young secretaries in summer dresses showing off their shiny tan bare legs. They flashed summer smiles at him and tossed their sun-burnished hair. "Oh, and there's this," he said, handing her Mick's Delta Force pin. "Alex planted it in my trailer. If you want the truth, ask him."

NORRIS DROVE ALONG THE GLACIER HIGHWAY loop trying to think. A patrol car came up fast behind her and she held her breath, thinking it might be Alex, but he hardly ever used a cruiser. The squad car passed her and she eased her grip on the wheel. Would Alex plant Mick's pin? It didn't make sense. The vest may not have shown up after all and he needed more? A desperate move. Not like Alex. Or was it?

If LuAnn was so helpful to Drew, maybe she lifted the pin from evidence and gave it to him. Maybe you could buy a pin just like it at Stanley's curio shop. Her thoughts were spinning. She should have asked Drew about the arguments Alex supposedly had with Jimmy over drugs. She could catch up with Drew and ask him. Or she could go to the police station and ask Alex. Or she could go to her apartment and lock the doors and pull the covers over her head. Now she didn't trust either of them. What she really needed was to go someplace and think. The glacier.

The parking lot was engorged with tour buses, the trails and viewpoints a chaos of people. No peace here. She parked in a striped-off no-parking zone and walked down the path to Mendenhall Lake and the glacier's edge. Clusters of seniors blocked her way, oblivious, comparing Mendenhall with Glacier Bay, Norwegian versus Greek cruise ship lines, the Mediterranean, the Greek Isles, the Caribbean, the Nile, the Amazon. And the food . . . The chatter gave her a headache. The serenity of the glacier, the urgent need to be there beside its immense silence was lost.

A raven dived toward the crowd at the rail. Shot straight out of the sky. What was it doing? It did it again and the crowd parted. It was playing, annoying them. Apparently she wasn't the only one upset.

Back to the car. Now what? Nowhere seemed safe. Father Davidovitch would offer sanctuary but both Alex and Drew could guess she'd go there. Eden's and the Baranof, obvious. Gayle would let her stay or Mimi but neither could keep their mouths shut. After Mick and Ole, she didn't want to put anyone else she cared about in jeopardy. Where?

Norris headed toward town and a patrol car passed, the officer waving. She didn't know him but had seen him around the office. Shoot, by now Alex would be looking for her after Drew's fake distress phone message. Now he would know she was driving Eden's car. Did she have anything to fear from him? From anyone? If Raven could take her to Jimmy, maybe they thought she had seen the killer.

She drove to the airport and left the Beemer in the long-term parking lot. Rather than catch a bus at the airport she walked a mile and a half using back roads, cutting across vacant lots filled with yarrow, lupine and scrub grass to the Valley Mall where she boarded with a group of shoppers and took the bus to the marina. The docks were quiet. A lazy afternoon. She thought about taking Ole's dinghy but realized it was too heavy so she walked down to Gil's *Misfit*. He wasn't on board and if caught, she was certain he wouldn't mind. She unhooked his inflatable outboard—a smaller version than Jimmy's Zodiac—and dropped it into the water.

She stayed in the middle of the channel where it was unlikely anyone would recognize her. She went south, out of site of town, and scanned the shoreline looking for Alex's place. There were few other homesteads along this southern stretch and she soon spotted his skiff on the familiar beach. She cut the motor and drifted in then pulled the dinghy onto the sand. She made her way to the house, where Ishi barked sharply then started jumping and stretching the length of his chain in greeting. Alex's pickup was gone so she figured she was safe. Besides, thanks to the cowbells, she'd have time to get back to the dinghy before he got to the house. She ruffled Ishi's furry jowls with "good boys" and went to the back door where she knocked as a formality before opening it.

The trailer was hot. She opened all the windows and doors and started the air conditioning fan. She went outside again, rinsed Ishi's bowl and gave him clean water which he gulped noisily, shoving his snout full in then looking up at her, water and slobber running down his face. She patted him behind the ears, the only fur that wasn't wet.

Back inside, she went through the bedroom drawers, the closet, the bookshelves and the kitchen cabinets. If there was anything hidden to find out about Alex, where would it be? What would it be? She didn't know what she was looking for. Drew had accused Alex but of what exactly? And there was Maya. What if Drew was right— that Alex did murder her? She went to the back room and looked through a closet of old clothes. Nothing.

She sat on the floor and opened an army trunk full of sports gear and old photos. She sifted through a box of photos. Alex sitting on a tractor. Alex and his sister dressed up for Sunday school, Bibles in hand. A trophy for raising bunnies. Baseball teams—Little League, Babe Ruth, American Legion. A prom picture. Oregon State baseball team. Alex lying in a hammock under an apple tree, the farmhouse in the background. Big smile. White T-shirt, blue jeans. He was a sunny kid. The Gulf. Norris looked at the young men tan and sweaty. Boys with guns grinning. Her heart skipped a beat. Jimmy and Alex arm and arm. Rifle-toting, bare-chested, desert fatigues and tan lace-up boots, a Humvee and the stark landscape behind them.

Why hadn't Alex talked to her about Jimmy when he was talking about Kuwait? Well, she hadn't asked either. Alex was never forthcoming.

His nature? Or a police thing?

The next photo was familiar to her. The Apache helicopter in the background, soldiers posed in front. The same photo she'd seen at Drew's place before their glacier flight. A different angle. Maybe she was mistaken. No, she was certain it was the same group. Wait a minute. Two helicopters. The other nose and rotor blades in the background. And there, off to the side. The pilots laughing, headsets in hands, arms around each other. Drew. And Alex.

Norris scrambled to gather the pile of photos she'd dropped. She knew Alex and Drew had served together in Kuwait but didn't know they were both helicopter pilots. She frantically stuffed the photos back in the box and placed it in the trunk. A bit of white caught her eye, just there, tucked beneath an old fielder's glove. She reached for it. OK, she thought, Alex has old sweat socks in the trunk. Only this one wasn't old. She pulled it out, praying there wasn't a red stripe at the top. She didn't have to examine it, didn't have to pull out the bloodstained down vest stuffed under it.

SHE HIT THE PORCH RUNNING, door banging behind her. She raced across the drive, Ishi at her heels nipping in play. She outdistanced him and he barked, jerking on his chain, leaping madly. She made it to the inflatable, stumbling and falling, trying not to throw up, shoving the dinghy into the water, falling into it and diving for the motor, racking her shin on the wooden seat. She set the choke and pulled the rope. Pulled again. And again. Damn you, she said and hit the motor on top with her open palm. One more time, pulling hard. The motor sputtered to life and she cranked it up, cutting through the bay, flying across the open chop.

33

NORRIS EMPTIED HER APARTMENT closet, shoving her few things into her canvas duffel bag. She was wrapping the mask of Raven in Jimmy's navy sweater when she heard her apartment door open behind her.

"What are you doing?" asked Warren.

"Get your things and meet me at the airport "

"Aren't we leaving a bit abruptly? Wasn't Alex going to arrest Drew? The big reveal?"

"No time. Go." But before he could, Drew walked in.

"They arrested Alex," Drew said.

"Arrested Alex? Norris, did you hear that?" said Warren. Norris bit her lip.

"They found Jimmy's socks and the bloody vest in an old army trunk at his place," said Drew. Smug. "Pretty foolish not to get rid of the evidence. Who knows why people do things."

"My god. It was Alex? And here he had us thinking it was you, Drew," said Warren.

"He'd like you to believe it was me."

Norris didn't respond. She stowed the last of her things in her bag and zipped it shut.

"You're heading back to Seattle?" said Drew. "Don't you want to know what happened?"

"I don't want to know anything," said Norris.

"Yes she does. She wants to know everything," said Warren.

She started for the door, almost pushing Drew aside.

"The least you can do is let me drive you to the airport," said Drew.

"Wonderful idea. We can swing by the hotel and gather my things," said Warren.

Reluctant, Norris let Drew take the bag from her.

"I can't believe it," said Warren.

"Well, at least it's over," said Drew.

"Yeah, it is," said Alex standing at the door, his Sig aimed at Drew's chest.

"Drew told us you were arrested," Norris stammered.

"Did he tell you he framed me?" said Alex.

Norris inched toward the Glock in her purse on the coffee table.

"Bad timing, bud," said Drew. "I took off before you got Jimmy's vest planted."

"Before we got a search warrant you mean. Couldn't leave well enough alone, could you, Drew? You couldn't just ditch the evidence. You had to make sure they found everything at my place. I don't suppose Humboldt asked you how you knew where to tell him to look for it."

"You can't get away with it, Alex," said Drew, calm, collected. "I think the best part was Waco's dead body showing up. Better to have a body than a missing person. Isn't that what you always say? And of course you counted on Smitty and Charlotte to identify the body. It couldn't be better for them: Jimmy's boat, property, the bank account. Man, with that kind of money they really become major dealers. How much was your cut?"

"You should know," said Alex.

Footsteps thundering up the stairs. Humboldt and the weasel in the doorway.

"Lower your weapon!"

Humboldt's automatic in Alex's back.

"Wrong man, guys," said Alex.

"Drop it or I'll blow your fucking brains out," said Humboldt.

"Yeah," said Farley.

"I'm telling you . . ."

Humboldt jammed his gun into Alex's back. Hard.

Alex lowered his Sig. Farley snapped it from him.

"Big mistake," said Alex. "Norris . . ."

"Shut up!" Humboldt gave him a whack on the side of the mouth, his lip cut and bloody, already swelling fat. He read Alex his Miranda rights as Farley cuffed him and pushed him toward the stairs.

Drew picked up the duffel and coaxed Norris, who couldn't move, down the stairs after them.

"My god, a real police drama right in your own apartment," said Warren. "It even sounded like a movie." He put his arm around her, "Just think, Norris, you could have made the wrong choice and ended up dead too."

"Thanks, Warren," said Norris.

"I never thought Alex would do it. He and Jimmy had lots of fights and I've heard Alex threaten him for years but I never thought it would happen," said Drew.

"Jimmy was dealing?" asked Warren.

"Big time," said Drew.

"I don't believe it," said Norris.

"People aren't always what they seem."

Outside, the street was full of patrol cars and officers with weapons drawn.

Humboldt shoved Alex into the back of a squad car and the officers relaxed, congratulating Humboldt and Farley, energized and hyper. A crowd began to gather.

"You'd think they were coming after a terrorist group instead of just one man," Warren said, appreciating the testosterone-filled spectacle.

Drew tossed the bag in the bed of his pickup and opened the passenger door. Warren maneuvered his lanky self into the rear seat. Norris climbed in front.

"He's finally getting what he deserved," said Drew.

Humboldt and Farley mingled with the other officers, relishing their moment.

"You told us they had arrested Alex before they did," Norris said to Drew.

"Did I? Humboldt must have screwed up. He told me they had him arrested," Drew said, shutting her door.

Since when was Drew pals with Humboldt? thought Norris, uneasy.

Alex was looking at her through the backseat window of the squad car. He looked like he was yelling.

She wondered if Alex still had his .38 hidden a second before she saw his cuffed hands raise the gun and aim it at Drew.

She ducked and the squad car's window exploded and blood splattered the pickup window next to her.

The shots kept coming and Drew rocked like a crazed marionette until it was quiet and Drew's face, a mass of red, contorted, inches from hers, slid down the window.

She was too shocked to scream.

34

BLOOD AND CONFUSION EVERYWHERE. The window of
the squad car shattered. A pile of cops on Alex. Norris
vomiting. Recovering, she slowly opened the pickup
door and stepped over Drew's body, a crumpled bloody
mass at her feet. And Sandy Humboldt, a flash of Cut 'n
Curl uniform pink, came straight toward Norris running
wildly screaming, flinging herself onto Drew, her hands
flying frantically to stop the bleeding. Norris would
never forget those metallic fingernails. Plum crazy.

FARLEY WAS REPRIMANDED and put on indefinite leave
for his bonehead handling of Alex—overcome with
excitement, he'd cuffed Alex's hands in front and
neglected to frisk him.

Charlotte, Smitty and the bank teller Anita Dorr got
slapped with forgery misdemeanors and a year of
community service but the charges didn't include
impounding the property or the money. Eden found an
actual will. Jimmy had left everything to Lauren except
Eden's place and the galleries. Whether Smitty and
Charlotte honestly thought the body was Jimmy's or not
was never concluded. They stuck to their story. Dix,
however, had a few things to say to the police.

Jimmy had tried to intervene in Drew's new
enterprise that would make them all very rich. It wasn't

only beer Drew was leaving the fishing fleets on the islands or at convenient contract assignments all over Alaska. It was heroin. Easy to conceal. Plenty of users.

That night after Jimmy took Norris back to the boat, Jimmy and Drew had a horrific argument. Jimmy had dumped the heroin stuffed in the two Coho before he left the fish at Eden's, nearly a kilo. Nearly a quarter of a million dollars worth dissolved in the channel. Jimmy left the bar. Drew followed. The next thing Dix, Smitty and Charlotte knew, Jimmy was dead. After that they did whatever Drew asked. Dix got scared after Drew made him dispose of Mick's body at the church, leaving the cap as instructed. It was his idea to have Quentin deliver the note and the pin to Norris hoping she'd take a hint about Drew while he, Smitty and Charlotte fled to Cabo out of harm's way.

Dix was suspected of Ole's murder and the disfigurement of Waco. Never proven. Waco's body was a timely convenience for Drew with no bullet to trace, no connection, unlike Jimmy's body. Smitty and his smashed lawn ornaments? Suspected heroin shipments. Rain-washed, no trace. Eden? Well, Edensaw was as cool as a glacier. And quiet as one too.

Norris didn't want to know about the soft tissue scramble, the freak ricochet that left the bullet in Jimmy's skull. Yet she was glad the bullet matched Drew's 9mm and exonerated Alex, much to Humboldt's dismay. Humboldt had enough bad news what with Sandy and all.

Alex was not put away for killing Drew, which he might have been if it hadn't been for his lawyer claiming he had acted in defense of Norris, who would surely have been Drew's next victim. Norris wasn't certain about that and neither was Alex but both kept their mouths shut and let the jury make its way to his acquittal.

Norris sat mute through the testimonies and was never called as a witness even though she had been at the center of it. Warren accompanied her through the maze and when it was over in less than two weeks insisted she come home to Seattle.

Instead, she stayed in the town of misfits and rebels and government workers, fishermen, Indians, artists and scavengers, frontier people all living on the edge of the continent. People who sometimes wore fishing boots to dinner.

35

NORRIS THOUGHT IT WAS A BAD DAY to climb a mountain. Overcast, socked in. But Alex said it'd be fine, just wait, they'd climb up 500 feet and be in sunlight.

They drove across the bridge and through Douglas, hardly a town at all, suburbs mostly, with the expensive homes terraced on the ridge facing Juneau, the low-rent single-family homes and apartments clustered along the highway and spilling down to the waterfront. A few miles out of Douglas and into the forested nowhere he parked.

"This is it," he said.

"Isn't there a parking lot?"

"This is a shortcut."

"Where's the trail?" she asked.

"Here someplace," he said, getting out of the truck.

He grabbed a rucksack from the back seat and slung it over his shoulders. When he stretched his arm, Norris saw that he had the .38 in a shoulder holster.

"A lot of bad guys up on the mountain?" she asked.

"Bears," he said.

"I may be naive but I seriously doubt a handgun will do anything to a bear except make it mad."

"We don't shoot them. We scare them off," he said.

"Does it work?"

"Sometimes," he said. "Hey, at least we don't have to

worry about grizzlies or browns. They haven't managed to get to the island yet."

"Yet."

"Only black bears and they're real small."

"How small?"

"Big dog."

She squinted at him.

"Really really really big dog."

Alex clambered up the dirt embankment and scrambled into the underbrush. Norris followed. The climbing was steep and the underbrush thick.

"Are you sure this is a trail?" she asked.

"It's supposed to follow a creek. You hear a creek?"

"How many times have you been up here?" she asked.

"Once, about six years ago and it did follow a creek."

Great. They were lost.

"Wait," he said, "Over to the left. I think I hear it."

They tramped over fallen branches, through blackberry vines and bracken fern, wound their way around snow-ravaged spindly firs and found the creek. Winded and hot, she leaned over a shelf of rocks to drink from a small cascade, the icy water stinging her face. Alex was right. They were climbing out of the cloud cover. Every once in a while wisps of cloud would disintegrate and she'd see blue sky. Everything below was still shrouded in gray.

A couple of yards from the creek they found the path, well trodden and obvious. They must have crashed near it several times. No matter, they were on it now and trekking along. The clouds cleared, the underbrush fell away and they were climbing on rock now. Not a bad hike. About two hours straight up. Norris was a casual hiker, no slouch, solid on a trail but no match for Alex's pace. She always hated hiking with athletic males.

They bounded ahead then rested up waiting for you and when you finally caught up they were ready to move on. But you hadn't had a rest, you could barely catch your breath, and there they were impatiently striding off.

At least going down she'd keep up.

"Listen." he said, stopping in front of her abruptly so she almost ran into him.

"The creek," she said.

"Not the creek."

She heard it. Low rumbling growls she didn't particularly want to hear. And little yipping noises.

"Bears," he said. "With cubs. They're down by the creek. If we're lucky we can sneak past."

"And if we're not lucky?"

"Don't ask."

They crept up the trail as silently as they could. It reminded Norris of playing cowboys and Indians with Rita. Rita was always the cowboy—she liked the fringed jacket and the guns. Norris was always the Indian. Stealthy, woods-savvy. She'd practice moving silently through the forest, not leaving a trail. Mainly to hide from Rita.

Now they could see the bears through the foliage, some thirty yards away. Black bears, three cubs and a mama. They tried to slip by unnoticed and would have, until Alex stepped on a twig and it cracked like lightning. Norris was glad she hadn't stepped on it since she really didn't want to be responsible for their being mauled. However, she didn't feel like being mauled at all no matter whose fault it was. Maybe the bears didn't hear it, she thought. Mama bear did. She reared up and sniffed. Luckily, the breeze was blowing away from them and she couldn't pick up a scent.

They stood motionless while mama bear sniffed. She appeared to look right at them and didn't see them.

Alex motioned to be absolutely still, whispered, "Bears have poor eyesight but keen noses. If the wind shifts, she'll be on us in a flash."

Mama bear, ears pricked, stayed alert, waiting for a sound, movement, a scent while the cubs rolled and played at her feet, one playfully batting at her hind paw. Mama bear didn't want to play just now and took a swat at the cub, batting it end over end. The cub licked itself, pouting, and the other two, lesson learned, sat at attention.

The mother bear found nothing on the air and relaxed, nudging her cubs toward the creek. Alex and Norris continued creeping up the trail, keeping an eye on her. A twig found its way under Norris' foot and snapped. They froze as mama bear reared on her hind legs sniffing furiously. The wind must have shifted because this time she got it and drew a bead on them. Alex pulled the revolver out of its holster.

"When I fire, run!"

Alex fired and they ran. Trouble was, the cubs did too. Ran right to them, sliding in the dust on the trail at their feet.

"Shoo!" said Norris to the cubs, waving her arms at them. "Go the other way. Go. Go. Thatta way."

"When I fire again," said Alex, "You go left, I'll go right. Find the nearest tree and go up it. Preferably a big one."

Luckily, part of her childhood cowboys and Indians phase was tree climbing. She went up the trees to scout and would stay there all day reading. Rita would yell at her to come down and play and she'd yell back, "I'm scouting, leave me alone," or better yet, she'd tell her that Indians have mysterious ways and shouldn't be interrupted. Anyway, she could climb but probably not half as fast as mama bear could.

Alex fired and the she-bear reared on her hind legs and let out a roar so loud and fierce, you could swear the world was ending. The cubs jumped about three feet straight up and Norris felt like she did too, running so fast she wasn't touching the ground. The cubs got the right idea and ran to their mama who hustled them off through the underbrush.

The bears disappeared into deep woods before Norris had time to get up the first branch of her chosen tree. She wandered carefully back to the trail.

"Did you hear the mother?"

Alex laughed, "Jesus."

"Cute, weren't they?" said Norris.

They were in sunlight now, the trees sparser, the ground rockier. Then suddenly they were out of the trees into a meadow full of buttercups. It wasn't a real meadow at all but a marsh in a wide bowl, the ragged cliffs on three sides like someone had taken a bite out of the mountain. The bowl was filled in with snow all year except for these few weeks of summer when it melted, leaving the illusion of a grassy emerald meadow. It looked like you could stroll out there and lie down in the flowers but what looked like grass was really an alpine meadow of moss. The ground wasn't solid but a bog, a network of squashy pods of earth and moss and rocks, with wildflowers spread all over the basin. They picked their way across, jumping from mossy pod to pod, relying on rocks for certainty.

In the middle of the boggy wonder was a ski hut on stilts, about twenty feet in the air, a primitive structure with a huge Plexiglas window on one side overlooking the meadow. They were headed to the hut for lunch. At first Norris thought it was foolish to hike all this way to eat lunch inside, but looking around knew there was no place else to alight. Oh, maybe they could perch on a boulder one at a time. It was unbelievably wet. If she wasn't careful, her foot would press right through the delicate flooring and squish ankle-deep in the sandy, silty residual muck of melted snow. Sometimes there were rocky sand bars and she gladly leapt for them. The sky reflected in the tiny pools of water networking the bog. Norris stood and watched the clouds drift by in the wildflowers.

She always was fascinated with looking at things upside down. When she was little she'd take a mirror and put it on the carpet, lie there and stare into it for hours, the ceiling now the base, pretending she was walking in a crazy place where the windows were inches from the floor and you had to step over door jambs.

Alex was already at the hut, on the top of the stairs waving. Norris picked her way across the meadow and climbed the stairs. The view was spectacular. The air was so clear, everything so defined. And so silent. The sky was excruciatingly blue. Norris laughed.

"What's so funny?" Alex asked, unloading the sandwiches from his pack.

"I was just thinking about Warren. We had this foolish discussion years ago about what makes the sky blue. I had told him how blue the sky was in Arizona when Bailey and I lived there, and he told me that he had decided the sky was bluest in the north. The fact that he'd never been out of the Northwest to test his theory didn't matter in the least. He figured that all the sunlight in the south diluted the blueness. I asked why it wasn't true in summer up north and he told me not to contradict him and then proceeded to change his theory. It's not refraction or short wavelengths that give the sky color especially, he said, it's reflection—everyone knows more blue-eyed people live in the north. Voila! A new hypothesis was born."

"Does he have any other theories?"

"Tons. How about his antidote for every known disease to man: Coffee and chocolate. Naturally, the medical community is indulging recklessly while hiding it from the general public so as to keep prices down and their business up."

"I think he'd better stick to buying and selling antiques. Anyway, to blue skies, however they get there," said Alex, pulling a bottle from his pack.

"Champagne?"

"Champagne," he said, popping the cork out the door. He handed her the bottle, she took a swig and handed it back. They passed it back and forth.

"How can ham and cheese sandwiches taste so delicious?" Norris said, gobbling like she hadn't eaten in days.

"Now for dessert," said Alex, pulling a thick hand-rolled joint the size of a small cigar from the backpack. "Remember the Jamaican rock group I helped get permits to film the video on Mendenhall?"

Of course she did, The Apes or something simian. Or was it insects?

"A gift." Alex lit up and took a deep drag then passed it to her.

She hesitated.

"A cop with hashish? Crazier things have happened in your life Norris. Come on. We deserve a bonus after everything this summer." He took another deep toke. "This is strong shit. Haven't had anything like this since Kuwait."

Norris looked at him.

"A little isn't going to hurt anybody. I don't indulge and I don't sell. I'm not tarnishing my image am I?"

"It just threw me."

"I'm human, Norris. Gimme a break."

She took a hit and he took another longer one.

Norris took another swallow of champagne.

"So are you going to move in with me?" Alex asked.

"I might. Now that it's all over."

"Yeah, none of us thought you'd stick it out."

Who didn't think she'd stick it out, thought Norris but was lost in the lovely numbness of champagne and a hit off the joint. They were high in a high alpine sweet flowered sweet water meadow, blue sky reflecting in pools everywhere and high in that alpine hut, looking out over the top of the world, Alex aloft on hashish and what did he say? Something about her almost figuring things out. Something about Drew blackmailing him, playing games, how sorry he was.

"I should have told you everything," he said taking another hit.

"What didn't you tell me?" gasped Norris.

Alex took a moment too long to answer.

He was staring at her. And then the revolver in his hands, passing it back and forth like it was too hot to touch. And he was pointing it at her and then at himself and at her and himself and he was high and he spun the chamber open, the bullets spinning out onto the floor and she was high, too high, and this wasn't happening. He dropped the revolver, chamber open and it lay like a broken skeleton on the rough wood floor. She stared at it lying there and he was already down the stairs running. Down, down the long stairs and out into the splashing alpine meadow, rock to rock and way out shipwrecked leaning bent against a boulder, his face in his hands until he stood up and looked back at her in the window of the hut where she stood frozen and he kept looking at her then she was quickly on the floor grabbing for the bullets, scrambling on all fours, snatching them all, counting, two, three, how many had he spent on the bears? Grab the gun, looking out again was he coming or still down there?

No not yet, still down there. She reloaded the revolver, forcing her fingers to work, to slow down, get it right, all in, snap it shut, both hands ready. He stood still by the boulder waiting for her and he wouldn't hurt her would he? He loved her she was sure of it. She put the gun in her pocket and went down the stairs cautious, watching. He didn't move, waiting still, far out in the meadow. She could run to him tell him it was all right, started toward him three steps on the rocks hopping, stepping toward him, blue sky underneath her feet. Stopped. What if he had his Sig? What if he did? Did she care? She started toward him, turned away. And ran.

Ran and ran, rock to rock, splashing and skipping across blue sky and wildflowers. She ran for life itself out of the meadow and down the mountain. No stops, skidding, leaps, waterfalls, across the creek, in a flash past the black bears eating berries, no fear of them now, nothing to stop her descent. Almost down, she heard him crashing behind her. She didn't know she could run like that. Downhill, downloping.

Norris reached the highway panting, the rig sitting where it should be. Keys. No keys. He has the keys. Extra keys hidden where? Fingers along the inside of the fenders, yes the little magnetic box. Now get it started as fast as her fingers could fly. Key in, ignition on, engine fired, she was in and behind the wheel and tore out gravel, spitting as she gained speed, almost gone when he flew out of the woods onto the hood. He hit and rolled on impact, an awful crunch, pitched off tumbling along the side of the road, dust billowing, half in the ditch, crumpled. Stopped. She saw him in the side mirror, a misshapen heap. Not moving. She couldn't leave him there.

She reversed. Slow and careful. Checked the side mirror. No movement. Out of the truck with the revolver, held it steady in both hands the way he'd taught her.

"Don't move," she said.

He didn't.

She kicked a shoulder. A muffled groan. Thank god, he was alive. Thank god he was alive so she could kill him.

But first, "What happened to Jimmy?"

"Drew killed him."

"Why?"

"Jimmy wanted it to stop. The heroin."

"And you knew," she said.

"I know, I know. I should have . . ."

"How long did you know?" she said, kicking him in the ribs.

He doubled up. Didn't answer. She kicked him again.

"How long did you know?!" she demanded.

"I knew they were meeting at the bar that night. I was going to bust them all. Had to handle an officer-involved shooting in Auke Bay and came back too late. I saw Drew loading Jimmy's body into his pickup."

"You saw? You covered it up? You let me . . ." Dissolving like she had no attachment to time or anything on this earth. Evaporate into a wisp and, whoosh, gone.

"He was blackmailing me."

Catching herself, regaining, "Because you killed Maya."

He flinched, shook his head no. "Opium running. Me, Drew, and Jimmy in the Gulf. A long time ago."

"And if anyone found out, goodbye hot-shot Investigator Tanner? How could your job be that important? How could you?! You faked everything."

"You don't understand. After the war and Maya, I was a mess. Drinking, dope, women. Anything to get me out of my own skin. Jimmy found me in San Francisco in a rat hole basement apartment more dead than alive. He saved me. Got me to Juneau. It isn't just the job. It's everything. I'm respected. I'm a good guy. I make a difference."

"You were going to kill me," she said.

"I couldn't think. You were suddenly a looming threat. I was fucked up. I couldn't . . . I don't know what happened. Fuck. Fuck. Fuck!" Anguish, coughing, spitting up blood, trying to get up, half crawling toward her. "Norris . . ."

"You lied to me the whole time!" Boot on his shoulder, shoving him back into the ditch. "He murdered Jimmy! And you did nothing!" Kicking dirt and stones over him in a fury.

Cowering from the barrage, "Jimmy was already dead. Nothing would bring him back. I had to stall until I could nail Drew once and for all." She stopped, stood over him and aimed the gun at his head.

"Everything'll be fine. We're happy aren't we? It's a good life," A choked plea.

She stared at him. He believed it.

"I couldn't let Drew ruin me. Law enforcement's all I've got. I can't face the fucking abyss again Norris. You wouldn't know what it's like. You have no idea."

No, she wouldn't, she lied.

And left him there.

Acknowledgements

Thanks to

Juneau P.D., Alaska State Troopers, John Corso, sharpshooter Paul Tekorius. Livingston Helicopters and especially Del Smith and Evergreen Helicopters all those years ago.

Betsy & James for the safe haven, a summer of writing bliss. Nick, you know why. Bob Schroeder for stealing your place. Ricardo for Ishi. John-John for being so alive once upon a time. Tom & Chris for all the meals over the fence.

And

Marcia Barrentine for your considerable gifts, not the least of which is patience, sister Sue, Marie Moneysmith and Angie Jabine for keen editing eyes, encouragement and guidance. Mom & dad for rivers and fish and oceans and boats. And all the friends & family I neglected getting this done.